D0877225

To Ambar
from
Manos :)

# THE CARGO

# THE CARGO

Trace Evans

Copyright © 2016 by Marios Ellinas and JM Olejarz (jointly under the pen name Trace Evans)

All rights reserved. Printed in the United States of America. No part of this book may be used or reproduced in any manner whatsoever without written permission from the authors, except in the case of brief quotations in critical articles or reviews.

First edition
Cover design: Sergio Barrera
ISBN 13: 978-0-692-80438-4
ISBN 10: 0692804382

*The Cargo* is a work of fiction, written for entertainment. The names, characters, places, and incidents portrayed in the story are either imaginary or have been used fictitiously. Any resemblance to actual persons living or dead, businesses, companies, governments, events, or locales is entirely coincidental.

*To the people of Singapore for their kindness and hospitality. And to the inspiring legacy of Mr. Lee Kuan Yew.*
–M.E.

*For my parents, who gave me books.*
–J.O.

# 1

# IN DEEP WATERS

***East of Somalia, somewhere in the Gulf of Aden***

The noon sun sparkled on the ocean's surface, forming shapes that leaped and danced across the water. Aboard the *Delfland*, a Dutch shipping freighter on a course from Singapore to Egypt, most of the sailors were oblivious to their surroundings, going about their assigned tasks with seasoned indifference. But one of them, a new recruit named Aileen Soh, was not. She and another sailor were supposed to be coiling thick lines on the deck of the *Delfland*, but Aileen couldn't go long without stopping to stare at the ocean.

"It's beautiful, isn't it?" she said suddenly.

"Hm?" the sailor grunted through his beard.

"The gulf," Aileen said, sweeping her arm toward the horizon. "It goes on forever—and that color! Such an amazing blue."

Now the man paused, wiping his forehead with a dirty rag from his pocket. He stared into the distance for a few seconds, eyes scanning slowly from right to left. Then he shrugged.

"It's just water," he said, returning to the lines.

Aileen turned her face skyward, letting the sun drench it. This was her first time working on a ship, and although her hands ached from the manual labor, the fresh air and the view made it all worthwhile.

She'd convinced the captain to bring her along as an entry-level sailor after a cousin who'd worked for the captain on a smaller, regional freighter had vouched for her. Now, several weeks after clearing Singapore Strait, Aileen was finally starting to feel at ease.

The change of scenery was perfectly timed. For months, Aileen had been feeling dissatisfied with her life, but she couldn't quite put her finger on the reason why. She'd quit her lucrative job as a user experience engineer at the Singaporean tech company ChiangComm, sold everything she could live without, and told herself she was going to try something totally new. A few weeks on a ship to clear her head seemed like just the thing. And she'd always wanted to see the Egyptian pyramids.

"Soh," a voice shouted from behind her. Aileen turned to see the captain waving at her from the ship's bridge. She jogged across the deck and up the stairs to the forecastle, just a few steps below the captain's position.

"Hi, captain. What can I do for you?" Aileen asked.

A burly man with piercing brown eyes and a no-nonsense demeanor, the captain was bent over a map of the *Delfland*.

"Soh, I brought you along even though you have no experience on a ship like this. I thought it might be a problem, but I took a chance. And now I'm glad I did. There are many experienced sailors on my crew, Soh, but I have a task that you, and only you, are qualified for."

"What is it, captain?" Aileen asked. "I'll do anything."

He tapped a section of the map and smiled. "Yes, you will. Do you know what this is?"

Aileen tried to decipher the map labels. "The crew quarters?"

His smile grew larger. "Close. The crew quarters' head."

Aileen knew exactly what that meant but hoped she was wrong. "The head is—"

"—the bathroom, yes," the captain finished. "One of the men isn't feeling well." He shuddered in mock horror. "There's quite a mess. I need you to clean it up."

"But the lines…"

The captain clapped her on the shoulder. "They'll still be there when you get back. You should find a mop in the storage room near the head. Return it when you're done."

As Aileen walked away, the captain called to her.

"Hey, Soh, welcome to the *Delfland*." The captain winked. "Glamorous life of a sailor, eh?"

\*   \*   \*

Several thousand miles away in Singapore, Monir Young walked out of an elevator and into one of the most opulent restaurants he'd ever seen. Demetra Bistro, perched on the rooftop of CapitaGreen at Raffles Place, in Singapore's business district, offered the organic Mediterranean cuisine of a famous Italian chef and spectacular views of Marina Bay.

Monir had been to Singapore a few times. He'd traveled the world in his previous job, as lead negotiator for CORE, a Swiss multinational that was under criminal investigation for the many dark corners its CEO had taken it into. The corner that had been the company's undoing was attempted bribery—specifically, of Cyprus government officials.

Six months before, CORE had sent Monir to Cyprus to secure the rights to an enormously valuable supply of lithium that had been unearthed on the island. A number of foreign groups were vying for it. Kidnapping, conspiracy, and murder were involved. Monir had been approached by Eli and Gina, two high-ranking Israeli intelligence agents who were trying to keep a handle on the situation. After the dust settled, CORE's illegal activities were exposed, and Monir had helped the Israelis do it. The grateful Cyprus government asked him to oversee any and all dealings for the lithium as they decided whom to sell the mineral to.

Now Monir was in Singapore, representing the Cyprus government. He'd always found the people here pleasant and hospitable, and this trip was no exception. He was on his way to meet William Tan, the polite Singaporean official who was overseeing the lithium deal for the Ministry of Trade and Industry. Knowing Monir's enthusiasm for the very best local food, Tan had suggested they meet at Demetra Bistro.

"Monir!" called a voice from across the restaurant lobby. Monir turned and saw William approaching, a smile on his face. They shook hands.

"How was your trip?" William asked. "When did you arrive?"

"Just an hour ago," Monir said. "The flight was uneventful, but Changi is one of the most incredible airports I've ever seen. I was so mesmerized by the *Kinetic Rain* sculpture that I almost missed my driver waiting in the lobby."

William chuckled. "Well, since you're here, shall we eat? It may be early afternoon in Cyprus, but it's dinnertime in Singapore. I asked for a table by the windows." He waved to the maître d', who led them through the main dining room. Monir realized that "by the windows" described nearly all the tables, as the entire outer wall of the restaurant was one continuous piece of glass, affording a panoramic view of Marina Bay Sands, the iconic hotel resort. They sat down and William handed Monir the wine list.

"I understand Cypriot wine is exceptionally good. Has that been your experience?" William asked.

"Yes, I've taken quite a liking to it, and to many other things about Cyprus," Monir replied, scanning the list. "My new wife, for instance, though unfortunately she couldn't be here tonight. How did you know about the wine?"

"Ah yes, you two met during all the commotion with the lithium, did you not? We'll toast your nuptials as soon as we have something to toast with," William said. "We in Singapore try to stay informed about our friends and their tastes. I haven't had the pleasure of trying Cypriot wines, as we don't import them. But I spoke to the *sommelier* earlier and he said he has just the vintage for you. Unless you see something else you'd like to try, of course."

"I'm smart enough to know when to put myself in the hands of a professional." Monir closed the wine list and stood up. "If you'll order the wine, I think I'll go wash up. I still feel grimy from the plane."

As he walked across the dining room, Monir noticed the other patrons for the first time. A young couple was sitting two tables over. The man was sipping a glass of red wine, and the woman was cutting into her steak. Neither spoke. A few tables away from them, two blonde women were waiting for their plates to be cleared. On the far side of the room, ten people sat around a large table, laughing and talking loudly. Monir guessed they were celebrating something. Looking forward to some celebrating of his own, Monir hurried into the bathroom. He was completely unaware that several pairs of eyes had followed him ever since he'd arrived at the restaurant.

On a rooftop fifty meters away, a sniper shifted her rifle slightly to the left, setting her crosshairs on Monir's empty chair and then on the man sitting across from it. The distance made it impossible for her to hear what was said, but the men's expressions and body language let her follow along well enough.

"In position. Assets just arrived." The sniper pressed a finger against her earpiece, waiting for a response.

"Copy," came the reply. "Keep us posted." The sniper moved her face away from the rifle's scope and continued scanning the room with a pair of binoculars. She'd been sent to the stakeout because an attack was imminent. When it happened, it would happen fast. She had to be ready.

\*   \*   \*

Aileen was beginning to regret her new job. Short sailing trips in the waters around Singapore were one thing; being on the *Delfland*'s deck on choppy high seas was another. She'd known vomit would be a factor, but she'd assumed it would be from her own seasickness, not someone else's. Mopping up the last of the floor, she grimaced at her boots and wondered if she'd ever get them clean.

Deep in the belly of the ship, she walked through the crew quarters to the maintenance closet where she'd found the mop. She was hoping to sneak in a quick shower and then return topside to finish with the lines. True sailors showered only once a day, if that often, she guessed, but she wasn't trying to fool anyone. And anyway, she couldn't finish her shift smelling the way she did now.

Aileen was closing up the maintenance closet when she heard a voice behind her. "Aileen Soh."

Turning, she saw an Asian man crouched behind a stairway, partially obscured by shadow.

"Uh, hi," she said. "Who are you?"

The man stood up and walked toward her. In the light, he looked vaguely familiar, but Aileen couldn't place him. He didn't look like a sailor. He was tall and slender with thinning hair. Aileen guessed he was in his fifties.

"You may not remember me, Aileen, but I know you," he said. "My name is Nicholas Tong. In your second year at university, you took a class on emerging technologies and digital ethics."

Aileen thought back to the class. She remembered the professor being a woman, she was sure of it. But as she looked at Tong, she recalled a man in a suit standing to the side of the class, watching the students.

"Have we met?" Aileen asked. "I remember the class—you were observing it, weren't you?"

"No, we never met. Not officially," Tong said. "But I know who you are. I've followed your early career, and I've been impressed by your work."

"Thanks, I guess," she said. "Why have you been doing that? And why are you on the *Delfland?*"

"Aileen, listen to me. We don't have a lot of time," the man said, stepping closer to her. "I used to work for the Singapore government. Part of my job was to identify promising young talent in the field of technology. You were one of the students I had my eye on. You have a great career ahead of you, I'm sure of it. But I need your help."

Aileen looked around. There was no one nearby. "My help? With what?"

Tong held out his left hand. In it was a metal thumb drive sealed in plastic. Aileen noticed that the back of his hand had a circular design tattooed on it. "I need you to take this thumb drive and guard it with your life. I can't tell you why, but please trust me. This drive is very important."

Aileen stepped back. "Whoa, hold on. What are you talking about? What's on that drive?"

"Please, you have to trust me. We don't have much time," Tong said. "Something significant and dangerous is happening in the technology industry, something with implications for the entire world, and I need your help to stop it. If anything happens to me, this drive is our only hope."

Aileen stared at the drive. It looked harmless enough. "This…isn't anything illegal, is it? I've got enough going on as it is. You may have noticed I'm a sailor now."

"Aileen, you and I are on the same side," Tong said. "Please, as a fellow Singaporean, believe me. I'm doing this for our country."

"OK, OK," she said, taking the drive. She put it in her pocket. "But you have to tell me what's going on soon."

"Thank you," Tong said, looking visibly relieved. "Yes, you'll know more before long, I can promise you that." He motioned to the stairs. "I'm sure you have tasks to do on the ship. Let's meet later and I'll explain everything."

"You better," she said. "I'm serious. I don't just accept thumb drives from strangers on the high seas."

"Soon," Tong said. "I promise. We'll share the king of the fruits together."

"King of the what?" Aileen turned to ask Tong what he meant, but he was gone.

\*　　\*　　\*

Monir rejoined William at the table, aerated his wine, and took a sip. "Mmm, very good. My compliments to the professional."

"2013 Penfolds Grange Hermitage. He thought you would like it. I took the liberty of ordering the chef's tasting menu for us as well." William lifted his glass. "Now, a toast—to your lovely new wife, to new friends and new business, and, most of all, to good wine."

"To all of those things," Monir agreed. They clinked glasses.

"Before we talk about the lithium, my superiors asked that I reiterate how pleased they are at the chance to work with Cyprus," William said. "Both nations are islands, commercial centers, tourist destinations, and former British colonies. But my superiors are especially pleased by the Cypriot president's commitment to establishing a corruption-free government. He demonstrated that with the way he handled CORE. As you may know, one of the achievements of our first prime minister, Mr. Lee Kuan Yew, and his cabinet was establishing an honest government. His legacy continues to be upheld by Mr. Lee Hsien Loong, his son, our current prime minister."

"Cyprus is equally pleased about Singapore's involvement," Monir said. "The road to this point was not exactly smooth. There were, to put it lightly, many bumps along the way."

\* \* \*

Climbing the stairs, Aileen heard muffled shouting above her. It continued for several seconds, then was drowned out by an air horn on deck giving three quick blasts. Instantly, sailors started rushing down the stairs toward her. The air horn repeated its cry.

"What's going on?" Aileen asked. She followed the sailors into the crew quarters, where the men were closing doors and securing anything with a lock on it.

"Three horns means pirates!" one shouted. "Lock down everything you can, and get into hiding!" Mind racing, Aileen tried to remember what she'd been told to do in the event of a pirate attack. The captain had said it was possible, though unlikely, for pirates to try to board the *Delfland*, especially near Somalia. They would approach in several small, fast boats and attach homemade ladders to the sides of the ship. Their goal was to take anything they could sell. And they wouldn't hesitate to shoot anyone who got in their way.

Already Aileen could hear boots clanging on the ladders as the sailors scrambled down from above. She looked around frantically, unsure what she should be doing. The room was filling with sailors, many armed with pipes and anything else they could find.

Someone turned the lights off and the room went dark, lit only by the sun drifting down the ladder from above.

Aileen felt her way to the maintenance room, where she grabbed the mop's wooden handle and held it like a club. It wasn't much, but she felt slightly more protected. Now all she could do was wait.

\* \* \*

The sniper glared at Monir and his companion through her scope. The two men clinked wine glasses, oblivious to the danger they were in. At a small table nearby, a man was being seated. He ordered immediately; the waiter wrote on a small notepad and then removed the second place setting. The two blonde women were gathering their phones and pocketbooks, preparing to leave. The sniper looked down at her watch and scribbled "19:45" on a sheet of lined paper, beneath her previous logs of "18:49" and "19:09."

\* \* \*

More shouts sounded from above as someone began descending the ladder, pointing a gun below him. Aileen peered around the maintenance room door.

Dressed all in black, the first pirate in view was Asian and cradled an automatic weapon in his arms. The sailors edged toward him, holding their makeshift weapons aloft. The pirate waved his gun at them and they stopped moving. "Do nothing," he said in English, repeating it in Malay and Mandarin. He shouted something up the ladder and three more pirates jumped down to join him. All three were dressed in black. One more followed them down. Aileen noticed he had a scar over his left eye.

Speaking louder, the first pirate said, "We will hurt you if we have to. Give us what we came for, we leave, and no one dies. Resist us, and things will get ugly very quickly. Everyone line up. Take everything out of your pockets and put it in front of you." He repeated it in the other languages.

Aileen looked on, wide-eyed. Tong had said he didn't have much time. She didn't see him in the room. She could hear sailors swearing as they started emptying their pockets.

"All of you, stand facing the wall," said the pirate. The other three started shoving the sailors against the wall, using their guns to prod anyone who didn't move fast enough. One pirate gathered up the items on the floor and placed them in a large bag. Aileen noticed the man with the scar was standing to the side. He started walking behind the sailors, stopping at each one. Looking through the darkness, Aileen realized the man was holding the sailors' left hands up to the light to inspect them.

\* \* \*

"Of course, we, too, have had our share of trouble already about the lithium," William said.

"What kind of trouble?" Monir asked.

"Mostly threats from different groups. They seemed to sense that we were likely to secure the lithium rights. There have been promises that if the deal goes forward, a number of government officials will be assassinated."

Monir frowned. "What have you done about it?"

"What can we do?" William said, sipping his wine. "The authorities are working on it. We move forward with the deal and hope for the best. Many people are nervous about what the future holds, but luckily nothing has been attempted yet."

The sniper watched a new waiter enter from the kitchen with a tray. "Different server," she said into her earpiece. "Can you check it out?" Using her scope, she looked around the room and waited for her colleague to reply. She watched Monir lean forward, both elbows on the table, while his host talked animatedly, waving his hands in the air. The sniper's crosshairs rested on Monir's chest.

At the other table, the young couple was well into their meal but had stopped eating. Conversation nonexistent between them, the woman stared at the city's skyline beyond the huge window. The man tapped on his phone.

"The dinner shift took over earlier," said the voice in the sniper's ear. "Is this the waiter's first appearance?"

"Yes," said the sniper, lifting the binoculars from the table.

"It could be them. How's the rest of the room?"

"The couple looks bored. The two women left. A man just sat down and ordered."

"My money is on the waiter to make the first move, but you should—"

"Wait!" whispered the sniper, readying her rifle.

\*   \*   \*

The man with the scar reached the last of the sailors and punched the wall in frustration. "What we came for is not here," he said to the other pirates. "Look everywhere." They spread across the room, kicking over chairs and pushing tables away from the walls. As one of them neared the maintenance closet, Aileen tensed, readying her mop handle. She wasn't sure what she could do against a gun. A pirate yanked open the maintenance room door and stuck his gun in Aileen's face.

"Join the others," he said, waving his gun toward the sailors. Aileen did as she was told while the pirates tore the room apart. When the man with the scar was satisfied, he shouted something and the pirates stopped. A new pirate dropped down the ladder and saluted the man with the scar. He leaned in and spoke quietly to the leader.

"No sign of Tong. We've searched the whole ship—he isn't here. And we've taken enough goods to make this look like a pirate attack. We have paint, ropes, personal belongings."

"Fine," said the man with the scar. "Let's go." He waved to the ladder and the pirates climbed up and out of view. "All of you, don't move," he said to the sailors. "We'll be gone very soon. Anyone who moves will die." Pointing his gun at the sailors, he climbed up the ladder.

Aileen had been close enough to overhear the exchange. *Tong isn't on the ship?* she thought. *Then where is he?* A few seconds later, she heard shouting from above. The sailors ran to the ladder and called up. "What's going on?" Aileen asked them. An ear-splitting alarm bell sounded, one Aileen hadn't heard before.

"They're scuttling the ship!" someone shouted. "That's the destruct alarm. The ship's going to explode! Everyone in the water!" The group of sailors began running for the ladder and scrambling up it. Hands grabbed Aileen and pushed her up. The alarm bell continued shrieking. Sailors were sprinting in every direction. A series of loud pops were followed by screams, and Aileen realized the pirates weren't gone yet.

The gunfire continued on the starboard side of the ship. Aileen climbed up to the deck, looking in all directions. Not seeing anyone wearing black, she ran for the port side of the ship. As she reached sight of the water, she saw three smaller boats bobbing at the front of the ship, more black-clad figures on them. The gunfire continued. The alarm bell was shrieking. Sailors were diving into the water as a series of explosions sounded below. Two people dressed in black appeared on the deck. Spotting Aileen, they raised their guns and started firing. She ran for the water, bullets whizzing around her. Aileen had no idea how high above water the deck was, but there was no time to worry about it. Reaching the edge of the ship, she jumped, arms and legs flailing. She heard a huge explosion behind her as she fell, and then she hit the water and everything went black.

\* \* \*

"Ah, our food at last," William said, eyeing an approaching waiter. "Was there a shift change?" he asked. "Someone else was helping us earlier."

"Yes, the dinner staff recently came on," the waiter said, handing them their plates. "May I get you anything else? Would you like more wine?"

"I'll take more," William said. He looked at Monir's half-empty glass. "So will my friend here."

"Right away," the waiter said. "And may I confirm your names for the reservation? You are Monir Young and William Tan, is that correct?"

Monir nodded. "That's us."

The waiter smiled. "Excellent. I will make sure you are taken care of tonight." He clapped his hands twice.

Time slowed to a crawl. Across the room, the couple and the man eating alone rose from their chairs. In one fluid motion, they pulled guns from beneath their tables. Monir stared, frozen to his seat. They pointed the guns in his direction. Monir heard the sound of glass breaking, soft and sharp. Again. A third time. The three diners crumpled to the floor, each with a dark hole in their forehead. The waiter had just enough time to glance at the bodies before glass broke again. Legs buckling beneath him, the waiter sank to the floor. It was over in seconds.

At the large table, several people screamed. Waiters and diners alike ducked beneath the tables for cover. William pulled Monir to the floor. After a long minute of waiting, Monir stood up.

"Monir, be careful!" William said. "It isn't safe!"

"No, I think it's over," Monir replied. "The way he asked our names—I think they were after us. And the way they were killed. Someone's out there. A sniper."

William stood up too. The maître d' was on the phone with the police. Waiters were helping people off the ground and covering the bodies with tablecloths. William looked at the window. Four small holes were punched through the glass. Beyond the window, he could see the lit-up side of Republic Plaza across the block, affording a perfect view into the restaurant.

"And good thing, or we'd both be dead," William said. "I suppose I should take back what I said about nothing being attempted." Seeing Monir still looking across to the next building, he asked, "Any idea who our savior could have been?"

"Maybe. I don't know for sure, but maybe."

"Well, who was it?"

Monir turned to look at William. "A true professional."

The sniper unbolted her weapon from its mount and packed it into a case. She worked quickly but calmly, watching a dozen police officers burst into Demetra Bistro and take up positions within the room.

"Four down. Assets are safe," she muttered into her earpiece. In the restaurant, the police officers were escorting patrons into the lobby.

16

"Nice work," said the voice in her ear. "See you at the rendezvous point."

*   *   *

Aileen awoke in a strange bed. The rocking motion beneath her revealed that she was on a ship. There was a small amount of light coming in through a porthole. Her wet clothes hung on a chair at the foot of the bed.

"Hello," a voice said. Aileen looked to her right. Next to the bed sat a gray-haired man and a woman with blonde hair. The man was smiling pleasantly.

"Where am I?" Aileen asked.

"You're safe," the man said. "You've been out for a while, but you needed to rest. My colleague here helped you into those dry clothes. We picked you up after the pirates left."

"Who are you?"

"My name is Eli, and this is Gina. If you can spare a few minutes, we'd like to talk to you. We need your help."

# 2

# TARGETS

Monir finished giving his statement to the police and walked out to the lobby of Demetra Bistro, where William was sitting on a couch. The other diners were talking to police officers or being served tea by the waiters.

"I can't believe the police response," Monir said to William. "Half the police officers in Singapore must be here."

"I would expect nothing less after an incident like this," said Tan, still shaken. "Such events don't happen here, ever."

"The police are certainly thorough. They questioned me for a while, but I didn't have much to tell them—it happened so fast. Are you all right?"

"I am deeply shocked, Monir. You grew up in the United States, so it may be hard for you to understand. But guns, snipers, murders in a public place—these things are unthinkable for us. Singapore is one of the safest nations in the world." William shook his head. "While the police were questioning you, I spoke with my superiors at the ministry. They are concerned about what this attack could mean. It must be someone trying to sabotage the lithium deal."

"I agree. But Cyprus has pretty much made up its mind to work with Singapore. What could an attack like this accomplish?"

"The usual goals—spreading fear. Making people afraid of the places they go every day. But there may be other motives."

William's face had a grim expression. "You are a central part of the lithium agreement, but I'm afraid that I am rather replaceable, as far as the deal goes. I can't flatter myself by thinking I was the target."

"I'm not sure I want that honor either," Monir said. "There's already been so much trouble around the lithium. I was looking forward to a nice, quiet resolution to it all."

William motioned to the bodies of their attackers, which the police were wheeling past them to the elevators. "They and whoever sent them had something else in mind. You told the police you don't know anything? I thought you had an idea of who saved us."

"Only the barest hint of an idea," Monir said, "and maybe less than that." He thought back to the events of six months before. "There is…someone I met in Cyprus when the lithium was discovered. He is a resourceful man. It may be wishful thinking, but the way we were saved…" He shrugged. "I don't know. Let me look into it before I say anything else."

"Very well. Get some rest, and we can meet at my office in the morning. We'll visit there for a bit, and if the timing works out, I will introduce you to some of the ministry's executives. Then I'll take you to Toast Box for breakfast. Even in these dark circumstances, you are my guest, and everyone should have a Toast Box experience in Singapore." William gave a small smile, and then continued in a serious tone. "Monir, you're an interesting man. I'm glad you, and your mysterious friend, are on our side."

\*   \*   \*

The sniper exited Republic Plaza from a side entrance and turned north toward the Raffles Place mass rapid transit station. Wearing a loose-fitting sweat suit, she walked at a moderate pace. Her long blonde hair, pulled back in a ponytail, was bouncing against the black-and-blue Wilson tennis backpack she had strapped on after leaving her stakeout. A tennis racket was poking out to fool any onlookers. Her earpiece was still in place, safely tucked inside her ear canal. It crackled momentarily and a voice spoke into her head.

"Car Two, do you copy?"

A half-smirk formed on the sniper's face before she responded. Even now, at the end of the operation, she still found the team's code names amusing. "Almost there, Car One," she whispered, bending to tie her shoe.

"Copy. Change of plan—police are moving into all MRT stations in the area. Take a cab. Meet us at the rendezvous point in an hour, over."

"Roger. Over and out."

A cab pulled up and the sniper got in. She called out the address and set her bag next to her, politely turning down the driver's offer to stow it in the trunk. The driver headed southeast for Marina Coastal Expressway. The sniper drifted into an internal debriefing session, retracing her steps from the moment she'd entered the building. Then she replayed the shooting. The waiter, the guns in the room, four kills, no cameras…and Monir Young. In her mind, things had gone as well as possible. Now for the official debriefing and a day or two of rest.

As the driver took the bend in the road where the Marina Coastal Expressway turned into the Ayer Rajah Expressway, the sniper looked to her left. It was her first glimpse of Singapore's massive port. Numerous ships were dockside and dozens of cranes were at various stages of the loading and unloading process. Stacks of colorful containers were scattered throughout Brani Terminal. The sniper mused that they resembled her nieces' Lego sets.

"They're moving this whole thing," the driver said, waving his hand around. "Building a huge new port on the reclaimed land by Tuas Bay."

The sniper momentarily met the man's eyes in his rear-view mirror, and then feigned a look down at her phone to check for messages. She could care less where they were moving the port.

\*   \*   \*

Jun Ai Boon alighted from her cab outside the Singapore Police Force headquarters on New Bridge Road and climbed the steps to the front entrance of Block C, the Criminal Investigation Department. Catching a glimpse of herself in the glass door before she swung it open, she nervously adjusted her jacket and ran her fingers through her hair. The twenty-seven-year-old had worked in Major Crime Division, specifically casino crimes investigation, and had handled a few difficult cases during her four years on the force. But none of them had even come close to the gravity of a mass shooting. With the exceptions of the 2006 murder of a nightclub owner by a single assailant and a handful of incidents involving air rifles, gun crimes were not just nonexistent in the Lion City; they were unthinkable. Firearms and ammunition were strictly prohibited. Violators faced the death penalty.

Jun cleared lobby security and swiped her ID by a metal door to enter the office complex. Her orders were to report straight to Director Phang Seng Low before the evening briefing. She approached the elevator doors and nodded to colleagues who were waiting. No one spoke, but everyone's faces wore the same expression: It would be a bad night at work.

\*   \*   \*

Aileen sat with Eli and Gina in the galley of their ship, ravenously eating a plate of boiled chicken and vegetables in silence. She tried to ask them questions from time to time, but they hushed her and insisted that she eat. She was too hungry to argue. When she'd finished, Eli leaned forward.

"Now, what would you like to know?"

"Where to begin?" Aileen said. "Where am I? Where are we going? How do I get home? Who are you people?"

Eli looked at her thoughtfully. "To answer in order, you're on a ship called the *Zen Shanghai*, south of Oman in the Arabian Sea. Where we're headed depends on you. We will take you home whenever you wish, but we hope you'll help us with something before you go. My name is Eli and this is Gina."

"I know your names, but who *are* you?" Aileen asked. "How did I get on this ship?"

"We're friends, Aileen," said Gina, "or we'd like to be your friends. We think we can offer you an opportunity that will interest you. In return, we'll ask you to consider working with us for a time. You're free to say no, of course, and we'll help you get home either way. As for how we found you in the water, that's simple. We were following you."

"You were *what*?" said Aileen. "Look, I want some answers. What's going on? Why were you following me? For how long?"

Eli raised his palms in surrender. "I understand this is confusing for you, Aileen, but we can't tell you exactly what's going on, because we ourselves don't know. Here is what we do know." He counted on his fingers. "One, cyber warfare, mass surveillance, and privacy are among the most pressing issues in the world today, with implications for global peace. Two, my job is to protect that peace. Three, you have an impressive background in the technology industry. You have skills and knowledge we do not."

"So you're in the military?" Aileen asked. "Which country?"

"Not exactly. Four, a great deal of lithium is about to be sold from Cyprus to Singapore, and the ripple effects in industry and technology could affect the balance of power in the world. Five, certain groups would like to have a say in how that happens." Eli stood up and walked across the galley. "Would you like some water?" He filled three glasses and brought them back to the table. "Those are the things I know. I also know those things are connected to each other. What I don't know is how. That is where you come in."

"Secret agents. You're secret agents, aren't you?" Aileen said. "You don't sound American or English or Russian. Do other countries even have secret agents?"

"That's as good a name for our job as any," Eli said. "As for our origins, we'll get to that. All in good time."

"You said you need my help. There's no way I'm helping you if I don't know who you work for. I'm not stupid, and treason isn't high on my to-do list."

"Of course. Let me tell you about the opportunity—"

"No. No more evasions. Who do you work for?"

Gina spoke up. "Aileen, there are things we can't tell you just yet, but the answers are coming, I promise you. Let's try this a different way. What happened on your ship? How did you end up here with us?"

"I was trying to get away from my life for a few weeks. Being attacked by pirates isn't what I had in mind, but it's definitely a new experience."

"What about the pirates?"

"They boarded the ship and started grabbing whatever they could find. That's all I know. I was busy trying not to get shot."

"Were they just looting, or were they looking for anything or anyone in particular?"

The question jolted Aileen's memory. "Wait, yes! I overheard a conversation between two of the pirates. One seemed to be the leader. They were looking for a man. The weird thing is, I know him, sort of. I talked to him just before the pirates showed up."

Gina and Eli exchanged a look. "Who was it? The captain? The first officer?"

"No, he was—" Aileen couldn't help laughing. "This is going to sound ridiculous, but it was someone who used to work for the Singapore government. He once observed a class I took. I have no idea what he was doing on the ship. What was his name…"

"Nicholas Tong," Eli said. "He had a circular tattoo on his left hand, yes?"

Aileen looked at Eli and Gina in disbelief. "Yeah. How on earth did you know?"

Eli smiled again. "We'll get to that, too. It's a bit complicated, I'm afraid."

\*    \*    \*

Jun knocked on the director's door and waited to be called in. She had met the man very briefly on two occasions—the ceremony that followed her Police Academy graduation and her first day on the job at Major Crime Division. The director was known for being quiet and introverted; he was also known for being ruthless with underperforming officers. Jun was wondering if he would remember her.

Low's authoritative voice interrupted her thoughts. "Enter."

Jun opened the door. "You called for me, Director?"

Low motioned for her to sit. "Officer Ai Boon, the night of your graduation, I presented you with the Cadet of the Year award, correct?"

"Yes, sir."

"And you were assigned to Major Crime due to the recommendation of the division's supervisor, a man I esteem as one of my most trusted colleagues." Low watched Jun, his eyes indicating he was waiting for a response. She nodded.

He looked down at a file on his desk, leafing through a stack of papers. "Just before 20:00, our force and nation suffered an unprecedented blow." He looked up at Jun. "Four dead, three carrying guns and multiple clips—by early indications, assassins from China. They were taken out within a few seconds by a sniper from across the street."

"I read the report in the cab on the way here, sir. It's terrible."

"Jun Ai Boon, it's time for you to prove yourself worthy of the award and your supervisor's trust. I am placing you in charge of the investigation. You have all the resources of the Singapore Police Force at your disposal. You report directly to me."

"I'm honored, sir, and happy to serve, but I have never led an investigation of this magnitude before."

"No one has, Officer Ai Boon, no one. I'm going to address everyone in there," he said, pointing in the direction of the assembly hall, "and I will name you as point on this investigation. Don't let me down. We have a shooter at large—we must start there. Find that sniper. Be sure to coordinate with our analysts who are looking into the victims. And figure out the connection to the government official who was dining with the man from Cyprus. Were they the targets of the assassins? If so, why did a sniper protect them? What's behind all this? Officer Ai Boon, we must cleanse our city of this bloody stain."

# 3
# PUZZLE PIECES

Aileen exhaled and sat back in her seat. "Nicholas Tong. OK. I have a whole new set of questions for you. Starting with, Tong was on the boat, and then he wasn't. Was that your handiwork?"

Gina nodded. "We got him off the boat before the pirates arrived. As you said, it was a bit ridiculous that he was on the *Delfland* at all. So it shouldn't be a surprise for you to learn he was there to help us."

"To help you with what?" asked Aileen.

Eli cocked his head to one side. "To help us meet you."

Aileen waved her hands around, trying to find the words for everything she wanted to ask. "Look, pirates, secret agents, random people from my past who vanish from boats…what is all this? What's going on?"

Now Gina spoke. "Aileen, as we said, there's a growing threat to global security. That isn't new. But right now we're still trying to figure out the full extent of the threat. Think of it like a puzzle—we've gathered some of the pieces. The lithium deal is one, this situation with Tong is another. You might be one yourself."

"Me?" Aileen said. "How?"

"But until we know how the pieces fit together," Gina continued, "we can't see the full picture, so we can't stop what's happening. That's why we need you."

"Need me for what?"

"Finding more puzzle pieces. Do you know Frontfacer?"

"The social network that half the world uses? Yeah, I think I've heard of it."

"What do you know about it?"

"Everyone and their dog has an account. It's one of the biggest companies in Silicon Valley, probably the world. It hooks up to mobile payments, games, pictures, chatting, everything. For a lot of people, it's their entire digital life."

A small smile spread across Eli's lips. "Have you ever thought about working there?"

The question surprised Aileen. "Well, sure, who in tech hasn't? It's a dream job. Why?"

"Then why haven't you applied?"

"I guess I never thought I would move to Silicon Valley. It's kind of far away, and my life is in Singapore. What are you getting at?" Aileen said.

"You have an interview there, if you want it. Next week with the head of human resources. It's a job I think you'll enjoy."

Aileen stared at him. "An interview? How? They must get hundreds of applications a month."

"They do," Gina said. "But only one from someone with your unique skill set, for a certain unique opportunity. Don't worry, it's a job you'll excel at. The application was based entirely on your impressive qualifications. You certainly could have gotten this interview without our help. We simply hurried things along because we're short on time."

"This is crazy!" Aileen said. "I'm supposed to trust you two? And even if somehow I did, I can't just leave my life here. My family is here, my friends."

"I understand, Aileen—you don't know us. We're strangers, you and Gina and I," said Eli. "But think about it this way: You were already looking for a change. We were hoping this would be one that interests you. You're free to turn it down, but I hope you'll think about it."

"You haven't told me what the point is," Aileen said. "Why are you doing all this?"

Eli cleared his throat. "Given our jobs, Gina and I, we like to keep an eye on things. That's more or less what we do, keep an eye on things."

"More or less," Gina echoed, amused.

Eli continued. "One of the things we're trying to keep an eye on is the technology industry. It's changing unimaginably fast, changing at a rate that no one could have imagined a decade ago. We need to know where it's going and how it affects our work." Eli's eyes were focused on something beyond Aileen, remembering. He looked slightly sad. "There was…an event a few months ago. I can't tell you exactly what happened, but we…we weren't as prepared as we should have been. Things went badly. We can't be unprepared next time, and that starts with us having more friends who know a thing or two about the tech industry."

"That's a bit vague," Aileen said, "but I think I get your point."

"All that said, remember the puzzle? Another piece of it is Frontfacer," Gina said. "We don't know what the connection is yet, but somehow there is a link from the company to the pirates, Tong, and the lithium. We'd like you to be a secret agent for us and find out."

Aileen's voice was skeptical. "What does a social network have to do with pirates?"

"Even pirates use the internet," Eli said. "It may sound outlandish, but our information is reliable. We simply need to figure out what the connection is."

Aileen was quiet for a while, thinking. "When did you say the interview is?"

Eli clasped his hands together and leaned forward. "Next week. We'll book a ticket for you. Of course, you're free to decline."

"You keep saying that. If nothing else, this is a great story you're telling me," Aileen said. "And my friends in Singapore will be so jealous when I tell them I was on the Frontfacer campus." Shifting in her seat, she felt the thumb drive in her pocket. "But wait. You never said what Tong has to do with it."

"We told you we need friends who know about technology. We, and some other friends of ours, were helping Tong...escape from something, let's say. In return, he pointed us to you. He thought we," Eli pointed to himself and then Gina, "and you could help each other."

"Just to be perfectly clear, this hasn't gotten less ridiculous," Aileen said. She took a deep breath. "Can I think about it? More important, will you throw me overboard if I say no?"

Gina raised her hand in an oath. "We promise not to throw you overboard. And of course you can think about it. Take as long as you need."

"But not too long," Eli said. "Gina and I are patient people, but the rest of the world is moving rather quickly."

\*    \*    \*

Back on his ship, Kong Li, the pirate with the scar over his eye, was pacing up and down on the bridge, furious about his dual failures in the Gulf of Aden and the Singapore restaurant. He was also nervous, a rare feeling for him. He knew that failure had consequences, especially when one answered to individuals such as Zhang Wei.

Li knew little about Wei's wealth and influence, which were both considerable, as far as Li could tell. What he did know was that Wei had a role in the Chinese government that was related to the country's technology sector. Wei had declined to tell him any details, but he seemed desperate to organize a deal for some lithium that Cyprus was selling. Asking around, Li had discovered that Wei had once held an important position in the government, but a series of bad decisions and worse luck had seen Wei fall from prominence. Li guessed he was intending to use the lithium to buy his way back into the government's good graces. Usually Li didn't get involved with people he knew so little about, but his criminal activities afforded him an expensive lifestyle—cars, wine, watches, prostitutes, and an unending supply of prescription drugs—and the mind-boggling amount of money Wei had promised him from the lithium's proceeds had won him over.

Li had also been warned about Wei's explosive temper. He hadn't had occasion to see it yet, and he didn't intend to anytime soon. Walking to the ship's intercom, he barked an order for his men to join him on the bridge. He had to right his mistakes, and soon—otherwise he might see Wei's temper after all.

\*   \*   \*

Jun lost no time. Within minutes of her briefing with Director Low, she had selected a small group of police officers to assist her in the field. She sent two of them back to the CapitaGreen building with orders to obtain all surveillance footage available from that property and nearby buildings. "The sniper left us with nothing at the Republic Plaza perch except for gunpowder residue. That means the shooter would have gone to the streets shortly after the incident with some kind of bag or case containing all his equipment. Get the feed and go over it in detail. I want close-ups of everyone walking or entering cabs with a bag or backpack, even cased musical instruments. We start there."

She waved to the other two officers to follow her and walked to the elevators.

"Where are we going?" asked one, a young male officer.

"Back to the restaurant, to examine every centimeter of it again. The attackers may have left something that could help us. We are going to need all the information we can get."

\* \* \*

Kong Li stood on the highest point of the ship's bridge, towering over his men. Some of them stared back defiantly; others were trying not to let their fear show.

Li's reputation was well known in Southeast Asia's criminal underworld. Born in China but raised in Kuala Lumpur, Li had started his criminal career early. His intelligence had made him bored in school, so he'd begun looking for other ways to amuse himself. Before long, he'd developed impressive skills as a pickpocket and petty thief, which, along with his good looks and charisma, had attracted the notice of the city's gangs, including the notorious Heavenly Kings.

A man named Kali, one of the Heavenly Kings, took a liking to Li and trained him. Li learned how to run teams of loan sharks and money launderers. He oversaw illegal gaming operations and was trusted by Kali to handle debt collections. After a turf war with a rival gang, during which he'd picked up a long scar over his eye, Li surrounded himself with bodyguards. He also began carrying a handgun anywhere he went. The penalty for possessing a firearm in Malaysia was death by hanging. But between being caught with a gun by the police and being caught defenseless by another gang, Li preferred his chances with the police.

"What the hell happened?" Li asked, anger in his voice. "We tracked Nicholas Tong to that ship after he ran from China. His own e-mails told us he was going to hide at his brother's house in Morocco. So how the hell did he disappear in the middle of the ocean?"

The gang members were silent, looking at each other. Finally, one spoke up. "Kong Li, you were there too. If Tong was ever on the *Delfland*, he was gone before we arrived."

"Are you saying this is my fault?" Li's voice was dark with menace. He took a few steps toward the man, putting their faces centimeters apart. "This is *your* fault. Do you understand? *You* must find Tong, or believe me, when it comes time for Mr. Wei to direct his rage, it won't be at me."

"But…you supplied our information," the man protested. "We were only following your orders."

Li looked at him for a long moment. In one swift motion, he grabbed the man by the neck and slammed his head into the wall, face first. The man stumbled backward, dazed. Li kicked his leg out, throwing the man to the floor, and then climbed on top of him, taking the man's head in his hands and slamming it into the deck until blood was spattered everywhere.

Li got up, wiped his hands on his pants, and looked at the rest of the gang. "Here are my orders. Find Nicholas Tong. All our setbacks are erased if we can produce Tong. I'll be speaking with Mr. Wei soon. I'll have fresh intelligence, and we'll get another chance at this. Do not fail me again."

The gang members nodded vigorously. "We won't fail you, Kong Li. We promise."

# 4

# LITHIUM KINGS

The next morning, Monir arrived at the Ministry of Trade and Industry's headquarters on High Street promptly at 9:00. William Tan's department was responsible for establishing and maintaining relationships with the various countries under its geographical purview. He had led the department for three years, rising to the post after twenty-three years at the ministry. The projects he had taken on had been fruitful, but the lithium deal promised to surpass them all. It was an extraordinary opportunity—for William, the department, and Singapore.

The lobby receptionist buzzed that William had a guest, and he walked quickly out of his third-floor office to meet Monir. William was out of the elevator before the doors had fully opened, his eyes searching for Monir, who was waiting in the easternmost corner of the vast lobby.

"Monir, good morning! We'll go up to my floor." Tan signed in his guest at reception, handed Monir a visitor pass, and led him to the elevators.

After a few minutes of small talk and a brief tour, Monir and William were alone in the office. Monir jumped into the most pressing subject. "I've been thinking about the attack," he said, "and about who could have been behind it."

"Any revelations?" William asked.

"Not exactly. I keep coming back to asking myself who benefits if the deal between Cyprus and Singapore is sabotaged. Who stands to gain from it?"

"That is the obvious question," William agreed. "There haven't been any other offers for the lithium, have there? Any other groups expressing interest?"

"Not since CORE. Maybe the point isn't who wants the lithium for themselves, but who doesn't want Singapore to get it. If you had to guess, who would that be?" Monir asked.

William took a sip of the tea an aide had brought in. He seemed to be formulating his answer.

"Singapore has had strong competitors and economic adversaries from the moment it was declared an independent nation in 1965. In the early years, Mr. Lee Kuan Yew—we often refer to him as LKY—and his administration faced enormous economic challenges from Malaysia and Indonesia, nations that had vast natural resources and strong economic alliances in the region, unlike Singapore.

"As LKY once put it, we were merely a 'little red dot' on the map. It took much diplomacy and exceptional leadership acumen for our tiny nation to gain a geopolitical foothold through trade agreements. Over a period of about four decades, Malaysia and Indonesia came around to working with us. Thailand, the Philippines, Myanmar, and Cambodia followed. And, eventually, China."

Monir noted how William lowered his voice when talking about the last country. He wanted to know what it meant.

"When you mention China, it almost sounds like…"

Tan raised his hand and looked around, indicating the need for discretion. His voice still low, he continued. "It's complicated, Monir. No other country has had a greater influence on Singapore's political development than China, the ancestral origin of more than half our population. The same applies to the economic sector. China has been a major force to consider for a very long time now."

Monir settled back in his chair, listening intently. He nodded for William to go on.

"The LKY administration led our nation with strong core values and insight into where things were heading technologically."

"What do you mean by 'core values'?"

"All Singaporean government agencies hail three attributes as their motto: integrity, service, and excellence. Everything that has been established from the late 1950s onward has been built on them. They are featured prominently on government websites and letterhead."

"I see. And what of Mr. Lee's role?"

"For many years, Mr. Lee emphasized the need for Singapore to establish strong trade ties with nations that produce raw materials for the manufacture of technology components. Long before laptops, flat-screen TVs, cell phones, and tablets, he saw it all coming. China had the raw materials we desperately needed to build our nation, namely crude oil. We had the precedent of successful infrastructure, along with progressive and brilliant minds that were making huge advances in technology. Through numerous state visits over the next few decades, Mr. Lee established strong, complex economic ties with China."

"Complex in what way?"

It was clear that William did not want to say much more. He grimaced, looking out his window. "China's political structure made technological advancement—*all* advancement, for that matter—slow and very difficult."

"This is very helpful, William," said Monir. "I'd like to learn as much about Singapore's history as you can teach me."

William continued, visibly reluctant. "At a Beijing summit in 1988, LKY was asked by General Secretary Zhao Ziyang for assistance with China's backward technology. The two administrations found their way to an amicable trade agreement. Millions of barrels of crude oil and lithium ore came our way from China, and Singapore provided expertise and investment opportunities for the Chinese. With the know-how gap narrowing due to Singapore's input, the Chinese turned their attention to exploiting their natural resources, while also acquiring foreign raw materials to boost their technology sector.

"Then, six months ago, Cyprus discovered its vast supplies of lithium, one of the most important minerals in tech manufacturing. In many ways, that has been the potential game-changer, Monir. The country with Cyprus's lithium could become the dominant technological country in Asia."

They had finally arrived where Monir had suspected they were heading all along. "William, are you saying China might have something to do with the shooting?"

"I'm not saying anything that would pin the events of last night on the Chinese government—I must make that clear. But we do have reason to believe there may be elements within the Chinese system that would pursue the lithium deal independently. That's why we need answers about last night's shooting, Monir. Have you had a chance to talk to your mysterious friend?"

"Er, no," Monir said, pondering the things he had just heard. "He's a little hard to get ahold of. But I'm guessing it won't be long before I hear from him."

"This friend only gets more intriguing," William said. "I look forward to knowing more about him."

"Have you heard from the police today? Do they have any leads about who was behind the attack?"

"No. They said they will inform me when they know something," William said. "But here's an even better question, one I hope you'll be able to help me answer: Who was the sniper that saved us?"

\*    \*    \*

Kong Li was in a car and headed to Zhang Wei's private plane at Djibouti-Ambouli International Airport. His ship had reached land a few hours before, and he was preparing to fly back to China to search for clues to how Nicholas Tong had vanished and where he had gone.

Li had been putting off calling Wei, hoping to have something besides bad news to report when he did. His men were working on it, but Li knew he couldn't delay any longer. Wei did not like to be kept waiting.

Pulling out his phone, Li dialed Wei's assistant, who answered immediately and asked him to hold for Wei. He felt the seconds tick by, heavy with dread.

"So, Kong Li, you finally had time to call me," Wei said.

"Mr. Wei, I am sorry for not phoning sooner. I only now got back to land and did not have cellular service on the ocean."

"I see. Please, tell me what is happening, if now is convenient for you."

"Yes, Mr. Wei. We are still searching for Nicholas Tong. He escaped from us on the ship. Some of my men are confirming that he was indeed onboard. Two others are going to see what information Tong's brother in Morocco has. The rest are following leads that may be useful. I myself am coming back to China to talk to Tong's colleagues at the project. One of them might know something."

"No, Kong Li. Tong was Singaporean. You are more useful to me in his home country. Find out who knew him, talk to anyone you can—friends, family, former coworkers. Tong can do tricks with computers, but he is not a magician. He must have had help to disappear. My assistants will follow up with Tong's associates in China. I have trained them to be quite persuasive."

"Very good, Mr. Wei. I will get in touch when I am in Singapore."

"See that you do, Kong Li. You were recommended to me as a man who knew how to get things done. The information Tong has could be very damaging to me. In the unlikely event that he succeeds in escaping, please do not make the mistake of thinking that you yourself will escape from what comes next."

\*   \*   \*

The interviewer looked up from her notepad and leveled her gaze at the man sitting across the table from her.

"Adrian Valencik, thank you for joining us tonight. You're the head of one of the biggest technology companies on the planet. You started Frontfacer after dropping out of Harvard, and a decade later the company has evolved from a social network into the central hub of our digital lives. Your stock price is at an all-time high, investors love you, and there can't be too many people left who don't use your services in one form or another. What's next for you and Frontfacer?"

The man put his hands on the table and cleared his throat. "You're too kind, Joan, as always. Frontfacer is doing well, yes, but we're only just getting started. The truth is, it's taken us more than ten years to get to the scale where we can do what I think we're really meant to do."

"What is that?"

"I want to save the world."

Joan gestured to the television camera pointed at them.

"A strong statement, to be sure. For our viewers at home, can you explain how a social network plans to save the world? Save it from what?"

The CEO's voice became a practiced blend of warmth and authority. "Joan, 'social network' is an outdated term. In the early days—MySpace, Facebook, Tumblr—we were all crawling around in the dark, figuring out what it meant for people to be connected by the internet. Fast forward to now, and we know a whole lot more than we used to."

He used his hands to articulate his words. "With Frontfacer, everything you need to do can be done in one place. Talking to your friends and family, ordering groceries, paying your bills, calling a car to pick you up—we're helping people do more, and do it faster and more easily. You hardly ever need to get off your phone."

"Unless you want to walk around outside," Joan said, winking.

"Don't worry, we're working on that, too," Valencik said, and the interviewer laughed. "But seriously, Joan, the internet is a sweeping force for change, especially in impoverished and developing parts of the world. Most people still don't have access to the internet, which means the world is missing out on what those people, and their children, might achieve."

"Which is where Frontfacer comes in," Joan said.

"Exactly. As we expand our reach worldwide, we can bring access, information, and convenience to everyone, no matter where they live. That's our goal, to see the future and to take everyone into it together."

Joan's voice took on a cautious note. "What about reports that—just like Google, Facebook, and Uber before you—Frontfacer is struggling to break into China, the next great market?"

Valencik didn't hesitate. "China is a challenge, of course it is. Their internet is walled off from ours, and their government supports local companies over Western ones. But that just means we have to work a little harder to prove our value. In fact, my most recent talks with the Chinese government have been very encouraging. I have every confidence that before long we'll be working hand in hand with China to create the future."

"One more question." Joan tapped a pen against her glasses. "Is there any truth to the rumors swirling about you and Stalker, the media gossip website? Some people claim that you secretly funded the libel lawsuit that bankrupted Stalker, all because of some articles it published a few years ago that were critical of you."

Valencik rolled his eyes in a show of annoyance. "I think you've answered your own question, Joan. There are internet rumors about everything. If there were any truth to them, they wouldn't be rumors, would they?"

"Well said, Adrian, well said." Joan faced the camera. "And that's all the time we have tonight, folks. Adrian, thanks so much for being here."

Valencik waved to the camera. "Joan, thank you."

"We're out," someone yelled, and Valencik's assistant hurried over, clutching a phone.

"Adrian, news from the project," she said, motioning him to follow her. She turned and walked away from the camera crew, Valencik right behind her. When they had some privacy, she handed him the phone, web browser open to a *New York Times* article. The headline read: "Four Dead in Singapore Restaurant Shooting."

Valencik looked at his assistant. "*Four* dead?"

"And none of them are Monir Young," she replied.

"What happened?" Valencik asked. "Police?"

She shook her head. "Details are still coming out, but it seems a sniper killed them before they could kill Young. I haven't been able to get Zhang Wei on the phone."

Valencik gritted his teeth in irritation. "This is going to draw too much attention. I told them. I *told* them."

"What do you want to do?" the assistant asked.

The CEO thought for a moment, thumbing through the *Times* article. "Tell Kong Li I need to talk to his boss at the first opportunity. Then find out who's in charge of the lithium for Cyprus." He handed the phone back to her. "Now we speed up my half of the plan."

# 5

# THE SUMMONS

Monir awoke late the next morning to his phone buzzing urgently on the nightstand. Reaching across the bed, he swiped to answer. "Hello?"

"Monir, it's Christakis Savvides from the Ministry of Commerce." It took a moment for Monir to place the caller. Then the name and thick accent sunk in.

"Oh, hi, Christakis. What time is it there?"

"Earlier than I usually wake up," Savvides replied, "but something has happened." We need you on the next flight back to Cyprus. There's a plane leaving Singapore for Dubai in a few hours. Then a connection to Larnaca will get you here the next morning."

Blinking sleep from his eyes, Monir looked at his watch. "I have meetings in Singapore the rest of this week about the lithium. What's so urgent?"

"Cancel them. Tell Singapore there's a family situation and you need to return home. It'll keep them from worrying, and I'm guessing Stalo won't mind seeing you."

"Why would Singapore worry? What's happened?"

"Just get back here, Monir. We'll fill you in once you arrive. The entire lithium deal could be at stake."

\* \* \*

Jun was at William Tan's office to talk to him about the shooting. She needed to ask him a number of questions about the events at Demetra Bistro, but she reminded herself to be especially courteous and gentle, taking into consideration Tan's shock from the incident.

Jun's first question was about Tan's relationship to Monir.

"I don't know him very well," Tan explained. "The two of us met for the first time on the night of shooting. We were beginning negotiations between Singapore and Cyprus for a large quantity of lithium."

"Do you have any thoughts about the motive behind the attack? Could it be connected to this lithium?"

"Yes, I expect so. The people sent to harm us were most likely trying to shut down the talks."

"How did they know where you would be meeting?"

"My only guess is they accessed my or Monir's e-mails. That is how we communicated to set everything up."

Jun took notes. "The sniper who killed your would-be assassins—is there anything you can tell me?"

"If I understood him, Monir said he has a faint idea of who it might be. He described the person as a very resourceful man."

"That could be anyone, Mr. Tan. Have you spoken to Monir since then?"

"Yes, but only about business. The last I heard from Monir was this morning. He called from Changi to inform me that he was flying back to Cyprus urgently."

"Monir left Singapore? Without telling us?" Jun demanded.

"Oh, I did not realize he hadn't told you. He told me he was going back for a family emergency."

Jun cursed under her breath, wrote a note for herself, and underlined it: *Sniper? Motive? Resourceful man? Talk to Monir Young.*

\*   \*   \*

The next day, Monir landed in Cyprus, his curiosity burning. Savvides had refused to tell him anything until they could talk in person, which intrigued and worried Monir—intrigued because whatever was going on had to be big, and worried because it clearly involved the lithium. He'd spent the trip thinking through the possibilities. Cyprus and Singapore had informally agreed to exchange the lithium's mining rights for payment to be determined; all that was left was figuring out exactly what the mineral was worth. What was significant enough to interfere with that? His mind kept returning to his conversation with William Tan about Singapore's place in the world.

A driver who was waiting at the arrivals hall in Larnaca drove Monir straight to the Ministry of Energy, Commerce, Industry, and Tourism in Nicosia, the capital. At the ministry, Monir ran up the stairs to the second floor and burst into Savvides's office. He dropped his bag on the floor and said, "All right, Christakis, what on earth is happening?"

"Thanks for coming so promptly, Monir," Christakis said, as cheerful as ever. "We didn't think it was wise to talk about this over unsecure phones, or in Singapore at all."

"Well, what is it?" Monir asked impatiently. "What did I just travel halfway around the world for?"

"Something very strange has happened. We aren't sure what it means. We'd like you to investigate it."

"Christakis, if you make me wait any longer, they may be investigating your untimely death."

Savvides grinned. "OK, Monir. Do you know who Adrian Valencik is?"

Monir frowned. "The CEO of that Frontfacer company? Sure, I know him. Why?"

"We received a phone call from Frontfacer's assistant, a woman named Siena, saying that Valencik wants to meet with you about the lithium deal."

"The lithium?" Monir said. "What's Frontfacer's interest?"

"That's just it—we don't know. She wouldn't tell us what Valencik wants to talk about. All we know is he wants to speak with the negotiator to Singapore. He mentioned you by name."

"That's odd. I wonder how he knows me," Monir said. "When does he want to meet? Where?"

Savvides winced. "He wants you to come to their headquarters in California. Silicon Valley."

Monir felt a pit forming in his stomach. Although he was originally from the United States, he hadn't set foot there in a very long time, for two reasons. First, he felt that the country no longer held anything worth returning for. Second, he believed that going back would put his life in danger.

Savvides continued laying out the plan, oblivious to Monir's reaction. "Valencik's people were very eager to talk to you. He says he'll make it worth our time. Don't worry, Monir, the meeting isn't for a few days, so you can rest up. Spend some time with your wife."

"Why did you bring me back to Cyprus to tell me this? You couldn't have told me over the phone?" Monir said, irritated at the turn of events.

"We thought it would be best to keep this situation quiet," Savvides said. "The pending lithium deal between us and Singapore is publicly known. Of course other parties are still interested, and there are eyes and ears everywhere. And now the billionaire CEO of one of the world's largest technology companies asks to talk with you about it. No matter what he wants, we should hear what he has to say. Who knows? Maybe Frontfacer wants to buy the lithium."

"I thought the government decided Singapore is the partner they want," said Monir. "Things didn't end so well the last time a company was involved."

"Ah, but CORE wasn't a company worth over $200 billion dollars," Savvides said. "Look, Monir, it's just a meeting, and even your skeptical nature has to admit the situation is interesting. Meet the man, hear him out, and report back to us. Simple. Maybe we move forward with Singapore and no one is the wiser. Or maybe we—but let's not get ahead of ourselves."

Monir sighed and picked his bag up from the floor. He descended the flight of stairs and headed to the cab that was waiting outside. The memories of his past had broken through; he couldn't push them away now. *Silicon Valley, here I come*, he thought.

\* \* \*

On the deck of the *Zen Shanghai*, Aileen watched the Cyprus coastline slowly come into view. She heard footsteps behind her and turned to see Gina approaching.

"Pretty view, isn't it?" Gina said, nodding in the direction of Limassol, Cyprus's largest port city.

"It isn't the vacation I was planning, but it's not bad," Aileen said. "I guess my career as a sailor is over. What happens now?"

Gina leaned against the railing and looked out at the water. "Now you interview for a job at a tech company that many people would kill to work for. You have a few days to look around Cyprus first, if you wish."

"Are you from Cyprus?" Aileen asked.

"No, but I've spent some time here," Gina said. "A few months ago I was on the island for work. I can suggest a few places to see. What do you like to do?"

"That's sort of what I'm trying to figure out. In my life generally, I mean. That's why I was going to Egypt. I thought being someplace new would be a break from everything. I thought maybe I'd travel for a while, do things I don't do, be someone other than myself." Aileen looked at Gina. "Does that make any sense?"

Gina nodded. "It sounds like you're feeling aimless."

"I don't know if aimless is exactly it. It's more…do you ever feel like you know exactly how your life is going to go?"

"It depends. In my work, sometimes I may know what I'll be doing next year but not where I'll be next week. It can be exciting or terribly dull," Gina said. "It can be hard to feel at home anywhere."

"My problem might be that I'm *too* at home in Singapore," Aileen said. "I've spent my whole life there, and the entire country is only half the size of Los Angeles. It doesn't take long for me to get a little bored. But I'm just venting now. Do you know Singapore at all?"

"I've been there once or twice. The architecture is incredible."

"You and Eli really get around," Aileen said. "You're right, it is nice. That's the problem. Singapore is home, but I know it too well. I want there to be surprises in my future. I don't want my life to be so familiar yet." She laughed. "I don't know why I'm telling you all this. I still don't trust you, and it's more than a little suspicious that you and Eli came along at just the right time."

Gina laughed too. "I'm glad you told me. Talking about these things can help, even with someone you don't know well. But I hope you'll grow to trust me. We really do want to help you."

"But why? That's what I'm still trying to understand. I get that you're spies or whatever, and you need people to help you do spy things, but why me? Assuming I do help you, that is."

"Being a spy…" Gina started. "It's not like in the movies—fancy clothes and guns and martinis. Yes, we have goals we're trying to accomplish, but our work is very collaborative. If we can help you get something you want, that might put you in a position to help us get something we want."

"Sounds a little manipulative," Aileen said.

"It's a matter of perspective. You and Eli and I are simply a few people whose goals might overlap. We will always be as honest and straightforward with you as we can. All we ask is that you do the same with us."

"That seems reasonable," Aileen said. In the distance, Cyprus was getting closer. She could make out fishermen and boats along the docks and cars crawling on the roads.

"I hope you find what you're looking for, Aileen," said Gina. "Something coming along at just the right time doesn't have to be suspicious. It could be fate."

"I don't believe in fate. Fate means I don't have control of my life—which, pirates or no pirates, I can't accept. By the way, what's with the name of this ship? You and Eli aren't Chinese, I know that much."

"You caught us," Gina said. "It's owned by an Israeli company, actually. We're borrowing it. The owner is a friend of ours."

"So many friends," Aileen said. "Wait, Israeli? So all this secrecy, all this mystery, your accent. I think I'm starting to connect the dots."

Gina put her hand on Aileen's shoulder. "Come on, I'll buy you lunch and get you set up with a suitcase and some clothes for California. Oh, and tonight Eli and I were hoping you'd have dinner with us. We're going to see an old friend."

\* \* \*

It was late afternoon by the time Monir got out of the cab at Stalo's house in Amiantos. It was small for two people, but he'd spent a lot of time traveling for work since their wedding. They were planning to look for a bigger house together in Limassol as soon as they had the chance.

He knocked on the door. "Ma'am? Special delivery for you."

The door opened and Stalo laughed. "I don't think I ordered this. You'd better send it back."

Monir swept his wife up in a hug and they went inside. He immediately plopped down on the couch. "I can't remember the last time I was this tired. I think I've gotten worse at traveling. I used to be good at it, didn't I?"

"You did," Stalo agreed. "You used to brag about your days of circling the globe without messing up your hair."

"Now look at me. My shirt is rumpled, for goodness' sake!"

"If I'd known I was marrying a man who wears rumpled shirts, I might not have said yes." Stalo sat down next to her husband. "It's nice to have you home. How long are you here for?"

"Only a few days, unfortunately. Cyprus is sending me to…to California for a meeting."

Stalo's eyes widened. "California? Monir—"

"I know," Monir said. "Frontfacer's CEO wants to talk to Cyprus about something. He insists the meeting happen at their headquarters. I don't know what I'm allowed to tell you, but I don't know much right now anyway."

"Have you eaten yet?" Stalo asked. "I was just about to make some keftethes."

Monir brightened immediately. "My favorite meatballs! I've been craving them for days. How did you know?" He pulled Stalo over and kissed her.

"If you'll behave, I can actually make them," Stalo said.

Monir kissed her again, slower and deeper this time. "How's that for behaving?"

"You're on the right track," she said. "I guess dinner will have to wait." She took Monir's hand and led him toward the bedroom.

# 6

# THE PROFESSIONAL

Monir and Stalo had thoroughly enjoyed their reunion. As one of her relatives had remarked in broken English at a family gathering, swatting Monir on the back, "The sex…much better when you go away a lot."

Stalo got up from the bed, dressed, and gave Monir a kiss on the forehead. "You can rest while I cook," she said.

Monir pulled on her arm gently, motioning her not to leave just yet. "Stalo, I'm afraid to go back."

She sat on the bed and put her hand on his cheek. "Why? Because of everything that happened with your family?"

"Yes. It's complicated, and it seems to get worse with time rather than better."

\*   \*   \*

Jun had not made much progress since her meeting with William Tan. She needed to talk to Monir Young, but he was in Cyprus. She'd repeatedly called the number Tan had given her, but kept getting Young's voicemail. There were only so many times Jun could leave a polite but stern message asking Monir to call her, but it was frustrating, and embarrassing, for Jun that he'd left the country during the investigation. She'd also e-mailed Monir several times, but all she'd gotten in reply so far was an out-of-office response.

Working overtime, Jun's tech team had produced dozens of pictures of people carrying bags near Republic Plaza on the night of the shooting, and Jun had blown them up and placed them on a bulletin board in the conference room. She and her superiors had gone over them thoroughly, setting aside a handful of persons of interest. The problem was with the technology. It was nearly impossible to identify potential suspects through blurry, pixilated stills from the CCTV video feed.

Jun reported the difficulties to Director Low, who told her to keep trying to contact Monir. He would appeal higher for assistance.

\* \* \*

After a long, hot shower, Monir headed to the kitchen. Glancing at his phone for the first time in hours, Monir saw the missed calls and e-mails from Jun. He wrote back a quick reply: *Officer Ai Boon, I'm very sorry for leaving Singapore. I should have told you my plans, but there was a family emergency. I will call you as soon as I return.*

Stalo was scooping the last of the meatballs out of the frying pan. She turned, wrapped her arms around Monir, and kissed him softly. "I don't think you have anything to worry about. Going back will help you get closure. I don't know how, but I know it."

"There is something else I have to tell you. It will be a shock," Monir said.

Stalo's hand went to her chest. "What is it?"

He took a breath. "My Singapore contact and I were targeted by assassins. A sniper killed four of them at the restaurant we were in. We know very little about the people killed or who sent them.

No motive has been nailed down yet. And we have no idea who the sniper was."

Stalo sat down at the table. She held her chin in her hand and looked at the floor for a long time.

The couple ate in silence. Neither said anything more about Monir's imminent return to the U.S. or the attempt on his life.

The doorbell rang. "Are you expecting anyone?" Monir asked.

"No," she replied. "See who it is."

He walked to the door and opened it. Standing outside were Gina, Eli, and Aileen, holding brown bags of food.

"Hello, Monir," said Eli. "Mind if we join you and Stalo? We brought Lebanese treats from the city." He motioned to Aileen. "There's someone I'd like you to meet."

\* \* \*

### Langley, Virginia, USA

Casey Margaret was pointing to a picture and the caption below it. John Harden was standing next to her, his eyes fastened on the face and name.

Margaret had joined the CIA as an analyst a few months earlier. That morning she'd stumbled onto an intriguing find. The face recognition software had singled out a series of face profiles that triggered alarms in the department. Within minutes, Margaret's supervisor, Sadira Hammad, had taken the elevator to the fifth floor to tell Harden, the deputy director, in person.

Harden's eyes contained a hint of bewilderment. "Good work, Margaret. Any news connected to this, Sadira?"

"Channel NewsAsia out of Singapore reported a multiple-fatality shooting at a rooftop restaurant on CapitaGreen at Raffles Place, the building across from Republic Plaza. Four dead. Single rifle shots to the head. Looks like a sniper, still at large."

"What do we know about the deceased?"

"Too early to know anything for sure," Sadira replied. "I placed a call to some of our Southeast Asia field offices. One preliminary assessment says independent operators—maybe Chinese. But we do know something about one of the survivors. The news identified him as an American citizen living in Cyprus. His name is Monir Young."

Harden's ears pricked up at the name. He locked eyes with Sadira. "And this one, Margaret?" Harden pointed at the woman on the screen.

"She exited the front doors of the building within minutes of the shooting. Republic Plaza cameras got nothing—she was definitely aware that cameras were on the premises. The shots we have were taken after she left the Plaza, by some surveillance cameras on an adjacent property. Do you recognize her?"

Harden shot a quick look at Sadira. "Our paths crossed a while back. As it happens, Monir Young was there too. Which is why it makes no sense for that woman to be the shooter."

"Why not?" asked Margaret.

"Because, based on their history, if Nadia Dryovskaya killed anyone that night, her first bullet would have been for Monir."

"*That's* Nadia Dryovskaya?" said Margaret.

"Right, they were on opposite sides in Cyprus, weren't they?" said Sadira. "Are you thinking what I'm thinking, John? It might be time to call our old friend Eli."

"My thought exactly. Wouldn't Jeff Collins be our best bet? The two of them worked Cyprus together, right?"

Sadira replied in the affirmative. Harden was already speed-dialing Collins.

*  *  *

Monir, Stalo, and their guests sat around the dinner table, food and plates spread in front of everyone. Stalo had been as surprised as her husband to find out who was joining them for the meal. She knew there was little chance the visit was merely social.

Aileen ate slowly, listening to her hosts make small talk with Eli and Gina. She didn't know who Monir and Stalo were, but they seemed nice enough. There had to be something more to them; why else would she be there? She glanced at Gina, who caught her look and gave her a reassuring smile. As Eli finished telling a story about a huge sea bass he claimed to have caught earlier in the week, Gina cleared her throat and turned to their hosts.

"Stalo, Monir, thank you again for letting us intrude on you like this. I know you weren't expecting company tonight," she said.

"It's our pleasure," Stalo said. "I wish I'd known you were coming, so I could have made more to eat. Thank you for bringing the extra food."

Gina put her hand over her stomach. "I don't think I'd have room for more. And it was the least we could do after interrupting while Monir is home for a few days."

"How did you know—" Monir said. "I guess I shouldn't be surprised you're keeping tabs on me." He grinned. "Same old Eli and Gina. Maybe I should start following *you* for a change."

"It's not 'following,' Monir," said Eli. "You're an important person right now, as that nasty business in Singapore shows. We want to make sure you're safe."

"Sorry, what nasty business was that?" Aileen asked Monir. "They didn't really tell me who you are."

"Yes, it sounds like you're here so we can meet each other," he replied. "Now seems like a good time to do that. Are you one of them?"

"A secret agent? No, I used to work in Singapore at a technology company. Then I was a sailor for a few days, but some pirates put a stop to that. Now I'm going to Silicon Valley to see a man about a job."

Monir blinked. "I don't know what I was expecting you to say, but that wasn't it. What's all this about pirates? And wait, you're going to Silicon Valley too?"

"Aileen is trying to change up her career, to try something new," Gina said. "Since you're both going to California, Eli and I thought you might travel together, to give you two some time to talk. You're both involved in the future of technology in different ways. Getting to know each other might be useful."

"Sure, it would be nice to have some company for the trip," Monir said. "I can only read so many issues of *The Economist*. Where are you going for this job, Aileen?"

"Frontfacer," she said. "I have an interview in a few days."

"You're kidding. I have a meeting there myself." Monir looked at Gina. "What a coincidence."

Eli laughed. "You know us. Coincidence is our business."

"What do you do?" Aileen asked Monir. "With the future of technology, I mean."

"Have you heard about the Cyprus lithium? I'm negotiating a deal for it with Singapore, though lately I'm spending most of my time trying not to get shot in restaurants."

"Whoa, what? Someone tried to shoot you in Singapore? Is that the nasty business Eli was talking about? I've been a little out of touch with the news lately."

"Yes. The police are looking into it," Monir said. "So this trip to California comes at a good time." He put his arm around his wife's shoulders. "Hopefully, the only people trying to shoot me there will be Hollywood paparazzi." He kissed Stalo's cheek. She rolled her eyes.

"It's really rare for shootings to happen in Singapore," Aileen said. "It's almost unheard of."

"That's what I've been told," Monir said. "Someone must have strong feelings about the lithium. Not much to do but let the police do their jobs." He jabbed some keftethes with his fork and pointed it in Gina and Eli's direction. "Luckily, I have my guardian angels to watch over me. Speaking of which, how do you know them, Aileen?"

"That's a good question. I guess you could say they fished me out of the ocean. Kind of like the fish Eli caught when no one was around to see it. Except I'm real."

"My sea bass is real!" Eli said. "It's stowed on the ship or I'd show it to you all."

"Too bad you didn't bring it with you, Eli," said Stalo, smiling. "I could have cooked it for us."

"Yes, too bad," Monir agreed. "That's quite a story you have," he said to Aileen. "I look forward to hearing more of it on our flight. Though I can't help wondering what else these two have in mind, with us meeting like this."

"We simply thought you two should get to know each other," said Gina. "Sometimes secret agents' motives aren't so secret."

"Let me propose a toast," said Stalo, raising her glass to the three guests. "To old friends and new ones."

"To old friends and new ones," Gina agreed. "The world is a smaller place than it seems. It can't hurt to have people by your side when you need them."

After dinner, the group lounged in the living room, talking and drinking wine. Aileen excused herself, saying she needed the bathroom. Walking down the hallway, she noticed a study at the rear of the house. Inside was a computer on a desk.

With a glance back at the others, Aileen slipped into the study and sat down. She pulled Tong's thumb drive from her pocket and plugged it into the keyboard. *Time to see what's on this,* she thought.

She opened the thumb drive and saw two folders, named "1" and "2." She opened the first folder. All that was inside was a plain text file named "Readme.txt." She clicked on it. A text window sprung up, containing three sentences: "Follow the clues. Enter the passwords. No second chances." She closed the file and clicked on the second folder. This time a window appeared, prompting her for a password. At the top of the window was a simple phrase: "Fruit from the ship." *Fruit? Didn't Tong mention something about fruit?*

Aileen had no idea what it meant, but she didn't have time to figure it out now. She pocketed the drive and headed back to see if there was any wine left.

\*    \*    \*

The next afternoon, Eli's phone buzzed while he was having a late lunch at a small café in downtown Limassol. Looking down at the screen, he saw a U.S. prefix and an area code he couldn't place; rarely did Eli or his colleagues keep contact lists on the temporary phones they used. He swiped to answer the call. "Hello?"

"Let me guess. You're drinking black coffee and having one of those almond croissants you love so much at a seaside restaurant in Tel Aviv."

Eli took a moment to process the voice. "Close enough, Jeff, close enough. How are you, my friend?"

After exchanging pleasantries, Collins got right to the point. "So, Eli. Nadia Dryovskaya popped up in a security camera feed in Singapore, right across the street from where a major shooting took place. Any of this ring a bell?"

"Someone did mention the shooting the other day. I'm on the other side of the world, Jeff."

"Come on, Eli, for old time's sake, if nothing else, don't give me that crap. What do you know about Nadia's involvement? Why did she protect Monir Young? Does any of this have to do with what we've been working on?"

Old time's sake went a long way among intelligence operatives. But because spies look after their employers' interests first, Eli answered with a question of his own. "Who's interested in the Russian, *if* she was involved in the shooting?"

Collins's tone got sharp. "It's high time we all get on the same page. The shooting was about the lithium. The lithium, Eli, that's what we've been working on for months now! Is Dryovskaya on your—on our side on this? If she is, what the hell? We've all been hunting her down since Cyprus. Did you conveniently forget to mention her while we were putting together the Tong escape?"

Eli replied coyly. "When don't we hold back some information? Don't act as if you don't do it yourself, Jeff."

"This is no time for games. We do need to know, now! How's Monir Young involved with you? Are you handling the Russian? Was that you in Singapore?"

"I'll answer your questions—all of them—but you'll give me something in return."

"What do you want?"

"For starters, Jeff, we're still waiting to hear about the files Tong turned over to you on the submarine."

All the cards were out on the table now.

"I really wish I could tell you something, Eli, but I can't. If you want me to say it again, there was nothing on Tong when we transferred him off the ship. He says he passed the info to a trusted friend. Believe me, we were all surprised. We're looking into what happened."

"So you've been claiming. Do you believe him?"

"I think so. The guy may be a lot of things, but a liar is not one of them."

"Hm. Let me know when you have something, will you, Jeff?"

"Sure. Your turn now. Singapore? Dryovskaya?"

"Yes, on all counts. And everything is under control, so relax. As for Monir, I can't say much now, but stay tuned. You'll be hearing from me soon. We may need your help, actually."

"Always nice to be needed, Eli."

"Sure is, Jeff." Eli hung up and took a sip of his coffee. Even the CIA would have to wait until he'd finished lunch.

# 7
# STORIES UNTOLD

Monir and Aileen met at Larnaca International Airport on the afternoon of their flight. Monir had always liked Cyprus's airports, especially Larnaca. Getting through security was a breeze, and the duty-free shops had an extensive selection of scotch. He and Aileen checked their bags and compared boarding passes.

"Looks like we're sitting right next to each other," Aileen said.

"Somehow that doesn't surprise me," said Monir. "I'd wager Eli and Gina have a good travel agent. Anyway, we have a layover in Abu Dhabi, so we'll have plenty of time to get to know each other. I'd like to hear more about this Frontfacer job you're interviewing for. Have you been to the U.S.?"

"No, first time," said Aileen. "I haven't traveled a lot in general, but that's another story. You?"

"Yes, you could say that. I was born there, actually."

"Oh, then that makes sense."

"What does?"

"Your last name. I thought it sounded American, or maybe English. But since you live in Cyprus, I didn't know what your background was. Did you grow up in the U.S.?"

Monir hesitated. "It's complicated. Yes, I did. But I've been away for a long time."

"It must be nice to be going home, if you've been gone."

He chuckled darkly. "America isn't home for me. I'm only going back for this meeting, and that's because my boss in Cyprus insisted. Otherwise, I'd be happy never to set foot there again."

"You and the U.S. have some history, I take it," Aileen said. "Can I pry?"

Just then, the airport's intercom announced a gate change for their flight.

Monir looked at a map of the airport on the wall nearby. "We're boarding on the other side of the terminal. Come on, I want to stop at Costa Coffee before we leave. I'll tell you more on the plane."


Watching the barista pour his steaming cup of coffee, Monir recalled what Eli had said to him after dinner, while the two men were making decaf in the kitchen.

"I hope you'll keep us in the loop about what happens in California, Monir. Gina and I would appreciate it."

"I'll try, Eli, but it depends what happens. Cyprus's business is Cyprus's business."

"Yes, of course." Eli poured a cup and handed it to Monir. "But do your best, would you? Friends help friends. And we would very much appreciate it."

\*　　\*　　\*

Zhang Wei looked at the telephone on his desk, which was signaling that his assistant was trying to reach him. He pressed a dial and spoke in Cantonese, his dialect of choice for conversing in his office. "Yes?"

"Mr. Wei, Mr. Valencik is asking for you once again. Are you available to speak with him?"

Wei knew why Valencik was calling; he'd been putting off talking to the CEO, hoping that Kong Li would find Tong sooner rather than later. He paused for a moment before picking up the line.

"Mr. Valencik, to what do I owe this honor? It is very late for business in California, is it not?"

"Hello, Mr. Wei. Thank you for taking my call. I must say, it doesn't inspire confidence in our partnership when I can't reach you for several days."

"My apologies. I have been attending to other matters."

"Yes, well, I'm concerned about the news coming out of Singapore. I thought you might be able to help me understand what happened."

"Nothing irreparable. A slight glitch, you might say."

"No, I wouldn't say that. Singapore hasn't had a mass shooting for decades—a "historical disaster," the news called it. A police investigation is under way, four of your hired goons are dead, and the shooter is at large. Monir Young is alive, and so are the lithium negotiations between Cyprus and Singapore. From my perspective, that is not a slight glitch, Mr. Wei. This is not the kind of history we're trying to make together."

"As I said, nothing we can't fix."

"And what of the whistleblower, Tong? Where is he? Are we on top of that matter as well? Last I knew, our pirate attack left a ship on the bottom of the Gulf of Aden."

"Give me a few days, Mr. Valencik. We are still on track."

"I hope you're right. There is way too much at stake for both of us. I'm bringing Monir Young here. I'll get the lithium for you; you focus on finding Tong. I don't think I need to emphasize how bad it would be for all of us if he has what he claims to have."

"Yes, of course. And since we are on the topic, allow me to make one request of you as well, Mr. Valencik."

"Certainly."

"I'm hearing from the U.S. media that your government is resisting Frontfacer's expansion into China. A concern with, as one reporter put it, unknown unknowns. There is some unease at the prospect of such an influential company working closely with China."

"Maybe, but that is a problem I'm addressing."

"If there is too much media attention on us, other parties may become interested—intelligence agencies, for instance. The last thing we need is CIA involvement. See to it, Mr. Valencik, that our mutual political allies clear the way for this deal to happen, without the media's spotlight shining on every segment of the process."

"Understood."

"One more thing. Be careful with Monir Young. My sources tell me he has relationships with American and Israeli spies. He may not be coming alone, so to speak."

\* \* \*

On board the airplane, Aileen and Monir were served water in their seats by a flight attendant.

"May I bring you anything else?" she asked.

"I'd love some coffee, please," Aileen said, eyeing the cup Monir had boarded with.

"Of course," said the flight attendant, walking away. "One moment."

"I hope they have good coffee in Silicon Valley," Aileen said. "I've heard the tech people there mostly drink Red Bull and beer."

"Beer at the office. I don't know if that would make negotiating easier or harder," Monir said. "On the other hand, there's a lot of money in those tech companies, so they must be doing something right. You should keep an open mind. Drinking

Red Bull will be your first step to becoming an American," he joked.

"I can hardly wait," she said. The flight attendant returned with a cup of coffee and handed it to Aileen.

She took a sip and looked at Monir. "OK, so what's with you and America? Why don't you want to go back?"

"You don't waste any time," he said. He sipped his own coffee and looked out the window. Cyprus was disappearing behind them as the plane flew southeast on the first leg of their trip. "Are you sure you want to hear the whole thing? It's a lot."

"I'm sure." Aileen tilted her seat back and waited.

"My parents met in the U.S. They were in law school at Georgetown. My father, Derek Young, is American. My mother is Iranian. Her name is—was—Suhir Farhad."

"*Was* her name?" Aileen said. "What does that mean?"

"I'll get there," Monir replied. "My mother is from a very wealthy family with real estate holdings in many countries. They had to flee for their lives during the Iranian Revolution, and my mother, aunt, and grandmother ended up in the United States."

"Where she met your father," said Aileen.

"Yes. The family fortune was stashed away in banks, so money wasn't a problem. But my mother never heard from her extended family again. Years later, she found out that the Revolutionary Guard took over the family's estate in Tehran. They sentenced her father to life imprisonment."

"I'm sorry. When did your parents get married?"

"About a year after they met. It was an odd romance. They met in class, but according to my mother, she didn't like my father at first. He was a smooth talker—charming, but sly. My grandmother didn't like him either."

"Yet here you are. He must have won them over somehow."

"During her first year of law school, my mother was home for the winter break. To her complete surprise, my father showed up at the house and invited himself to stay for dinner. By all accounts, it was an awkward evening. My aunt even told him that my mother wouldn't go on a date with him. But soon after that, she did. His persistence got the better of her," Monir said, smiling. "My mother used to say his persistence is what made him a good lawyer. Later that year they were married."

"The mysteries of love," said Aileen.

"Unfortunately, my father was persistent in every area of life. That's how he got the family into serious trouble later on."

*     *     *

Jun pulled into the parking lot of her flat building and found the only open spot, all the way at the back. She'd been at work for almost twenty-four hours straight, so Director Low had ordered her to go home and sleep. As an investigator on assignment, she could have parked on the street, right in front of the building, but Jun had decided long ago that she would never abuse the privileges of her job. Both her training as a police officer and her upbringing had taught her the value of humility.

Police work ran in her family. Jun's father, a police officer for thirty years, had died of cancer when Jun was thirteen. Her uncle, retired from overseeing the security detail for the prime minister, had stepped in to help raise her. Jun's uncle had always emphasized that character must be esteemed above position or accomplishment.

Jun was deep in thought during her walk to the elevator. It felt as though everything was at stake with the shooting investigation, professionally and personally. She had to bring the criminals to justice for the shootings. She needed to show her superiors that their faith in her was not misplaced. She intended to show her colleagues, most of them men who still hadn't accepted women as equals, that she was every bit as capable as they were. And she wanted to make her family proud.

Jun opened the door to her flat and caught her reflection in the hallway mirror. A tired version of herself stared back. She looked at her reflection, narrowed her eyes, and whispered, "You can do this, Jun. Just don't give up."

\*    \*    \*

"What kind of trouble did your father get into?" Aileen asked.

Monir sipped his coffee. "After law school, my parents moved to a big estate in Teaneck, New Jersey, and opened a law firm, with my mother's family as one of their biggest clients. Handling my mother's finances brought my father into contact with powerful bankers, government agents, and even organized crime groups in a few countries.

"After the revolution in 1979 and the hostage crisis, America imposed unilateral sanctions on Iran, including five Iranian banks. They were forbidden from transferring money to and from the United States."

"And your father…" said Aileen.

"Was very persistent," Monir continued. "Even though the family had plenty of money, it was all from my mother. He wanted to make something that was his alone. He and his shady contacts created an underground exchange that let Iranians illegally transfer money among foreign countries. One of them was the U.S."

"I take it that didn't end well."

"You could say that. Toward the end of 1998, the FBI caught up to them. One Saturday morning, just before Christmas, a SWAT team showed up at the front door and arrested my parents. I don't know if my mother was involved, but her name was on the accounts that funded the whole thing. The FBI said my parents had two options: spend a few decades in a federal prison in Wyoming, or turn in the rest of their network and enter the Witness Protection Program." Monir's face was calm, but his voice carried a hint of sadness. "I was old enough to take care of myself. It wasn't much of a choice for them."

"Wow," said Aileen. "How old were you? That must have been so hard."

"I was twenty-two and finishing university. My parents assumed I would join them in Witness Protection, but I was too angry at my father for what he'd done. I had to get away."

"So that's what you meant when you said your mother's name changed."

"My parents got new identities and vanished. I packed a bag, flew to Europe, and got a job. I haven't seen my mother or my father in over twelve years."

# 8

# ARRIVALS

Since arriving in Singapore a few days before, Kong Li had received bad news from his men in Morocco. Their search for Tong's brother had turned up little, as the man had gone out of town. A neighbor said he had packed a car and left in a hurry. Other efforts to locate Tong or find out how he disappeared off the *Delfland* had also been unfruitful, infuriating Li. Wei's men who'd investigated Tong's workspace in China had found nothing but a few mystery novels and a map of Morocco. The hard drive in Tong's computer had been erased and had half a dozen holes drilled in it.

Normally, Li entered a city's nightlife scene to gather information. He was excellent at poker, and at drinking; between the card players and the bartenders he would have gotten some answers. But the atmosphere in Singapore was different since the shootings. He could spot CID officers from a distance, and there were plenty of them in most of the bars Li had visited. Asking a lot of questions when the police were doing the same could backfire.

Li's other go-to source for unofficial intelligence-gathering was brothels, but prostitution in Singapore was not exactly commonplace. Through an old friend, Li was introduced to an escort service, and not long after, a European woman came to his hotel room.

After they'd finished having sex, Li and the escort had a few drinks and talked. He asked her how she found working in Asia.

"I like it. Most of the people I've met have just been looking for a little company. There's been quite a few white men lately, actually—Americans."

"Americans?" Li asked. "Did any of them say what kind of work they do?"

"Who knows? Consulting, according to some of them, but they all had guns on their dressers. Guns are hard to come by in Singapore, unless people are big-time criminals or have special licenses. My clients didn't seem to be criminals. But they definitely aren't consultants."

"How did they find you?"

"I have a friend who bartends at Drop. A lot of Westerners go there. He directs business my way."

\*    \*    \*

The plane landed in Abu Dhabi, and Aileen and Monir disembarked. They followed the crowd out the plane and wove their way through the massive terminal to the food court near their next departure gate. Low clouds reflected shades of gold and auburn as the sun set in the distance.

Monir looked at his watch. "We have some time until our flight to San Francisco. I think I'm going to take a nap. Sorry for talking the whole flight. I really do want to hear your story."

Aileen shrugged. "There's a second flight for that. I wanted to hear yours." She yawned and looked at her phone. "I need to find somewhere to charge this thing. I told some friends about this trip, and they'll get worried if they don't hear from me for too long."

"Are your friends back in Singapore?" Monir asked.

"Yep. We're all a part of this…sort of a religious group, I guess you'd say. It's how I met them."

"What kind of religion?" Monir asked.

"The group is Christian, though I don't know if I'd call myself that. Like your background, it's a long story. Are you religious?"

Monir pursed his lips. "I'm not sure what I am, but I'm open to the idea of religion. There are times when I think there must be more to life." He thought back to the Cypriot priest he'd met while pursuing the lithium rights. The man had encouraged Monir to look for deeper meaning in a way that was comforting without being pushy. The priest had shown him how faith could be not about judgment or guilt, but about hope.

"That sounds about right," Aileen said. "My parents grew up in the church in Singapore, so I did too. I just don't know if church is where I belong. My mother says I worship at the altar of technology now."

"What do you say?"

"That's a question for the next flight. Go take your nap. Despite Gina and Eli assuring me that I'm qualified for this job, I still need to prepare for the interview."

"Let's meet for dinner," Monir said. "We can compare notes on Frontfacer and you can tell me your story."

\*   \*   \*

Li had dismissed his escort early and was taking a cab to Hongkong Street, where Drop, the bar she'd mentioned, was located. His mind was replaying what the woman had said about her American clients. They had to be in intelligence or law enforcement, and their presence in Singapore could be connected to Tong. It was a long shot, but it was something.

\*   \*   \*

Refreshed from a nap in the airport's business lounge, Monir went to look for Aileen. He found her sprawled across three seats in an empty boarding area, thumbing through news stories about Frontfacer.

"Anything interesting?" he asked, sitting down next to her.

"Sort of," she said. "Adrian Valencik went on TV the other day to say he's hopeful about the company breaking into China. He says recent talks with the Chinese have been encouraging. And, of course, he thinks he's saving the world."

Monir laughed. "Don't all you tech types think that?"

"It's mostly a Silicon Valley idea, as far as I know. Obviously, technology runs the world, and there have to be people who run the technology. But it's one thing to want to make a better product. It's another to think your hot new app is anything more than that."

"Doesn't Frontfacer count as more than a hot new app?" Monir asked. "What do they have, a billion users?"

"Closer to two billion. Don't get me wrong, Frontfacer's technology is amazing," Aileen said. "For a while, WeChat was the gold standard—one app plugged into everything you need. But Valencik is combining that kind of functionality with a social network and Frontfacer's global reach. He's really trying to *be* the internet for people."

"How can one company be the internet?"

"Think of it this way. There's an app for everything you do, right? Everything has its own link to the internet. Frontfacer lets you hook all those things up to one central location. The more you can do from within Frontfacer, the less likely you are to log out, and the more data the company can gather about you."

"But how is that different from WeChat?" Monir asked.

Aileen thought for a moment. "Ambition, I'd say. Frontfacer is trying to set up internet connections in poor and remote parts of the world, so that when residents of those areas get on the internet, they'll be doing it through Frontfacer. That all sounds good for anyone who wouldn't have the internet otherwise, but it means Frontfacer has a ton of control over the information people see, which is a little scary."

Monir grinned. "You mean we shouldn't hand over our brains to a huge tech company and hope for the best?"

"You catch on fast," Aileen said. "But that's why Valencik's comments about China worry me. The bigger Frontfacer gets, the more control it has over information. If the company could succeed in China, it would have a huge—well, *huger*—amount of control. Most people don't understand how thoroughly these companies can watch them and affect what they see online. If privacy is a thing of the past, it's because we've let it become that."

Monir looked at Aileen seriously. "For a sailor, you're pretty paranoid about this stuff."

She laughed. "I am! You're right. That's why I'm getting more and more excited about this interview."

"I was just about to ask, why do you want to work at Frontfacer, given your feelings about it?" Monir said.

Aileen sat up beside Monir. "Obviously I wasn't planning to until very recently. But it's a chance to work with the best technology and the smartest people, and maybe to make a difference in the world. And it just so happens that the big companies are starting to pay more attention to an area of tech that I specialize in."

"What's that?" Monir asked.

"People." Seeing the confused look on Monir's face, she laughed. "That's enough preaching for now. Come on, let's get some food."

\*　\*　\*

Jeff Collins and John Harden rarely spoke in person, mostly because they tended to be on opposite sides of the globe. That morning the two men were in the same building, so they met in the small cafeteria at the eastern end of Langley's executive floor.

"John, some of our agents in Singapore said CID is stuck—they have no leads in the investigation. We might want to think about giving them a hand."

"How?" asked Harden, stirring cream into his coffee.

"By offering our services, our equipment."

"You're feeling generous today. Since when are you so benevolent with other people's investigations?"

Collins took a bite from his sandwich, chewing slowly. "It isn't generosity. We need to be close to Singapore's police force in case they get to Tong before we do."

"We hold their hand until they find Tong? Then what?"

"Grab Tong's files and get out of there."

Harden was wary, and his whole face said so.

"What's the problem, John?"

"The problem is Eli. We're working on Tong with the Israelis, Jeff. We can't just cut them out of whatever Tong has."

"Sure we can. Just like they cut us out of Dryovskaya."

"I don't like it."

"With respect, you need to toughen up, John. You're getting soft in your old age."

"Maybe. But you're the one who always says there are some people you should never screw over. Don't you think Eli is one of them?"

\*   \*   \*

Aileen and Monir bought plates of hummus and shawarma in the airport's dining area and sat down by the picture windows, with views of the city just beyond.

"You're in the technology industry, but your specialty is people?" Monir asked. "How does that work?"

"There are tons of engineers and developers already," Aileen said through a mouthful of food. "Companies like Frontfacer don't need more talented coders. What matters now is knowing how people *use* the technology. That way you can design your product to people's needs."

"I've read about that," Monir said. "The field is called user experience, right?"

"UX is part of what I do, yes," said Aileen. "But it's also about having empathy for the people who will spend money on your product, and understanding what their needs are. That seems obvious, but for a while the tech industry, especially in the U.S., was all about who could build the coolest product."

"I see. It doesn't matter how cool your product is if it's too complicated to use."

"Exactly. My specialty is helping companies build user-friendly versions of their ideas."

Monir dipped his pita bread in the hummus and took a bite. "That's what this job is?"

"It sounds like it. According to Eli, who's my personal recruiter, Frontfacer is pretty interested in my background of doing this kind of stuff in Singapore. Which may be my ticket in. Maybe you've heard how it's really hard to get a job in Silicon Valley if you're female or not white."

"May I have your attention, please," said a voice over the loudspeaker. "We are now beginning our pre-boarding for Etihad Airways flight one-eight-two to San Francisco International Airport."

78

"I've read that white men are biased toward hiring more white men, yes," Monir said. "I hope your experience will be different. Shall we go?"

\* \* \*

The phone rang, and the woman picked it up. The caller ID was blank. "Do you have them?" she said.

"Yes," said the voice on the line. "They're on a plane coming here from Abu Dhabi. They're sitting next to each other—did the same on the first flight. Coincidence?"

"Not likely," she said. "So, they know each other. I wonder how much they know about each other, and about Tong."

"What do you want to do?"

She thought for a few seconds. "Reach out to Young after his meeting. We'll see what he says and go from there."

"Think he has any idea what's coming?"

"Not a chance. Like most people, he has no idea what Adrian Valencik is capable of."

# 9
# THE RECRUIT

The white SUV had just crossed the bridge over Singapore's Marina Reservoir and was entering the East Coast Parkway. Inside the vehicle were three people—two of them Israeli, one Russian. Eli, their katsa, or field intelligence officer, had just told them that sometime in the next day or two they would be picking up an arriving passenger at the airport. They were en route to the house where the person would be staying, to make sure it was secure.

In the front of the vehicle sat Jael Efrat, who was driving, and Itai Pardo, riding shotgun. Jael and Itai were close in age, mid-thirties, and had worked together on several missions in their nation's intelligence service. In the back, sitting directly behind Jael, was the Russian operative Nadia Dryovskaya. Her head was turned to the back window as she looked out at the spectacularly lit Gardens by the Bay.

"Beautiful city," she muttered, turning to face forward.

"It is," agreed Itai. "And to think everything we see here has been built over the last fifty years—amazing."

Nadia glanced at Jael. She had both hands on the wheel and was driving the speed limit. During all the times Nadia had been around her, Jael was quiet and reserved. Unless the mission called for her initiative, Jael never started conversations, not even with Itai, whom she had known the longest. A few nights earlier, Nadia had heard Jael's voice loud and clear through her earpiece during the sniper mission. Jael hadn't said much to Nadia since then.

Nadia leaned forward slightly and said, "Itai, how do you guys always end up with such nice cars—a brand-new Infiniti QX80, of all things?"

To anyone listening in, it would have seemed like a simple question. Not to Itai. He smirked out of the corner of his mouth and said, "This one belongs to a friend of Eli's." But Itai's mind was processing Nadia's question, noting her use of "you guys," which implied that she was not one of them, and "always," which showed that Nadia had some knowledge of previous operations. Itai wasn't surprised. Nadia Dryovskaya was a fellow professional from a rival intelligence agency. She could be counted on to get the job done, based on the terms of her recruitment, but she could not be trusted with sensitive information.

"Good old Eli," Nadia said, hoping for a comment from Jael. "He's quite the character, isn't he, getting in with all the rich people and fancy cars."

More Nadia content for Itai to process; another baiting question he would never respond to. After a few seconds of silence, Nadia placed her hands in her lap, giving up her inquiries. Moments like these, when other operatives gave her the bare minimum of information and nothing further, underlined the fact that she was an outsider.

Jael spoke up, drawing a sideways look of surprise from Itai. "Eli is a legend in our agency, perhaps the most respected katsa in the field."

It was true. "Eli" was actually a nickname. Only his wife, Sylvia, called him by his real name. Jedidiah Abrahamson had become Eli for two reasons. The first was that "Jedidiah" was too long, and Eli had always insisted that no one shorten it to "Jed." The second was his outstanding operation in the late 1980s, when, through the exceptional direction of a high-ranking Iranian asset, Eli had almost single-handedly taken down a team of six nuclear scientists who were engineering a bomb that could have leveled

Tel Aviv. His triumph reminded old-timers in the agency of Eli Cohen's legendary infiltration of the Syrian military in the 1970s. Cohen had ascended almost to the position of defense minister before he'd been caught and hanged by the Syrians. After Iran, some of Abrahamson's colleagues started referring to him as "the new Eli," and before long the nickname had stuck. Most people in the agency didn't even know Eli's real name, and no one used his last name.

Nadia was Eli's recruit. They had worked against each other in Cyprus six months earlier but had never met, not until a summer evening at a bar in Paris. Convinced that Jael and Itai had no intention of talking to her, Nadia looked out her window at the lit-up rain trees along the ECP median, her mind drifting back to the night she'd been recruited.

\* \* \*

On the plane, Aileen watched the Pacific Ocean slowly pass beneath them. Monir sat beside her, rereading some of the news stories Aileen had found about Frontfacer. She glanced over at his phone.

"Getting ready for Valencik?" she asked.

Monir nodded. "It isn't every day that I'm in a room with a tech gazillionaire. Whatever he says about the lithium, I want to seem like I have a clue about Frontfacer's business."

Reaching the end of an article, he closed his phone and looked at Aileen. "OK, your turn. Who are you, and why is Eli scheming to get us to work together?"

"I've only known Eli a few days, so you'd have a better idea," she said. "But my story? Normally I'd say it isn't what you'd call a thriller, but there have been some real twists lately. Born in Singapore, went to university, started working in the technology industry. That's the normal part. Now here I am, flying to Silicon Valley because some spies found me floating in the ocean."

"Right, and what happened there?" Monir asked. "You mentioned something about pirates."

Aileen looked out at the ocean again. She closed the window shade. "Do you know what it's like to grow up in a place where everyone knows you and everything about you?"

"Singapore, you mean?" Monir asked.

"Yes. I stayed for university because I didn't feel the need to leave. But one day I woke up and I'd spent my entire life in the same place. I had to get out."

"You mentioned not knowing where you belong. Is that what you meant? Moving elsewhere?"

Aileen laughed. "More like moving to another planet. Mine is a bit of an existential crisis."

Monir laughed too. "I know the feeling. What about the church stuff? How does that factor in?"

"It's a pretty standard thing, I imagine. Growing up and realizing that maybe you don't believe everything your parents believe. Which is fine and all, but then you have to figure out what you *do* believe."

"That's a little bit scary. Almost like starting your life over."

"Yeah. Hence the trip to Egypt. Being on a boat in the middle of the ocean seemed like a decent metaphor for my life."

"You sure picked an interesting change of pace," Monir said. "What happened on the ship?"

"It seemed like your run-of-the-mill pirate attack, for the most part. They boarded the ship, they waved guns around, they yelled. Except…"

"Except what?" Monir asked, intrigued.

"Well, pirates want loot, right? Like, by definition. But they were after a person."

Monir frowned. "Eli didn't mention that at dinner the other night. Who did they want?"

"That's the weird thing," Aileen said. "It was someone I knew from a while back. Nicholas Tong."

"Who is he? How do you know him?"

"I think he's a technology adviser for the Chinese government, and did something similar for Singapore before that. I've been reading about him—he's a big name in certain circles of tech. It was totally random that he was on the ship. I don't really know Tong, but he once observed a class I was in during university."

Monir rubbed his chin, thinking. "China just keeps popping up these days. Strange. I wonder what the pirates wanted him for. Ransom?"

Aileen's mind flicked to the thumb drive Tong had given her, safely tucked in her pocket. "No clue. It's really bizarre."

"It is. Maybe I'll ask Valencik about it," Monir joked. "He must know things."

"By the way, how long will you be in Silicon Valley?" Aileen said. "It's nice to be traveling with someone, even if you're basically a stranger."

"Likewise. I'm not sure," Monir said. "It depends how this meeting goes."

"Well, if you stay for a few days, we should have lunch, or whatever people do in Silicon Valley. Power lunch?"

"You can tell me about your interview over a Red Bull," Monir said, and Aileen laughed. "But yes, let's talk more soon. Having a friend at Frontfacer can only be useful. My computer skills are a mixed bag, so it won't be long before I need you to help me reset the password on my Frontfacer account."

"If I get this job, I'll be able to do a *little* more than that," Aileen said, smiling.

"I'm teasing. Anyway, whatever Eli had in mind, I have a feeling that our paths are going to cross again soon."

\*    \*    \*

### Paris, two months earlier

Nadia arrived at Pour Toi, a trendy restaurant in the 11th arrondissement, a few minutes before noon. At her request, she was seated in the far corner of the room, from which she could maintain a degree of privacy and keep an eye on the bar and the door. Only one table nearby was occupied: a middle-aged man and a younger woman were smiling at each other and holding hands while waiting for their food. Nadia settled onto a semi-circular couch and ordered a cappuccino. She set her purse on the table and searched for her lipstick, planning to make a quick stop at the restroom before the meeting she'd come for.

Her eyes focused on the purse, Nadia felt a presence. She looked up.

A man was standing across from her, average-looking except for his gray eyes, which conveyed strength and resolve.

"May I have a seat?" he asked. "This shouldn't take long." He sat across from her.

She regained her composure almost instantly and gave him a cold look. "What is this about? I have a meeting, and frankly I do not wish to speak with—"

"He's not coming, Miss Dryovskaya. Your meeting is canceled," said the man. Nadia looked past him, to the other end of the restaurant. A blonde woman was standing by the entrance, eyes locked on Nadia, her posture giving no doubt that she was part of this.

Still trying to seem poised, Nadia asked again. "What is this about? Who are you?"

"Eli is my name, and this is about giving you a chance to walk out of this restaurant alive." He spoke slowly, calmly, with a fatherly tone, making clear that he knew something she didn't.

Nadia was searching through years of faces in her memory, hoping for a match. Nothing. "What the hell are you talking about? I have to go." She grabbed her purse off the table and slid out of her seat.

Quickly, Eli said, "You don't want to walk out of here without me, Nadia. A sniper every bit as capable as you has her sights fixed on the door. You either walk out between me and my partner, or you'll die as soon as the restaurant's front door closes behind you."

She sat down, starting to panic. "You have the wrong person."

"Is that the standard SVR evasion technique, or did your former employer coach you?"

"I do not know what you are saying."

"No? Then do you know about the murder of Davin Valois in a silver Mercedes at the Vienna airport's long-term parking facility? Or about Karl Braun and CORE's activities in Cyprus? Or what about your attempts on the life of Monir Young? Not to mention one of your colleagues and two garbage truck operators being found dead in Cyprus."

"I have no idea about any of this."

Eli smiled patiently. "We aren't the only ones who know your former exploits, or your current whereabouts. Farrouk Ahmadi's ISIS brothers have been on the prowl as well. They're just a few steps behind us in locating you. Pointing them in the right direction wouldn't be difficult."

Nadia looked away. The reflections on dozens of liquor bottles behind the bar helped her fade out of the moment, back to that night in Vienna. Blood was everywhere, including her knife-bearing hand. Farrouk Ahmadi, gasping for air, was holding his punctured throat. "Sorry, Farrouk, but Moscow doesn't want any survivors," she'd said to the dying Jordanian. Nadia had been Ahmadi's colleague at CORE, but no one—not Farrouk, not anyone at the Swiss-based multinational—had known that Nadia's ultimate loyalty was to her bosses at the SVR, one of Russia's elite espionage units.

"What do you want?" she asked Eli.

He folded his hands and put them on the table. "The simplest thing in the world, Nadia: your services. Work for me for a little while, and we'll keep Farrouk's friends away from you. You help me, I help you. How does that sound?"

\*     \*     \*

As the SUV drove on, Itai watched Nadia out of the corner of his eye. He remembered the day Eli had walked into the office in Tel Aviv to tell Itai about their newest asset.

"Eli, you never cease to amaze me. Some of your operations have been works of art, but recruiting someone from another agency is a masterpiece. Just like that, Nadia Dryovskaya is working with us."

"She had no choice," Eli said. "But she made one thing very clear from the beginning."

"What was that?"

"She would never work against her country."

"Meaning?"

"She told me she would cooperate fully, as long as she was never made to participate in an operation against the SVR or Russia."

"They would view her as a traitor for leaving the restaurant with you, no?"

"I asked her that. Her response was that having her hand forced by an Israeli katsa is one thing, but actively opposing her country is another. She said she is willing to die for Russia. I believe her."

"I see. Model patriotism."

"Maybe, but also fear."

"Fear?"

"Deep inside, beneath the front she puts up. I saw it. She was afraid, not of us, but of Russia. Nadia would rather we put a bullet in her head than let her fall into the SVR's hands for treason."

# 10
# FRONTFACER

San Francisco thrummed with the energy of disruption. Dense fog and a cool breeze floated in off the water as Aileen and Monir walked out of the airport. They'd arrived very early that morning, so they'd gotten rooms in a hotel nearby to sleep for a few hours. A line of cars sat by the curb, people waiting to pick up their friends and family. Farther up, in a separate area, was a long row of sleek black shuttles bearing the names of companies—Google, Apple, Oracle, and more. Outside each one was a driver holding a sign with someone's last name. Looking to their right, Aileen and Monir spotted a shuttle with tinted windows and Frontfacer's name on the door. The man outside it had a sign that read, "Young and Soh."

Walking over, Monir introduced himself. Aileen followed and did the same. The driver grabbed their bags and put them in the shuttle. "Please make yourselves comfortable," he said.

As Aileen and Monir got in the car, the driver pointed to the armrest between their seats. "There's water and some light refreshments in the panel below there," he said. "Please help yourselves. Would you like the radio on?" He turned a knob and classical music filled the car.

Aileen took a water bottle and raised her eyebrows at Monir. *Fancy*, she mouthed. He grinned and winked. "Nothing but the best for the guests of Adrian Valencik," he whispered.

Neither of them noticed the green sedan that pulled away from the curb and followed them out of the airport.

The Frontfacer campus looked like it was on another planet. Aileen and Monir stared out the window as the shuttle turned onto the company's private street, named after an obscure programming term. In a clearing, set back from the street, a dozen identical multistory domes were clustered like spokes around a central hub. The buildings were white at the base, their top halves made of clear, polished glass that was crossed with thin lines of silver metal arranged in an intricate spiral. Concrete walkways were laid between strips of grass and trees at precise intervals. It all looked more like a futuristic greenhouse than a technology company.

As if on cue, the driver nodded toward the buildings and said, "We like to think we're growing the future here."

"It's certainly something," Monir said. "I'm more used to corporate buildings that look like white-collar prisons."

"Adrian likes to say that being creative requires creative surroundings," the driver said. "He built the new offices a few years ago as a symbol of innovation and progress."

"Progress is a word for it. I feel like I'm on Mars," said Aileen.

The driver laughed. "That's intentional. Adrian likes to say that you have to build the world you want now, and let everyone else catch up to you later."

Continuing toward the central hub, he told them more about the campus. Several thousand people were onsite every day, more worked remotely, and even more were at Frontfacer sites around the world. The campus had been based on the very latest research on office design, using open layouts that were engineered both for quiet acoustics and to encourage serendipitous encounters between employees—a hallmark of the most-creative companies. Plus, the driver added excitedly, every building had private nap rooms, a twenty-four-hour cafeteria, laundry, exercise facilities, showers, and more. "You never need to go home!" he said.

"How exciting," said Aileen, throwing a look at Monir, "never leaving the office. I think I'm going to like it here."

Missing her sarcasm, the driver told them that he hadn't been in his apartment since last week. "Why bother? The food here is free, and the chefs are always on call." The car stopped in front of the center building. "Mr. Young, this is you. Adrian's office is in the middle of campus. He likes to say it helps him keep an eye on everything that's going on."

Monir got out and grabbed his bag from the trunk. "Good luck," he said to Aileen. "Let me know how it goes." She waved and the car pulled away. Monir turned to face the entrance. Up close, the buildings were surprisingly intimidating, reaching up and away into the sky, giving the impression of being endless. He took a breath and walked inside.

\*     \*     \*

Retracing their steps from the previous night, Jael, Itai, and Nadia were headed to the safe house. Their guest, whose name was Nicholas Tong, Eli had told Jael and Itai, was scheduled to arrive in Singapore soon, but first they needed to drop Nadia off to keep an eye on Tong's destination. Jael took the exit for Siglap Link, which immediately led to Siglap Road. There was a tall condo near the safe house that Nadia would set up in. The plan was to keep Tong out of sight until Eli arrived. The katsa would take it from there.

The house was at the end of Bedok Drive. Once they'd taken a look around and agreed everything was in order, they turned around. Two right turns at the end of Bedok and the Infiniti was halfway down Towner Road, a street that ran parallel. Jael drove for a few hundred feet and then turned right into the ornate drive of Highline Residences. Nadia exited the car and walked around the vehicle to the trunk. She retrieved a small handbag and her Wilson tennis bag with a racquet sticking out the back. Walking to the lobby, she nodded at the two security guards at the door. She handed the bellhop her luggage but held onto the tennis bag.

Nadia checked in using a fake name and ID and took the elevator to a room on the sixth floor. She tipped the bellhop, locked the door, and pulled the curtains apart at the large window. With a pair of binoculars from her tennis bag, she had a clear view of the safe house. She spoke out loud, and a mic in her earpiece transmitted: "In position. Good vantage point on the house."

"Copy. Pulling away now." Jael put the car in gear. Itai sent a text to Eli: *Surveillance is in place. Changi jet terminal is the next stop.*

\* \* \*

Aileen got out of the car in front of a building whose sign read "People."

"This is human resources?" she asked the driver.

"Adrian thinks that label is too impersonal," he said. "Why not just name the department for what it's focused on? People."

"Ah. Well, thanks for the ride," she said.

"It was my pleasure! Have a great day." He drove off.

Aileen walked into the building, looking up at the glass dome. Two large, circular staircases connected the floors of the building on either side of the lobby. Walkways crossed from one side of the building to the other, a handful of people on them. A glass reception desk sat in the middle of the floor. Behind it was a man wearing a Frontfacer T-shirt and a blazer. He looked up from his computer as Aileen approached.

"Hello! How may I help you?" he asked.

"I'm here for an interview," Aileen said. "Aileen Soh."

He tapped a few keys. "Welcome, Ms. Soh. I see you're meeting with our vice president of people, Jackson Weller. If you'll please take a seat over there," he gestured to a few couches behind Aileen, "I'll let him know you've arrived." He looked down at her bags. "I'd be happy to store those for you during your meeting. We have a coat room just off the lobby."

"Thanks, that would be great," Aileen said. She sat down to wait, using the time to take in her surroundings. Everything was very clean and quiet. In some ways, it didn't look too different from the place she'd worked in Singapore.

Behind the reception desk, an elevator door opened and a man—not older than Aileen, and possibly younger—walked out. He, too, wore a blazer over a Frontfacer T-shirt. He walked over to Aileen and offered his hand. "Ms. Soh? Jackson Weller, head of people. How was your flight in?"

She stood up and shook his hand. "Nice to meet you. The flight was fine. This is an impressive office."

"Thank you, we're proud of it," Weller said. "Adrian worked on the designs himself. He says a leader should have a part in all the important things a company does."

"Huh. Adrian sounds like quite a guy."

"He is. A lot of people who end up here applied specifically because they wanted to work for him."

"And now here I am."

"And now here you are," Weller said. "Usually we would start with a video interview for someone living so far away, but Adrian said he had a good feeling about your application. He really appreciates you coming in. He said he just had to meet you himself."

"He's seen my résumé?" Aileen asked, surprised.

"Oh, yes. Adrian reviews all the most promising hires himself." Weller leaned in and whispered conspiratorially. "I probably shouldn't tell you this, but he's very interested in your background. Your résumé was very impressive, perfectly tailored to our needs. It was like you knew exactly what we wanted to hear."

"Good news for me. So what's the next step?"

"Right! I'm sure you're ready to get started after traveling all this way." Weller waved toward the elevator. "If you'll just follow me, we can begin."

\* \* \*

Jael parked the car on the second level of the parking garage. Itai got out and walked to the terminal alone. He came out twenty minutes later, sprinting. Jael jumped out and hissed a question in Hebrew. Itai's reply was punctuated with curses. They darted back into the car and weaved out of the garage and back to the ECP. Once on the highway, Itai called Eli.

"He's gone, boss. Never came out of the airport with the Gulfstream crew. Obviously, I didn't ask questions. I looked every place I could. Tong is nowhere to be found."

\* \* \*

Weller led Aileen into a glass-walled conference room on an upper floor of the people building. Outside, she could see Frontfacer employees sitting at desks and lounging on couches that were spread around.

"Sit anywhere you like," Weller said. "Coffee? Water? Tea? Something else?"

"I'm fine, thank you," she replied, taking a chair. She was surprised to find it was pretty comfortable. "How long have you been here?"

"I've been at Frontfacer for my entire career," Weller said. "I started here after business school, and was lucky enough to rise quickly." He gestured at the building around him. "At the time, Frontfacer's people department was underperforming. I specialized in human resources in B-school, so I helped Adrian get us where we needed to be."

"Where did you go? Harvard?" Aileen asked, guessing the only business school she could name.

Weller wrinkled his nose. "Wharton, actually. Adrian tries to distance himself from Harvard and people who went there. He dropped out, as you may know. But enough about that. Tell me what made you want to work here."

Aileen looked around, taking in the office as she thought of her reply. She couldn't very well say *a secret agent sent me here*. The obvious answer seemed to be the right one.

"It seemed...obvious. I needed a change, and Frontfacer is the best. I wanted to work for the best." She paused, watching Weller's face. "There were other opportunities, other companies, but no one has Frontfacer's reach or user base or technology. Really, once I decided to leave Singapore, I couldn't see myself anywhere else."

Weller nodded slowly, listening. "Nice! Adrian likes to hear that people can't imagine themselves working at another company. That's why he invested so much in making this," he swept his arm toward the glass wall, "an amazing place to spend time, whether you're working or not."

Aileen looked out through the wall again. Groups of Frontfacers were playing Ping-Pong and standing around talking, holding bottles of beer. She glanced at the clock on her phone. *A little early for a drink*, she thought.

Weller followed her gaze. "We offer a variety of food and beverages in all our buildings, day and night. A lot of our employees work odd hours. We don't monitor when people are coming and going as long as the job gets done. Some of them work from midnight to noon, which means this," he glanced at his watch, "is early evening for them, in a way."

"Is it OK if I keep normal hours? If I'm hired, I mean."

"Of course. Now, tell me more about your background. I've read your application and done some research about you. Connect the dots for me. What makes you right for Frontfacer?"

Aileen had spent part of the plane ride from Cyprus drafting answers to this exact question. Given how many people wanted to work for the company, having a good reply seemed essential.

"To be honest, Frontfacer needs me," she said.

Weller couldn't help smiling. "A bold statement. Go on."

"It's no secret that you guys want to keep growing. I saw Adrian Valencik was talking about it on TV a few days ago. You're already huge, so what's going to take you to the next level? What *is* the next level?"

Intrigued, Weller nodded. "All true. What are your thoughts?"

"It's not that complicated, really. Everyone uses Frontfacer, but the core Frontfacer app and website aren't the future. The things coming next are the future, and you need to get your users onboard with everything you want to do—virtual reality and giving people free internet access, for example. I know parts of the world that are valuable to the company, and I specialize in understanding people's needs. Global thinking, local context. My skills and knowledge would be useful in all kinds of areas."

"We think so, too," Weller said.

"Plus, China," said Aileen.

Weller raised his eyebrows. "China."

"You guys need in. I'd like to help make that happen."

"It's no secret that we've struggled to succeed there. Most American tech companies have."

"But you aren't giving up, of course," said Aileen. "You can't. A billion new users is too juicy to pass up. From what I hear, the question isn't *whether* you'll be there. It's simply what Frontfacer will look like in China's censored internet."

"You've done your homework," Weller said. "I'm impressed." He stood up. "I'll be back in a minute. There's someone I'd like you to meet. He had another meeting, but I'll see if he's free."

"Who is it?" Aileen asked as Weller walked out.

He stopped and looked back, his hand on the door. "Adrian Valencik, of course."

\* \* \*

Nicholas Tong was riding in the backseat of a car on the airport connector to the ECP and TPE. Just minutes before, he'd slipped out of the airport with the help of James Chan, a longtime friend who worked in customs and immigration. Before Tong had boarded the *Delfland* for Egypt, he'd enlisted Chan for tonight's action. Tong hadn't known exactly how the Americans and Israelis would get him off the *Delfland*, but he'd convinced them to help him loop back around to Singapore, where he thought his Chinese pursuers were unlikely to look for him. All he'd told Chan was that he would be arriving at Changi in a few weeks and would need help leaving the airport without being seen. Knowing what Tong did for a living, Chan hadn't asked any questions.

Sure enough, when the Gulfstream carrying Tong showed up, Chan moved ahead with their plan. After boarding the plane, Chan and his customs officers ordered the crew, Tong, and his two CIA escorts off the vessel for an inspection, citing tighter security measures as a result of the recent shooting. Chan had been conducting similar searches over the last few days so his team wouldn't be suspicious.

Once they walked across the disembarkation bridge into the terminal, each person was ushered into a private room for a "personal inspection." The CIA agents protested, but Chan's authority prevailed. He assured them he would soon reunite them with Tong in the arrivals hall.

While his team performed an intentionally long questioning and search, Chan rushed Tong through a series of hallways and a storage facility to a remote car park by the westernmost part of the terminal. They exited through a side door, walking out to the car park and straight to the rear door of a Toyota. Just as Itai was running to his car with news of Tong's disappearance, the Toyota with Tong in it was leaving the airport from the opposite direction.

# 11
## ADRIAN

After checking in at the reception desk, Monir had been shown to a sitting area outside Valencik's office containing two couches and a glass coffee table. He'd been offered all manner of food and beverages, enough that he felt like a guest of honor. But he still didn't know why he was at Frontfacer in the first place. Across the room, Valencik's assistant, a dark-haired woman in a black sweater, sat at a desk, typing on a computer. Every so often, she looked in his direction, as if checking on him. He smiled when their eyes met, and she returned to her typing.

He'd been waiting about 15 minutes when the woman stood up and walked over to him.

"Mr. Young? Thank you for your patience. Adrian is ready for you now. He was coming from across campus."

Monir glanced at the office door, which had a stylized map of the world engraved on it, with California at the center. "Thank you. I'm sorry, I didn't catch your name."

"It's Siena, Mr. Young. You can go in whenever you're ready." She returned to her desk and sat down, watching him as he approached the door.

Monir opened it and walked inside. Valencik's office wasn't as fancy as he'd expected. Most of the walls were glass, affording wide views of the Frontfacer campus. A small desk sat by the far wall, with a computer and a dozen books on it. Opposite the desk was a simple brown leather couch. Closer to the door were two reading chairs. Everything but the couch was decorated in shades of gray and white. Sitting in one of the chairs was Valencik, who looked up from a book as Monir entered. He stood up and shook Monir's hand.

"Mr. Young, welcome! Do you mind if I call you Monir? Please, call me Adrian." He motioned to the chair next to his. "Join me."

Monir sat down, taking a moment to see Valencik up close. The CEO was in his early thirties and intelligent-looking, with bright brown eyes that didn't seem to blink very often. Monir found the effect slightly unnerving. He wondered if it was intentional.

"Your office is, well, a little bare," he said, wishing he'd said something smarter.

"I'm obsessed with order," Valencik said. "The less I have in my office, the easier it is to keep clean. I do my best thinking when I'm not surrounded by clutter. That," he tilted his head toward the couch, "is my thinking spot. I only use it when I need to solve a problem or find a new angle on something. Otherwise, all I really need is my desk and these chairs. And my books." He held up the book he'd been reading, whose title was something about disruptive innovation. "Never stop learning. If you stop learning, you're dead."

"I think my wife would appreciate your approach to decorating," Monir said. "She's the organized one. I'm a bit of a slob in comparison."

"Speaking of your wife, I've been eager to find out more about you, Monir. You're an interesting man."

Monir was curious where this was going. "Is that right?"

"You were born in the U.S., but you've spent your adult life working in Europe and Asia. How did you go from New Jersey to Cyprus? I need to know more."

"It sounds like you know a lot already, Adrian." Monir's tone was friendly, but he was wary that the CEO very clearly researched him.

"Force of habit. I *did* start a company based on collecting information about people." He put a finger to his temple. "I'll get right to the point. The reason I'm interested in you is you're handling the Cyprus lithium."

"Yes, I know that much," Monir said. "But why? What would Frontfacer do with it?"

"It isn't for us," Valencik said. He leaned forward, looking Monir in eye. "I'd like Cyprus to sell the lithium to China."

Monir was taken aback, but his poker face had been perfected over years of negotiating. The head of one of the largest U.S. tech companies had just asked him to help the country's chief rival. He needed to find out what was going on.

"Oh, yes?"

"Yes." Valencik kept his eyes locked on Monir's, his gaze intense. "That's the reason I asked your superiors to send you here. I needed to convince you, and I could only do it in person." He chuckled to himself. "Imagine if I'd called you in Cyprus and asked you to back away from the deal with Singapore. You'd have hung up on me."

"You're probably right," Monir said, and both men laughed. "OK, you've got my attention. Tell me why Cyprus should sell the lithium to China instead of Singapore."

"Simple," Valencik said. "China knows what to do with it."

"Hmm. Is that all?"

"Ha! I'll elaborate." Valencik stood up and began to pace beside the chairs. "It's no secret that China's economic growth is slowing. Some experts think it's for good. Others think China needs to figure out how to push beyond its current plateau." Valencik stopped. "I'm in the second group, and I think the lithium is the answer."

He continued pacing, waving his arms as he talked. "Silicon Valley is stuck in a rut. Most companies are focused on pipe dreams like sending people to Mars, or useless technology—self-driving cars, glasses that record a few seconds of video, apps that help you carpool to the dry cleaner." He grimaced. "Sure, a few companies are actually trying to do some good. Look at Zuckerberg, running around the globe, trying to make sure people in the jungle can get birthday notifications on their wooden phones. Have you heard his speeches about wanting to create internet access for the four billion people who don't have it? Charming."

"But that's a good thing, isn't it?" Monir asked. "People having the internet seems like a worthwhile goal. Besides, Frontfacer is working on that, too, aren't you?"

Valencik became even more animated. "Yes, yes, it's fine, but is that really all we're going to do? Give it a decade or two, and everyone will be online. Period. It's going to happen. What then?"

Monir tried to remember anything he'd read about the future of technology. "Virtual reality? Isn't there a company working on it in Florida?"

"Who cares? That's what I'm trying to say, Monir. I don't care about the next decade; we have that under control. I'm thinking much further ahead, and what I see is our useless 'innovations' continuing indefinitely. U.S. companies need a reason to work harder. Right now there's no competition for a lot of them, so why shouldn't they be content making gif keyboards?"

Valencik sat down and looking at Monir intently. "China has some of the world's biggest tech companies, and for a while they were growing at an incredible pace. Even with the slowdown, they have the infrastructure to keep growing—they just need some help. Almost every computing device in the world uses lithium batteries.

Before the Cyprus lithium was discovered, experts were predicting a lithium shortage of 46,000 tons by 2021. Now they're saying whoever Cyprus sells the lithium to will become a technological superpower."

Monir was confused. "I follow all that, but I still don't get why you want China to have it. Shouldn't you want the lithium to go to the U.S.?"

Valencik snorted. "China's government overseeing Chinese companies—"

"You mean censoring and controlling them?" Monir cut in, testing him.

The CEO had an amused expression on his face. "You know, Monir, what China's government does isn't so different from how Lee Kuan Yew ran Singapore for decades. His approach accomplished a lot, but it didn't exactly leave room for second opinions. The same kind of approach is what's made Chinese technology succeed so quickly and emphatically. Are there downsides to it? Of course. But the upside is that business and government are on the same page. They have to be. That lets China move fast when it needs to."

Valencik pointed to his wall, where Frontfacer's unofficial motto was stenciled in stylized letters: *Fuck up the present, create the future.* He grinned. "We used to have that on walls throughout the office, but some visitors didn't like the language. But that idea is what China still knows how to do. Our own government is hopelessly behind the times. A lot of U.S. policymakers don't even use e-mail, let alone understand things like net neutrality. They're clueless when it comes to what the future looks like and how to get there. I am not."

Listening to Valencik articulate his position, Monir couldn't help wondering whether the CEO was right. Should Cyprus work with China after all? He was sure that the Cyprus government preferred Singapore as a business partner, but he felt confident he could sway them if it came to that. Some of what Valencik was saying seemed to make sense. Monir would be the first to admit that he himself was no expert on technology.

"OK, but you still haven't told me what's wrong with Singapore," Monir said.

"There's nothing *wrong* with Singapore," Valencik said. "It's made some great strides in the last few decades, and there's a lot of cool stuff happening there. But it doesn't have the industrial and manufacturing capabilities to use the lithium to its full potential." He thought for a moment. "Do you like movies, Monir?"

"Sure, who doesn't? Why?"

"Think of it this way. Hollywood, another industry whose future is in China, has a much easier time making money with a $100 million movie than with a $10 million movie. Blockbusters are too big to fail, you might say. If a $10 million movie does spectacularly well at the box office, the studio might see a profit of $40 million or so—not bad. But when a blockbuster does spectacularly well, everyone at the studio buys summer houses." Valencik held up his hands, as if surrendering to the cold logic of economics. "Singapore is the $10 million movie here. China—"

"Will buy the world summer houses?" Monir said.

Valencik chuckled again. "I like you, Monir. You get it. Yes, China is what will bring the technology industry, and the world, into the next age of prosperity. Silicon Valley has already created more wealth than anywhere in the history of human civilization. Imagine what a little global competition could push us to do next."

Monir was surprised to find that he wasn't sure what to think. Was Valencik onto something? He was still confused that the CEO was so in favor of China, but he didn't know enough about the technology industry to pick sides.

"But wait, Monir," said Valencik. "I think I've buried the lede."

"*That* was burying the lede?"

Valencik laughed. "What I meant is, I don't expect Cyprus to do what I want, no matter what line of reasoning I lay out. Right? So here's what I'm offering. This is how much I believe in what I'm saying." He leaned forward, his hands folded, fingertips touching. "If Cyprus agrees to sell the lithium to China, I will invest $100 million to bring Cyprus's digital infrastructure into the twenty-first century. Schools, banking, high-speed internet—whatever the government wants. In addition, I have contacts in the Chinese government. Whatever Singapore is offering for the lithium, I'm sure I can get China to pay more."

Monir was working hard to keep his face neutral. "Adrian, that is…very unexpected. But I'm sure Cyprus will want to consider it."

"I merely want the government to know I'm serious about the offer," Valencik said. "All they have to do is say the word, and the future is theirs."

"Adrian, this has been very interesting. I'll admit I was skeptical about coming here, but you've given me a lot to think about."

Valencik rubbed his hands together. "Good! Good. All I ask is that you consider what I've said. I know it may sound strange, but I honestly have the world's best interests at heart."

Monir wasn't sure he bought that, but he did want to find out more. "Can we meet again? I need to check in with Cyprus and tell them what we've talked about."

"Of course, Monir. Why don't we chat again tomorrow? Just let Siena know what time works for you, and I'll be there. While you're in town, Frontfacer would be happy to cover your hotel bill. We have some excellent sleeping facilities on campus, too, if that interests you."

"I may not be a billionaire, but my Cyprus expense account is good enough," Monir said. "But thank you." He stood up.

Valencik walked him to the door and they shook hands. "Until our next talk, then," he said. "Now, if you'll excuse me, I have another meeting to go to."

\*   \*   \*

Tong directed his driver to get on the PIE and bear right for the TPE. They took the first exit, and then Tong asked to be dropped off at the corner of Loyang Avenue and Loyang Lane.

"I can find a ride from here," he said to the driver.

But no further travel was needed. After thanking his driver, Tong started in a northwesterly course up Loyang Lane, walking a few blocks to a location that was undisclosed to everyone except a small group of trusted friends. His mind was working. The events of the last few weeks were like a dream to Nicholas, the kind he often had, half-conscious, in the hazy realm between sleep and consciousness. But the fact that he was walking on the streets of Singapore proved that what he had just experienced was very real.

\*   \*   \*

As Monir walked through the lobby, he briefly locked eyes with Valencik's assistant, who was watching him with a curious expression on her face. He couldn't figure out what it was, but then he was outside and into the California sunshine. *Hard to beat the weather here*, he thought.

Pulling out his phone, he saw a text from Aileen. He opened it. *Waiting to meet Valencik next. Seems like it's going well.*

Monir decided to kill some time by walking around the campus. He'd only taken a few steps when his phone rang. He looked down, but the number was blocked. He swiped to answer it.

"Hello?"

"Monir Young. Do not trust Adrian Valencik," said an electronically distorted voice.

"What? Who is this?" Monir demanded.

"Anything Valencik told you is a lie," the voice continued. "Do not believe him. Whatever he's doing is for his own gain, not the world's."

"Why should I trust you over him?" Monir asked.

"You shouldn't. Meet us. We will explain in person. Then you can choose who to believe."

"I'm not going anywhere because a mysterious voice told me to," said Monir. "Why should I meet you?"

"The future depends on it. China, the lithium, Singapore. There is much at stake. We must speak with you before you see Valencik again."

"Fine. Where do we meet? Somewhere public, so I know I'm not about to be murdered."

"There's a park two miles directly west of where you are. We will meet you there in one hour."

Monir spun around, scanning in all directions. "How do you know where I am?"

"The park, one hour. Do not be late," the voice said. "And remember, do not trust Adrian Valencik."

# 12
# SLIPPING AWAY

***Sri Lanka, two weeks earlier***

The *Delfland* was anchored a few nautical miles south of the Colombo International Container Terminals. The captain had chosen the spot to blend in with the other freighters waiting to refuel at the port, while being far enough away that the ship's activities would avoid detection.

Nicholas Tong had flown from Shanghai to Bandaranaike International Airport in Sri Lanka. After being driven to the coast and ferried to the *Delfland*, he was ascending the last flight of stairs to the bridge. He was running through a list of tasks in his head to be sure he hadn't forgotten something. The most important item of all had been checked and checked again over the last few days, to be absolutely certain: Aileen Soh was onboard the *Delfland*.

Tong didn't know how or when he would be transferred off the ship. During a phone call earlier that day, a man named Jeff Collins had told Tong that his pursuers from China had taken the bait and were making plans to intercept the ship on its way to Egypt. Collins had said the ship's captain would tell Tong where to meet his ride when the time came. He would be given further instructions soon.

\*   \*   \*

A week later, the time had come. Tong had been hiding in the captain's quarters, out of sight of the crew, since boarding. The captain signaled him that they'd picked up his pursuers approaching in the distance and his rescuers coming up behind the *Delfland*. Tong had to pull off the rest of his plan right now. The captain added that he'd found a way to get Aileen Soh alone for Tong to talk to her—she was below deck in the crew quarters, cleaning up some vomit. Tong didn't have time to question the oddness of the situation. He grabbed his thumb drive, opened the door, and went to find Aileen.

At 12:14, a small rib boat pulled alongside the *Delfland*. Tong used a rope ladder on the side of the ship to climb down to the rib boat. His belongings were lowered down after him on a rope with a hook on the end. Two sailors were in the boat waiting for Tong. One of them handled the motor; the other held a radio and was communicating with someone in Hebrew. The outboard motor started and the rib boat took off. It sped away from the *Delfland*, splitting the waves in lurching up-and-down motions. Tong was worried he was about to produce some vomit himself. Five minutes passed before he asked a question, shouting over the motor noise. "Where are we going?"

One of the men pointed a finger at the horizon. At first, all Tong could make out was a black object that looked like a smokestack. But as they got closer to it, Tong realized that the smokestack was the conning tower and sail plane of a massive submarine—Seawolf class, 353 feet long—the *USS Connecticut*.

Tong saw four men emerging from a topside hatch. They all wore life vests and harnesses, but three of them were in U.S. Navy uniforms and the fourth was in civilian clothes. One of the sailors on the submarine shouted orders to the rib boat, which immediately slowed. A rope ladder was draped down the side of the vessel. The men in the rib boat helped Tong climb the ladder to the submarine, where he was pulled up to the deck by the three sailors.

"Welcome aboard, sir," said the submarine commander, extending his hand.

Tong nodded politely but didn't put out his hand. His eyes darted from the faces of the sailors before him to the officer on the submarine's conning tower to a sailor with binoculars in the lookout beneath the bridge. The quick escape had put him on edge, and what he saw next didn't help. Tong glanced back in the direction of the *Delfland* but saw nothing but plumes of black smoke in the distance.

"Hello, Nicholas," said the man in civilian clothes. "I'm Jeff Collins. We spoke on the phone."

Tong looked at Collins intently and raised his hand. "Hi." Pointing to the smoke, he asked, "What happened? Are Eli and Gina here?"

Collins shook his head. "No, the pirates did something unexpected—set off explosives on the *Delfland*, probably to cover their tracks. Eli and Gina went to get Soh out of there, but they radioed and asked me to let you know they have her. She's unconscious but alive."

Tong breathed a sigh of relief. Against all odds, the plan was still on track. The first lieutenant escorted Tong down the hatch and the other sailors followed. The rib boat roared to life and took off toward the *Delfland*.

The *Connecticut* opened its main ballast tanks to begin its dive procedure: the sound of air escaping the tanks; water rushing into the ballasts from below. The submarine dove quickly, sinking toward its safe operating depth of 200 feet; then, on the chief of the watch's command, the *Connecticut* leveled out and set its course in a northwesterly direction.

In a few days' time, the submarine surfaced. An MI26 helicopter approached and hovered one hundred feet above the sub, lowering a round cage by winch. Collins and Tong got into the cage and were hoisted up to the chopper. Later that day, the helicopter landed in Mumbai's Chhatrapati Shivaji International Airport. From there, Collins led Tong to a private jet terminal, where two men shook hands with Collins and took Tong to a Gulfstream IV jet. Tong and the Gulfstream departed from Mumbai a few minutes later, setting a southeasterly course for Singapore.

\* \* \*

Valencik walked into the conference room, Weller close behind him. The CEO sat down next to Aileen and shook her hand. "Nice to meet you, Aileen. You're hired."

"Just like that?" she said.

Valencik jerked his thumb at Weller. "Just like that. I trust his instincts. We know you're smart, we know you have skills, otherwise you wouldn't be in this room. What I really wanted to know, what I ask everyone I interview, is why you want to work here. Jackson says I'd like your answer."

"Great. When do I start?"

"We've had a change of plans," Valencik said. "You applied for the user experience job, but I have something of a special project that I think you'd be a great addition to. The team can get you up to speed. The people working on it are some of our best, and they report directly to me."

"That sounds awesome. What would I be doing?" Aileen said.

Valencik waved his hand as if brushing away a fly. "We'll figure out your title. When it comes to hiring, I like to get the best people onboard now and figure out their job descriptions later. I want to surround myself with people who really, really care about my mission."

"Huh. I've been onboard a lot lately," Aileen said.

"What do you mean?" Valencik asked.

Aileen shook her head. "Just a little joke. I was doing some sailing before this. Anyway, I'd love to join this special project."

"That's great to hear. It's something that I think is vital for the future of the company. I think you'll find it very interesting." Valencik stood up and shook Aileen's hand. "OK, I think we're done here. Welcome to Frontfacer."

\*    \*    \*

The elevator couldn't ascend the ten floors fast enough. Jun had been on a call with one of her colleagues when she received a message from the tech deck upstairs. A match had been found for an individual who had been carrying a bag in the vicinity of the CapitaGreen and Republic Plaza buildings after the Demetra Bistro shooting. Jun darted out of the elevator and nearly ran into the sliding doors to the control room. "What do we have?"

A young police officer with a goatee pointed to the screens in front of him. On the left was a picture of Nadia Dryovskaya with a Wilson tennis bag, about half a block from Republic Plaza; on the right was a picture of her with the same bag in the lobby of Highline Residences. "A very close match, Officer Ai Boon. That woman could be the shooter," he said.

Finally, the break Jun had been hoping for. Grabbing her radio, she ordered several patrol cars near Siglap to the Highline complex and issued an all-points warning for a tall Caucasian female with long blonde or light brown hair, possibly carrying a Wilson tennis bag. Exiting the control room, she called Director Low and told him she had a lead and was heading to Siglap immediately.

Jun didn't have the patience to wait for the elevators. She ran down the ten flights of stairs to the car park.

\*　　\*　　\*

Itai and Jael's orders from Eli were to retreat and regroup. "Leave it to the Americans to lose him," he said in frustration before hanging up. Jael immediately called Nadia, who was settled into her surveillance position at the condominium. She told Nadia to pack up and wait outside for the car. They would be there in less than fifteen minutes.

Jun sped away from headquarters, down New Bridge Road. She turned onto Cantonment, then Keppel. She entered the MCE and continued north until it merged into the ECP. Radioing the patrol cars she had deployed, she asked for an update. Two were almost at Highline Residences. "I just got on the ECP," she said. "Light traffic, but I'm still ten minutes out. Establish a perimeter and wait for me."

Nadia walked out the front doors of the condo and stood along the curb, looking up and down the road. Jael and Itai pulled up moments later. Nadia put her bag in the trunk and took a seat in the back. As the Infiniti was exiting the driveway, two patrol cars were pulling in. Itai saw another cruiser in the opposite lane, two streets down, and a fourth one as Jael turned onto the ramp for the ECP. The cars were not on a routine patrol, he knew that much.

Four cruisers in close proximity and moving quickly was highly unusual for Singapore.

"Tong's no-show at Changi may have been a blessing in disguise," Itai said.

Nadia turned from looking at the last cruiser. "Who's Tong? What no-show?"

Itai seemed oblivious to her questions. He turned to Jael and spoke in Hebrew. "They're onto her. We may have pulled her out of there just in time. We have to switch vehicles immediately."

Jun was frustrated but optimistic. Her team's search of the condominium complex turned up nothing, but security cameras in the lobby and front entrance confirmed that the woman with the Wilson bag had indeed been there and had been picked up by a white Infiniti. Jun issued an all-points warning for the vehicle and sped back to headquarters.

\* \* \*

Monir got out of a car on the edge of the park, a few miles away from Frontfacer. He looked around, alert for any sign of whoever had contacted him. The park was large and green, with trees and ponds dotting the space. A few paths cut through the grass, occasional benches beside them.

He started walking along one of the paths, keeping an eye on his phone in case the mysterious voice called again. He didn't have to wait long. He swiped to answer on the first buzz.

"The tree by the largest pond," the voice said.

Monir followed the path past a few smaller ponds until he saw the one that had to be the biggest. A few people were having a picnic nearby; on the opposite side, a man was pushing a baby stroller on the path. Monir kept walking. Soon he spotted two people in jeans and metallic gray hoodies standing beneath a thick maple tree that stretched out over the pond. They watched him approach, and then motioned for him to follow. Monir fell into step beside them, walking across the grass.

Sneaking glances at them, he tried to make out who they were. The one closest to him was a man with brown hair and a scruffy beard. The other was a woman with long black hair that peeked out from the folds of her hoodie. Both wore their hoods up. Their eyes constantly flicked left and right, watching the edges of the park. *Are they hackers?* Monir wondered, thinking of the voice on the phone. He decided to ask.

"Are you hackers?" he said.

The man snorted. The woman responded slowly, as if speaking to a child. "'Hacker' is a meaningless word that the media uses to lump together everyone who does anything cool with computers." She paused. "That said, yes, you would probably call us hackers."

"Do all hackers wear the same hoodie?" Monir asked. "Matching clothes might give you away in public."

"They're made of a fabric that blocks thermal imaging," the man said. "If drones have a harder time seeing you, they have a harder time killing you."

"Are you seriously worried about being killed by a drone?" Monir peered up at the sky, shading his eyes with one hand. "Maybe I need one of those hoodies."

"It's a precaution. You'd hope the U.S. government wouldn't target its own citizens," the man said with a sneer, "even ones who work outside the strictest boundaries of the law, but I'd rather not take any chances. Not that long ago, no one thought automated drone strikes would be the default tool for killing terrorists. Now the government uses them all the time."

"The hoodies are less for drones than for other modes of surveillance," the woman said. "You must know that at least half a dozen satellites are tracking you right now. Some are the government's. Others are privately owned. We can't avoid them all, but we try."

"Um, yes, I know that," said Monir, who was continuing to realize just how little he knew about cutting-edge technology. Thinking about the phrase "strictest boundaries of the law," he had a feeling similar to when he was talking to Valencik earlier: *Were these people paranoid? Or was he not paranoid enough?* Suddenly Monir couldn't help noticing that the man with the baby stroller was walking in their direction on an adjacent path. The hackers noticed it too. They immediately turned and walked in another direction. Monir jogged after them to keep up.

# 13
## COMMON GOOD

The hackers led Monir away from the other people in the park, not saying anything. Once they had put sufficient distance between them and anyone who might be listening in, the woman spoke.

"Mr. Young, we don't have a lot of time. They might be watching you, which means they might be watching us."

"Who might?" Monir asked, eyeing the man with the stroller, who was chasing a toddler around a tree.

"Frontfacer. Valencik. I wouldn't put anything past him. However suspicious you are of him now, it's not enough."

"I'm not suspicious of him at all."

"That's a mistake. He's dangerous."

"You said that on the phone, but why? Help me out—you guys live in a different world than I do. I'm only here to talk to Adrian about a business deal."

"The lithium, we know," she said. "Cyprus absolutely can't sell it to China. You can't listen to Valencik."

"First, stop telling me what to do," Monir said. "Second, to me, you two are a couple of tinfoil-hat-wearing weirdos in a park in California. Start telling me what's going on or I'm out of here. Maybe I'll sell the lithium to China on my way back to the hotel," he said with a smirk.

"This isn't a game," the man said angrily.

The woman touched his shoulder to calm him. "OK, Mr. Young. Here is what's going on. We're part of Clandestine, a watchdog collective of, well, hackers. We're all over the world, and we make sure the technological superpowers aren't abusing their access."

"Superpowers?" Monir said. "You mean the U.S.? China? Access to what?"

"The superpowers of today include more than governments. We keep an eye on what they're doing, but we're interested in the companies that have sprung up in the last decade, collecting as much personal data of as many people as they can. That's what I meant by 'access': their access to you."

Monir thought back to his conversation with Aileen in the airport. "I see. But what's so bad about Instagram knowing where I went on vacation? I like Instagram."

"Do you have any idea what the company does with your pictures and the data attached to them?"

"No, but I'm guessing it's bad."

"That's my point—you don't know. Almost no one bothers to pay attention to how much these companies know about them, and their lives, and who they know, and where they go every day, and what they're doing. People are oblivious, which lets these companies record and store anything they want. It would be nice to think the worst-case scenario is that Instagram sells your information to advertisers, but the worst-case scenario might be much worse."

"Like what?" Monir said. "Selling it to telemarketers?"

"Not selling it, being forced to give it away," the woman continued. "And not to telemarketers. To the government. The worst-case scenario is an authoritarian surveillance state where the people who write and enforce the laws know every detail of your life: exactly what you're doing, exactly where you were on Tuesday, exactly who you were with, and so on. There goes any shred of privacy you had left."

"What does this have to do with Frontfacer?" Monir asked. "I've had my fill of technoparanoia in the last few days."

"Frontfacer is the focal point of it all," the woman said.

"Meaning what?"

"Mr. Young, do you know a man named Nicholas Tong?"

\*   \*   \*

The phone call from Director Low could not have come at a better time. For the last forty-eight hours, Jun's investigation had failed to provide more leads, as both the white Infiniti and the tall woman who had entered it at Highline Residences had disappeared. Nothing from police stakeouts at MRT stations, malls, and main thoroughfares. Footage from hundreds of security cameras across the city had found nothing; the immigration posts by the Malaysian border had fared no better.

Jun cringed at Low's voice, expecting him to be angry.

"Officer Ai Boon, the PM's office has received a call with an offer for assistance in the shooting investigation."

"What kind of assistance, sir? From who?"

"The Americans. The deputy director of the CIA, to be exact. They will run our surveillance footage through their facial recognition apparatus at Langley and make available their NSA voice collection capabilities to sift through radio and cell phone traffic. I have read about their technology in these areas. It is far more advanced than anything we have here."

"That will be a great help, sir."

"John Harden will call you directly to coordinate the effort. Our orders are to give the Americans everything they need."

"I understand, Director Low. May I ask a question?"

"Of course."

"How does the CIA know about our investigation, and what is their motivation for offering to help?"

"According to Harden, the CIA identified our chief suspect before we did. They must have received security footage from their station chief's office. Harden said they recognized the suspect as someone they've had dealings with before."

"Did he give a name?"

"He said he will share that information once we agree to their offer."

"And the motive for their assistance?"

"Harden wasn't clear about it. All I could deduce was that the shooting is connected to a potential lithium deal between us and Cyprus, and that the CIA has been after this suspect for some time now. Perhaps you will find out more when you speak with Harden."

"Thank you, Director Low." Jun breathed a small sigh of relief. As much as she liked to do things her way, she could use all the help she could get.

\*　　\*　　\*

"Nicholas Tong," Monir repeated. He did know the name, but all he knew about the man was what Aileen had told him. "I might know him. I might not. Why?"

"Don't play dumb," the man said. "You know who he is."

"Mr. Young, we're going to be frank with you," the woman said, "because time isn't on our side. I'm sure you have to get back to Singapore before long, and there are things you need to know before you do."

"What things?"

Their conversation had brought them around to the far side of the park. A few people were playing soccer in a large open area, and a few more sat watching. Monir saw the hackers size up the crowd. He did the same. Nothing out of the ordinary, as far as he could tell. To his right, a green sedan slowly rolled down the street beside the park.

"Tong was a technology adviser to the Chinese government," the woman said. "He contacted us a few weeks ago, saying he needed help. Something bad is happening in China, and Valencik is connected to it. Tong wouldn't say how, but if Frontfacer is involved, it must be big. He wanted us to help spread the word."

"But you don't know what he found. Why you?" Monir asked. "Why not go to the police, or a newspaper?"

"Who do you think controls the newspapers in China?" the man said. "Tong's employers. He needed us to help him get the evidence of what he'd found into the right hands. It's disgustingly easy for the authorities to bury something like this."

"Clandestine mostly works behind the scenes," the woman added. "We connect the people with information and the people who can use that information for the common good."

"Who decides what the common good is?" Monir asked. "Though I can probably guess."

"We do," the man said. "We know what's best for the world, and we help it happen."

"How generous of you," said Monir. "So you're like WikiLeaks?"

"Don't make me laugh. Julian Assange wants to be a celebrity, and WikiLeaks has an agenda now. Besides, they're in bed with the Russians. Our only agenda is the truth. We don't need fame or awards along with it."

"Mr. Young, Tong told us he had evidence of a cyber threat whose scale is unprecedented," the woman said. "He called the evidence 'the cargo.' He was making plans to escape from China with it, but then he vanished. We haven't heard from him since."

Monir shrugged. "I don't know what to tell you. I sure don't know where he is."

"I believe you, but someone you know might know where to start looking."

"Who?" Monir said, guessing the answer but wanting to see how much they knew.

"Frontfacer's newest employee: Aileen Soh."

\*　　\*　　\*

A few miles away at Frontfacer, Aileen was following Siena, Valencik's assistant, on a tour of her new home. She'd been given a laptop and introduced to a few people who weren't working at the moment. No one at Frontfacer had an office except for Valencik, but even that, Siena was quick to point out, was only for meetings or when Valencik needed to think or meditate. There was no assigned seating, so everyone else found some open space at the rows of white tables that were surrounded by all kinds of distractions: game rooms, lounges, kitchens, nap alcoves, and more.

Aileen's project team, which Valencik called his "digital ninjas," was clustered at one end of the long room. They were the only employees with assigned seats, due to the secretive nature of their work. Their space was cordoned off with gray panels, the sole work area that had anything resembling walls. Aileen was already realizing the open seating plan would present some noise challenges.

The team reported to Valencik, but Siena was the point person for the team members, as she explained to Aileen, since the CEO had a lot to deal with. The ninjas were essentially a special task force, thrown at obstacles that needed Frontfacer's best and brightest.

"What's the team working on right now?" Aileen asked Siena.

The assistant waved toward the walled-off area of the room. "Come on, I'll introduce you. The team members can tell you more about their roles, but no one knows the full extent of the project except Adrian. And me, to a lesser extent."

"Really? How does anyone get work done in silos like that?"

"Adrian gives them enough to work with. It's that simple. He breaks the project into chunks and lets the team loose on their pieces. Then he reassembles it at the end. It's a little cumbersome—no one knows what anyone else is working on, and team members are forbidden from discussing their work. That's why only the best people make the ninjas." Siena smiled. "Yes, the name is a little silly."

"No, it's great," Aileen said. "I always wanted to be a ninja when I was a kid."

"One of Adrian's heroes is Steve Jobs, who also used secrecy to get things done. Sometimes you have to control who knows what. Frontfacer is involved with some sensitive things, as you'll find out."

"What's this one?" Aileen asked again, following Siena toward the rest of the ninjas.

"The biggest prize left in the world," Siena said. "China."

# 14
## CLANDESTINE

"Aileen Soh," said Monir slowly, as if trying to remember who she was. The hackers knew plenty already; he wasn't sure he wanted to give them any more information until he knew whose side they were on. "Yes, I know her. We met on the plane. She knows Tong?"

"That's the odd part," the woman said. "We think she does, but we aren't sure how they met. But that's irrelevant. Tong is hiding somewhere, and he has the cargo with him. We think he's afraid for his life, but we need to get that evidence."

"How do you know all this?" Monir asked.

"Uh, we're hackers, remember?" the man said sarcastically. "We hack. We know things."

The woman took a step toward Monir. "Please, Mr. Young. Something bad is happening at Frontfacer, and Soh may be able to help. Talk to her. Find out if she knows where Tong is. She might have a way to contact him."

"No promises," Monir said. "But I'll try to talk to her."

"Thank you. We really do have the world's best interests at heart. We're trying to help."

"You know, I've been hearing that a lot lately," Monir said. "How do I contact you? If I decide to."

"You don't. We'll contact you," the man said. "Three days from now. Try to have something for us."

"I might need more time than that," said Monir. "Things are a little busy at the moment."

"Fine. A week. Just get it done."

"Please, Mr. Young," said the woman. "So much is at stake."

"I know," Monir said. "Believe me, I know."

\*　\*　\*

### Ismailia, Egypt

It had been a quiet evening at the Suez Canal Authority headquarters. Admiral Magdy El-Aziz Saleh, the SCA managing director, was busy signing documents when his phone started buzzing. He looked down, saw the number, and groaned. Things were never simple after a call from John Harden.

"Good evening, Magdy. It *is* night there, right?"

The admiral chuckled. Harden was a stickler about taking time changes into account.

"Yes indeed, John. Is it morning for you?"

"Early afternoon. I just got back from lunch. You would have liked it—rice, lentils, garlic, a few other things."

The two men had met in 2011 in Cairo, shortly before the Day of Revolt protests. After a year's worth of research and surveillance, the CIA station chief in Egypt had recommended the admiral to Harden as a high-level asset. The admiral had been an outstanding military leader, but he aspired to a life of wealth that thus far had been out of his reach.

Harden hadn't needed much convincing to recruit the admiral, and he flew to Cairo to do it himself. By the end of a two-hour lunch at El-Fishawi café, an agreement had been reached. The admiral would supply a list of names and e-mail addresses of up-and-coming Muslim Brotherhood leaders in return for a handsome sum in a British bank and an American-induced promotion to head of the SCA. Things had progressed well for both sides from that point.

The admiral closed his office door and sat at his desk. "What can I do for you, John?"

"The *Delfland* shipwreck is causing some ripples that we're trying to monitor."

"How did I know this would be about the *Delfland?*"

"There seems to be particular interest for the type of information that ships normally submit to the SCA before going through the Canal."

"You mean the crew list and cargo manifest?"

"Yes. Has anyone been asking for that information?"

"Not to my knowledge, but I can ask my deputy."

"Thank you, Magdy. We believe the ship was carrying primarily Mitsubishi air conditioners from Singapore, and the freighter was en route to Egypt."

"I heard something about it. I can look into it for you."

"Please do. Oh, and this is unrelated, but I'm interested in a marine mechanic by the name of Nicholas Tong. Can you confirm he was on the *Delfland* crew list when the ship left Singapore?"

"Give me a day or two. I'll get back to you the usual way."

The admiral ended the call and looked up at the ceiling for a few seconds. Then he shoved some papers in a briefcase and walked out of his office and through the cubicle-lined hallway, not making eye contact with any of the staff. He needed to make some calls, and his car had always been the safest place for that.

\*   \*   \*

Taking a car to his hotel, Monir thought about his next move. He needed to talk to his bosses in Cyprus about everything that had happened. Whether Valencik was right about China or not, his offer to vastly improve Cyprus's technology was something the country had to consider. In some ways, Cyprus not being involved in the global technology industry was now an advantage. The lithium was so in demand that Cyprus could afford to be choosy about what to do with it. Singapore had seemed the obvious country to make a deal with, but Monir's conversation with Valencik had suddenly made that outcome seem far less obvious.

Monir shifted in his seat. Eli and Gina, too, would want to know what had happened at Frontfacer, but Monir wasn't sure how much to tell them. After all, he didn't work for the spies. They were something like friends, and without a doubt they had helped Monir in the past, even saved his life, but that didn't mean they were privy to everything he knew. Monir watched the suburbs of Silicon Valley roll past. He had to tell them something; sometime soon he'd figure out exactly what that would be.

And, of course, there was the matter of Tong. Whatever was going on with Frontfacer, if China was involved, the whole lithium deal could be at stake. Aileen's connection to Tong seemed to be the best place to start asking questions.

Pulling out his phone, Monir checked the time and texted Aileen: *When are you done today? I need to talk to you ASAP. Dinner?*

\*　\*　\*

The admiral turned onto the Nile Corniche highway and drove along the southeastern rim of the city to the Qasr al-Nil Bridge. He got off the highway one exit before the bridge and weaved his way through narrow streets to a gravel parking area directly under it. He'd found the spot when he and his wife were courting, and he always returned there when seeking privacy from potential drone surveillance.

Magdy remained in the driver's seat, looking around cautiously to make sure he hadn't been followed. He confirmed that the doors were locked and retrieved a cell phone from the glove compartment. He turned it on and pressed two keys. It rang once on the other end.

"Just as you expected, sir. The Americans are starting to ask questions."

"About the ship?"

"Yes, the *Delfland*."

"Who was it, CIA?"

"Yes."

"What did they want?"

"Something about the *Delfland*'s cargo and a Nicholas Tong."

"What did you say?"

"That there were no inquiries about Tong yet and that I'd look into what the ship was carrying. You have Tong, correct?"

"No. He seems to have been transferred off the ship before we boarded it."

"I see. Sorry to hear that, sir. What can I do to help?"

"Call the bosses of major ports within a two-thousand-mile radius. See if they heard anything or have video we can use. We have to find Tong as soon as possible. You may double your fee if you help us find Tong quickly."

"Thank you, Mr. Li. I will do my best."

Magdy hung up. He exhaled deeply and smiled. Certainly, the Americans had put the admiral in a position of power and influence, but his pay was still miniscule in comparison with other port and canal bosses around the world. Side deals with men like Mr. Li made up the difference. His perch at the SCA let the admiral work both ends from the middle. And in the middle was a big payday. Magdy had no idea who Nicholas Tong was or what the Americans and Chinese wanted with him. But if that's who they wanted, that's who he'd find. He switched phones and began making calls.

*   *   *

Aileen was settling into her work area when Monir's text arrived. She called to Siena, who was talking to one of the other ninjas. "Hey, not to run out the door on my first day, but how long do you need me here? I still have to find a hotel and drop off my stuff."

Siena walked over, typing on her phone. "I just sent you instructions on how to reserve a sleep space here on campus, if you'd like to do that. The nap rooms are first come, first served, but the overnight rooms require a little more planning, since there are fewer of them. We set aside a few for visitors and new employees, though. Adrian plans to build more this year."

"Thanks, but I think I'd like a little work-life separation for now. A hotel is fine," Aileen said. A few of the ninjas laughed. She wondered whether they agreed with her plan or thought it was silly. Silicon Valley's culture of your work being your whole life was legendary, but Aileen didn't love the idea.

"Suit yourself," Siena said. "Let me know if you need any help finding a place."

"Thanks. Should I be here at nine tomorrow?" Aileen asked.

"Whenever. My hours tend to vary with Adrian's, so text me when you get to the office and I'll get you started on your project."

"Will do." Aileen looked over at the other ninjas, most of who were staring at their laptops, headphones on, typing away. She'd met the team members who were there that day, though Siena said a few ninjas worked remotely most of the time. There were about a dozen people on the team, mostly men, mostly white. The ninjas greeted her with a mix of professional friendliness and skepticism.

Siena explained privately that most of them had been working with each other at different companies for years; the U.S. tech industry was a small world. The competition for jobs at the "coolest" companies was fierce, and it wasn't unusual for in-demand employees to be lured to a competitor with more money and stock options. Sometimes whole teams were poached. Everyone knew everyone else, which made Aileen an outsider. Siena told her not to worry—before long, the other ninjas would view her as one of their own.

Anyway, Aileen thought with a little thrill, now she worked for Frontfacer. Having the name on her résumé would open doors in the future, and of course the job itself was exciting. She was looking forward to finding out what her China project would be.

Aileen pulled out her phone and texted Monir. *Leaving FF now. Where are you staying? Meet there?*

He texted back immediately. *The Oxford Hotel. I'll wait for you in the lobby. A lot to tell you.*

*OK. See you soon.* Aileen gathered up her things and headed outside to call a car. Whatever Monir wanted to talk about, it sounded like it couldn't wait.

An hour later, Aileen had checked into a room at the hotel, changed clothes, and gone downstairs to meet Monir. They were talking quietly in a corner of the hotel's restaurant, away from the other diners.

"What happened today?" Aileen asked.

Monir exhaled slowly. "Where to start? Valencik wants the lithium to go to China. He thinks Singapore can't do enough with it. He wants me to convince Cyprus to abandon the deal with Singapore. Oh, and then there were the hackers."

"The hackers?" Aileen said.

"Have you ever heard of a group called Clandestine?"

"Yeah, they call themselves watchdogs for global technology, or something like that. Why?"

Monir held up his phone. "After meeting with Valencik, I got a call. Turns out, it was Clandestine. They told me not to trust him. I went to a park to meet them, and two of their people walked me through a story that's either really crazy or really interesting. Or maybe both."

"What story? This is already sounding a little crazy."

"I'm not sure how to put this," Monir said. "They were asking about Nicholas Tong. And about you."

Aileen looked around the restaurant. Most of the other diners seemed to be tech people, if their jeans and T-shirts were any indication. Some of them were in suits. Lunch meetings, she guessed. "What did they ask about me?"

"I'm still wrapping my head around it, but it sounds like Tong was into some bad stuff. Clandestine said Tong contacted them about a situation he had some evidence about."

"A situation."

"I don't know more than that, because Clandestine doesn't know more. Before he disappeared, Tong wouldn't tell them what's actually happening, but something big is going on with Frontfacer and China. He needed help getting the information to the right people."

Aileen's mind was whirling. "Monir, Valencik put me on a special project today. They haven't told me what I'll be doing, but it's about China. That can't be a coincidence, right?"

"There's more. They know you know Tong. And I don't know why, but they think you might know how to find him." Monir paused. "Then again, these people were a little nuts. You should have seen their hoodies."

"Well…" Aileen said slowly. Could she trust Monir? She hoped so. Gina and Eli trusted him, and Aileen trusted them, more or less. "I might know something. But I don't know what it is."

Monir smiled. "That was delightfully vague."

It was now or never. "Tong gave me a thumb drive. I've been carrying it since I was on the ship. I'm not sure what's on it, but he told me to keep it safe. I've been waiting for a chance to figure out what it is."

Monir couldn't hide his surprise. "Have you looked at it?"

She nodded. "There are a bunch of files, but they're either encrypted or locked. That's as far as I've gotten. Getting past encryption isn't really my area."

"Huh. Interesting. That is interesting. Maybe those hackers aren't a bunch of crackpots after all." Monir was thinking. If the thumb drive was connected to all this, it might be connected to the lithium. He needed to know what was on it, and soon. "To be honest, I'm not sure what our next move is. I'd guess Gina and Eli have the resources to figure out what's on the drive, but that could take time, and I'd rather find out more about this before telling them everything."

"Really?" Aileen said. "I sort of thought you all were the very best of friends."

"We aren't *not* friends," Monir said. "I'm friendly with them, but I work for Cyprus. I'd like to know what we're dealing with before going back to them."

"I agree," Aileen said. "Eli asked me to check in with them in a few days, once I'm settled here. I don't have to mention this stuff with Tong yet, but it's going to come up eventually." She looked hard at Monir. "Hey, I can trust you, right? I know we haven't known each other for long, but I think we're on the same side. Or at least we aren't on opposite sides."

Monir nodded. "You can. If there's one thing the last few days have reminded me of, it's that there are way more than two sides to this. We definitely aren't on opposite teams." He grinned. "And even though you're now one of Adrian Valencik's top lieutenants, I'll still trust you."

"Ha. It may take a few weeks before I know all of Frontfacer's secrets, but I'll get there," Aileen said. "Just you wait."

"Looking forward to that. Tong, Valencik, China—I freely admit I can't figure this out alone. I'm glad we're working together."

"Actually, I had an idea about that. I have a group of friends in Singapore, tech friends. Some of them qualify as hackers, and there's one in particular who I'd trust to look at Tong's drive. Maybe he can figure out what it is. He'll know more than we do."

"Great. Any hacker friend of yours is a hacker friend of mine. Who is it?"

"Remember how I said I grew up in the church? He's a friend from a church group I used to belong to. His name is Dominic."

"Churchgoing hackers. What will they think of next?" Monir said. "I'm most likely going back to Singapore in a few days. How do I meet Dominic?"

"Let me talk to him first. I'll explain what's going on and tell him to keep it quiet. If he says it's OK, I'll send you his information."

"If he's anything like Clandestine, this should be educational," said Monir. "OK, Tong, watch out—we're coming to find you."

\*     \*     \*

The long-awaited call came from Mumbai, a friend who worked at Chhatrapati Shivaji International Airport. Video surveillance showed two white men and one Asian man boarding a plane.

"Nice work, my friend," said Magdy. "The plane they boarded, where did it fly?"

"Singapore."

# 15
# ON THE JOB

The next morning, Monir woke up early. He had two phone calls to make, and he was calling many time zones ahead.

First was Christakis Savvides, who sounded very pleased to hear from him, nearly shouting into the phone.

"How did things go with Frontfacer, Monir?"

Monir told him about Valencik's proposal, keeping his tone even to avoid revealing how he felt about it.

Savvides listened and then said, "OK, let me see if I understand this. Valencik wants us to sell the lithium to China, who he says will pay us a better price than Singapore, and he's offering to invest a huge amount of money into our technology infrastructure as well?"

"Exactly."

"I don't get it, Monir. That's good for Cyprus, but what's in this for him?"

"That's the part I'm still figuring out. I have some connections in California that are looking into it right now. I need some time to research this more carefully."

"How much time?"

"A week. Two weeks at the most."

"OK, Monir. Stay in touch. I'll talk with the president in the meantime so he knows what's happening. This sounds too good to be true, to be honest. But then again, who knows, eh?"

"I'll be in touch, Christakis. Take care."

Monir hung up and started dialing William Tan's number. "So far, so good," he muttered. As expected, Savvides was too interested in the financial prospects of Valencik's offer to challenge Monir's request for time, even if the Cypriot was skeptical about it. Monir hoped his next call would go just as well. He was hesitant to call so late—it was past dinnertime there—but William had said he often worked into the night. The last that the Singaporean knew, Monir was flying back to Cyprus for something urgent; a lot had happened since then.

William picked up on the third ring. Monir apologized for calling so late and for being out of touch, explaining that Cyprus had sent him to California, and the reason why. Although William was quiet, Monir could feel tension mounting as he told the Singaporean about his meeting with Valencik. "That's where things are, William. Cyprus wants me to talk to Valencik more before moving forward in any direction."

William spoke slowly, his voice sounding tired and just a little angry. "Monir, first of all, it would have been appreciated if Cyprus, or you, let us know why you left Singapore, and just as negotiations were starting, no less. Then this development with Valencik—the fact that an American executive wants to influence a deal with China! Isn't this alarming to you?"

"He explained his reasoning, and it intrigued me. I'm not saying I agree with him, William, and I share your concerns. But I need to investigate what he said, to do my due diligence for Cyprus. I have some people digging into the situation for me. Why don't we talk when I return to Singapore? I'll be there in a few days."

"May I send for you at the airport? Actually, I'll come myself. We can talk about everything."

"I already have a ride, William, but thank you."

"Very well. Please let me know when you arrive. I'd like to speak with you at the earliest opportunity. Singapore remains fully committed to the lithium deal, Monir. We hope Cyprus is, too."

"Don't worry, William, I'll be in touch once I'm settled in. Talk soon." Monir hung up and took a deep breath. He'd expected William to be upset, but it couldn't be helped. For a deal as big as this one, Cyprus had to explore all its options. That was just good business.

He had one more call to make. Monir dialed Siena and asked to meet with Valencik later that day.

On her way to work, Aileen texted Dominic from her cab, explaining about Tong and the thumb drive. She told Dominic she was sending the drive back to Singapore with Monir, and asked him to trust Monir with whatever he found on it.

At Frontfacer, a few of the other ninjas were already at their desks. Siena was nowhere to be seen. Aileen sent her a quick text to say she'd arrived, and then sat down at her station, trying to look pleasant and approachable. "Hi, everyone. I'm Aileen, if we haven't met yet."

One of the ninjas rolled toward her on his chair.

"Hey, Aileen, I'm Priyansh," he said. "Welcome to the team." He pointed to the other ninjas one by one. "That's Andrew, that's Tanya, and that's Carlos. Carlos is the newest, besides you."

"How long have you been here?" Aileen asked.

"About a year," Priyansh said. "I was at Facebook before, doing pretty much the same thing, but Adrian offered me a 30% raise to come to Frontfacer, so I did." He shrugged. "Not exactly rocket science. Though one department here does that, too."

"How do you like working for Adrian? He seems to know what he wants."

"He's been pretty hands-off lately. We've been reporting to Siena. She says Adrian has some new venture he's obsessed with." Priyansh grinned and shook his head. "He's a maniac. Barely leaves the office, as far as I can tell. Some people say he used to sleep in a trailer in the parking lot."

"Yeah, I've heard this place isn't the biggest fan of us going home at night," Aileen said. "How's your workload? What are you working on right now?"

"Sorry, can't say. It's pretty much the only rule of the ninjas."

"That's right," cut in a voice from behind them. Aileen turned to see Siena walking up. "Adrian is serious about it. You're working on delicate projects, so keeping things under wraps is paramount. It's part of the nondisclosure agreement you signed when you were put on this team. The ninjas have their own unique version of the NDA." Siena clapped her hands. "Anyway, enough paperwork talk. Let's get to work."

\*   \*   \*

According to Kong Li's sources in Singapore's nightlife, some Americans had been asking around for any information they could get about Nicholas Tong. It sounded as though Tong had disappeared yet again. Li was told that Tong had been flown to Singapore by the Americans, only to get away shortly after arriving at Changi. It confirmed what Magdy had said about Tong being on a Singapore-bound flight from Mumbai. Li didn't know how to tell Zhang Wei that he still had no solid leads on Tong. He was more than a little confused himself—who was this computer expert who was managing to stay a step ahead of him?

When Li finally called Wei, he conveyed the news and braced for Wei's famous temper. He was surprised to find that Wei was calm, and almost sounded amused.

"Kong Li, do you know where I am?"

Warily, Li replied, "No, Mr. Wei. Where are you?"

"I am sitting in my office, where I am asking myself many questions, many questions indeed. One of these questions is, 'Is Kong Li not an experienced criminal?' Another is, 'Am I mistaken? Am I demanding too much of him?' Perhaps this is your first time finding someone who does not want to be found. Perhaps that is why you did not have your people waiting at the airport after your Egyptian informant told you Tong was flying there."

"Mr. Wei, by the time I learned the information, Tong's transfer had already taken place."

"Kong Li, I have only two ears, so I can hear only so many excuses. You know the larger aims of my work. If your newly discovered ineptitude remains a hindrance to them, there will be more questions asked about you. For example, 'Where is Kong Li's body buried?'"

"I understand, Mr. Wei. But I have an idea. You told me that Adrian Valencik brought Monir Young to California. I propose we follow Young night and day when he returns to Singapore. I have a strong feeling that he will lead us to something useful."

"Perhaps I spoke too soon, Kong Li. You may have a brain after all. Find out when Young is returning, and do not let him out of your sight."

\*   \*   \*

When Monir arrived at Frontfacer, a group of people was playing a game involving hoops and balls on one of the lawns. They were straddling brooms and running back and forth between the hoops. Monir watched, clueless about what was happening. "California," he muttered, walking into Valencik's building.

He greeted Siena outside the CEO's office. "Sorry, I'm a little early. Happy to wait until he's free."

"Actually, he's ready for you now, Mr. Young," she said. "He's been looking forward to talking again. You can go in."

"Oh, perfect. Thank you," Monir said, opening the door with the map of the world on it.

Valencik was sitting in the same chair as the previous day, legs crossed, sipping from a bottle of water. "Monir, come in. Glad you could make it today. How are you finding California? Can I get you anything to drink? I try to be eco-friendly," he held up the bottle of water, "but this brand is my weakness. I can't get enough of it. I don't know where they get the water, but it's incredible."

Monir held up a hand. "Thanks, but I had coffee on the ride over, and I need to keep it in my system as long as possible." He yawned. "Generally I don't feel like I'm getting older, but I've noticed jetlag is worse than it used to be."

Valencik laughed. "I know what you mean. I don't have many indulgences, but my private plane is essential for all the traveling I do. For the life of me, I can't sleep on commercial flights. And I can hardly expect myself to create the future if I'm too tired to stay awake for it."

"A private plane, that's what I need," Monir said. "I'll talk to Cyprus about it when I get back."

"You're heading back soon?" Valencik asked. "Have you talked to the government about my offer?"

"I have," Monir said.

"And?" Valencik said, his eyes bright with confidence.

"Well, they're interested, of course."

"Do I sense a 'but' coming?"

"But…Adrian, I'm not sure how to say this."

Valencik spread his arms reassuringly. "Just say it, Monir, whatever it is. We're friends now, and I demand complete and total honesty from my friends."

"OK. To be blunt, Adrian, Cyprus doesn't trust you," Monir said. "You're some foreign billionaire who's promising to swoop in and solve a bunch of local problems you don't really care about."

"I can't care about a country's technological well-being if I'm not from that country?"

"Come on, Adrian, you know it's not that simple."

"Why not? To me, it is. Besides," Valencik said, his expression halfway between a smile and a leer, "doesn't Cyprus trust *you*, Monir? Wouldn't the government be swayed if their negotiator told them to trust the foreign billionaire?"

Monir laughed uncomfortably. Suddenly the conversation wasn't going the way he wanted. "They might."

"Is there another 'but' in there?"

"To be honest, Adrian—"

"Yes, please, be honest."

"Everything you say sounds great—about Cyprus, about the world and competition and all that—but I'm still thinking through your position. I need some time to look into your claims about China. It's my job to be thorough."

Valencik's face was a mask of calm. "I see."

"It's a formality," Monir said. "Cyprus intends to sell the lithium to the best partner. We need some time to figure out who that is."

"I wouldn't expect any less. You're smart, Monir. You'll figure it out. But be careful. It's a big world out there. Things change. My offer might be off the table in the not-too-distant future."

Monir wasn't sure what to make of that. Was it a bluff? A threat? "Thanks for the tip, Adrian. I'll be in touch as soon as Cyprus is prepared to move forward."

"Good." Valencik stood and offered Monir his hand. "Safe travels back to Cyprus. Do let me know when you're ready to talk."

"I appreciate your understanding," Monir said, shaking his hand. "So long, Adrian."

"Wait! Monir, I almost forgot. I have something for you."

The CEO reached behind his chair and handed Monir a tall, thin bag. "A gift, to thank you for coming all this way. I would never want you to think I don't appreciate it. Believe me, I know what it's like to fly around the world because someone who wants to do business with you prefers to talk in person."

Monir reached into the bag and pulled out the most expensive bottle of scotch he'd ever held.

"Adrian, this is incredibly generous. I don't know what to say."

Valencik waved away the compliment. "It's nothing. A gift from me to you. But promise me you'll think about my offer while drinking it."

"I promise. How did you know I like scotch? I don't remember mentioning it," said Monir.

Valencik burst out laughing. "Have you forgotten who you're talking to, Monir? I read it on your Frontfacer profile."


Monir left the office and sat down on the couch in the waiting area. He texted Aileen: *I'm just about finished at FF. Any word from your friend?* Until he heard back from her, and until she heard back from Dominic, Monir had time to kill. He noticed Siena watching him, but she looked away quickly. The assistant seemed a little odd, but she worked for Valencik, who was a little odd himself. *Like attracts like*, Monir thought.

He stood up and walked over to Siena. "This may be the last time we see each other. Thank you again for all your help."

"It was my pleasure, Mr. Young," she said. "Are you headed back to Singapore?"

"Soon, yes. I have a few more things to do in California first." He thought for a moment. "Can I ask you something? What do you think of him?" He motioned to Valencik's office. "What's it like working for this place?"

Siena's tone never wavered from complete professionalism. "It's a dream job. Frontfacer is creating the future. Adrian is a visionary, and I'm lucky to work for him." Then she smiled. "What did you think I was going to say?"

"Right, right, of course. Can I ask you something else? How long have you been here? In Silicon Valley, I mean. I'm still trying to get a handle on it. Adrian has a lot of opinions about it. I don't know what to think."

"I've lived in the Bay Area for most of my life," she said. "I grew up in Oakland and got a job here after graduating from Stanford. It's home for me, though a somewhat fancier home than I'm used to."

"Do a lot of Stanford grads do this kind of work?" Monir asked, trying to word the question carefully.

"You mean, are there a lot of Stanford-educated assistants?" Siena said. "I started at Frontfacer as a software developer, actually, but I took some business classes in college. When Adrian was looking for a new assistant, it seemed like an opportunity to do a lot of different things and learn closely from him. It's paid off—I've gotten to see how Frontfacer operates up close. And in some respects Adrian trusts me more than anyone."

"Very impressive," Monir said. "What about his claims that you all are going to save the world? Do you think he's right?"

"I think it isn't always clear what the world needs," she said. "But smart, driven people trying to make a difference is the best-case scenario for the planet. Adrian really believes what he says. Whether he's right is for history to decide."

"You might have missed your calling as a PR person," Monir said. "You're good." His phone buzzed, and he looked down to see a reply from Aileen: *Yes, I have news. Come to my building, I'll meet you in the lobby.*

He looked back at Siena. "One more thing. You know about this lithium situation?"

She nodded. "Yes."

"Who would you sell it to?"

"Whoever can do the most good with it."

"And who is that?"

"Isn't figuring that out your job, Mr. Young?"

Monir rubbed his chin. "I suppose you're right. I was hoping you could make it easy for me. Well, take care. See you in the future."

"Goodbye, Mr. Young," Siena said. "Have a safe flight."

Monir walked across the lobby and went outside. Next to the building's front doors was a map of the Frontfacer campus. He found Aileen's building and set off in its direction.

After Monir had gone, Valencik called Siena into his office. "I need you to do a few things, please. First, find out what flight Monir is on. Tell the airline you're his wife if they give you any trouble. Second, send the flight itinerary to Kong Li. Tell him not to screw things up this time. You can tell him I said that. Third, would you find out what the cafeteria is serving? I'm famished."

"Sure thing, Adrian," said Siena, heading for the door.

"What would I do without you?" he called after her. One way or another, China would get the lithium. If Monir tried to get in the way, well, that's what Kong Li was for.

# 16
## STORMS AHEAD

Monir reached the lobby of Aileen's building and texted her to say he was downstairs. She appeared from an elevator a few minutes later and pulled him into a nap room off the lobby.

"I'm heading back to Singapore in a few hours. What did you hear from Dominic?" he asked.

"He's ready to look at the drive. I told him he can trust you." Aileen reached into her pocket and handed the thumb drive to Monir. "Here it is, the source of all our joys and sorrows. I'll text you the information about the church group Dominic and I attend. He can be a little skittish around strangers, so you'll meet a woman named Mae Mae, who will take you to the group. I've known her a long time. You can trust her, too."

"Great. I'll keep you posted about what happens. Hopefully we'll know what this drive is soon."

Monir and Aileen stared at each other awkwardly.

"Well, goodbye," she said. "It's weird that I didn't know you until recently. Now we're solving global mysteries together."

"The sign of all true friendships," he replied. "Good luck out here. Keep an eye on Valencik for me."

"Will do. Actually, can I ask you something? Any tips for dealing with Eli and Gina? They've been texting to ask for an update."

"Tell them however much you're comfortable telling them. They aren't paying your salary. You don't have to do anything you don't want to do."

"You're right. Thanks. OK. Have a safe flight back, Monir. Hey, if you happen to see Tong anywhere, say hi for me."

Waiting for the elevator, Aileen saw she had a text message from an unknown number. She opened it.

*Aileen, Valencik is hiding something. I need you to help me find it. The whole world depends on it.*

The elevator arrived. Aileen got in and reread the message. She typed a reply: *Yusri, is that you? I told you I don't want a second date.*

A response appeared almost immediately.

*Take this seriously. Your boss is involved in something very big and very bad. I need your help to stop him.*

She wrote back. *I dunno, Yusri, it sounds like you're into some bad stuff. Not sure I want to join in.*

The next response got her attention.

*This is why Tong sent you to Frontfacer.*

Aileen got out of the elevator and found a chair away from other people. She sat down to think, and then typed: *How do you know Tong?*

*We're working together. He said you're reliable. Don't make him a liar.*

"I knew there had to be more to this," Aileen muttered to herself. "California, you were too good to be true."

She typed: *Out of curiosity, just because I have some time to kill, who are you and what help do you need?*

\* \* \*

Eli was watching the moon illuminate some cloud formations over Cyprus when his phone rang. "Hello?"

"Eli, it's Monir. I'm on my way to the airport in San Francisco, so I thought I'd check in. Since you asked me to. Where are you?"

"I appreciate the thought, Monir. Still in Cyprus, finishing up some work with another friend here. How was Frontfacer?"

"It was fine." Monir wondered if he could get away with not mentioning Valencik's offer, but he figured Eli would find out somehow. "Adrian Valencik wants Cyprus to sell the lithium to China. He's willing to sweeten the deal if we do."

"That is…troubling." With the phone pressed against his ear, Eli began to walk along the brick sidewalk by the seafront. "What did you say?"

"That I'd think about it. Why is it troubling? The offer has nothing to do with Israel."

"I understand the offer, Monir. That's not the problem."

"What is the problem?"

"The fact that he's willing to go to such lengths to broker a deal for China. Along with the fact that a powerful Chinese commercial presence in this region could complicate things, geopolitically."

"It's all about geopolitics, huh?"

"Always."

"What's Israel's issue with China? I've never heard of them clashing in any way."

"We haven't yet. But China is continually expanding its commercial alliances, enough to incorporate several of our enemies in their dealings. What are your next steps?" Eli stopped walking and turned to face the sea.

Monir couldn't dodge the question, but he wasn't sure how much to reveal. A version of the truth would have to do.

"There are some former colleagues of mine in the mining industry," he lied, "trustworthy consultants. I put out some feelers to them about the deal, discreetly, of course."

Eli scanned the horizon. "Feelers about what?"

"China, the lithium, supply-and-demand stuff. Also a little research on what cheaper lithium components mean to Frontfacer and other companies. Give me a week or two to work with them on getting some information. I'm sure it will be helpful." Monir bit his lip and hoped Eli would buy it, keenly aware that the Israeli's job involved seeing through fabrications.

"OK, Monir. Get back to Singapore and we'll discuss things further. Someone will pick you up at the airport. A woman who works for me."

It sounded like Eli was telling, not asking, and Monir didn't feel like arguing.

"Sure, Eli. Whatever you want. Talk later."

Eli put the phone back in his pocket. The wind had picked up and the clouds had moved farther west. Lightning flashed inside the clouds like a fluorescent bulb that had been switched on and off again. Thunder followed. The katsa glanced at his watch before heading for the car park. It was very late in Singapore, but he had a call to make, and it couldn't wait.

\* \* \*

Priyansh noticed the strange look on Aileen's face when she came back to her desk.

"You OK?" he asked.

"Yeah, I'm tired. Jet leg is still pretty serious," she said.

"Right, right, you're from Singapore, aren't you? Siena said that. I really want to go to Singapore. One of my friends who was at

Twitter got poached by a company there. He loves it, says it's a futuristic city."

"He's right," Aileen said. She motioned to the office around them. "But now I get to create the future here."

"Haha, totally. I'll let you get back to it." Priyansh put on headphones that wrapped around his entire head and started typing on his laptop.

Siena had given Aileen a lengthy documentation file to read on her assigned project, which turned out to be making what the file called "localization optimizations" for a Chinese version of Frontfacer. In other words, Siena had explained, Aileen's job was to help envision what Frontfacer would look like in China's walled-off internet, and maximize what it could do within a pretty specific set of restrictions. It wasn't a surprise that Frontfacer was preparing for entry into China, but Aileen hadn't known the company was this far along.

Before getting to work, Aileen hid her phone beneath her desk and reread the most recent texts from the unknown number:

*I'm a concerned global citizen who has a vantage point into Frontfacer.*

*To prove you can trust me, Tong asked me to tell you he's sorry for vanishing off the ship.*

*What I need right now is for you to earn some goodwill at FF. Do your job, keep your head down. I'll have more for you soon.*

\*     \*     \*

Monir's car pulled up to the departures area under the sign for Singapore Airlines at San Francisco International Airport. He stepped out and waited for the driver to unload his luggage and place it on the curb. A green sedan pulled up behind the car and a woman in a dark suit got out. Monir thought the car looked familiar, but he couldn't quite place it.

The woman made eye contact with Monir and kept her eyes on him while approaching. She held a small white card in her hand.

"Mr. Young, right?" She didn't wait for Monir to respond. "My boss wants you to have this. He told me to tell you everything will make sense soon." She walked back to her car and got in.

Monir started to say something but was interrupted by his driver, who had finished with the bags and wanted Monir to sign a receipt. By the time he did, the green sedan was pulling away. Monir looked down at the card. A cannon was embossed in the middle of it. He looked up, but the car was speeding away, nearly out of sight. Sighing, Monir put the card in his pocket and walked into the terminal.

# 17
## UNLIKELY ALLIES

Monir's flight from San Francisco landed on time in Singapore. As he exited the plane and made his way to the immigration queues, he wondered what he would say to Eli, who lately seemed to be assuming Monir would share any and all information about his work. Monir rounded the corner to the arrivals area and froze. Across the hall stood Nadia Dryovskaya, who six months earlier had been trying to kill him. Spotting Monir, she jogged over, smirked, and put out her hand. "Hello, Monir. Did you have a nice flight?"

Monir was baffled, his eyes wide. He had never expected to see Nadia again, let alone here.

She put her hand down. "I know, this makes no sense to me either, but apparently we are on the same side for now. Eli will explain later, I'm sure. But I was sent for you, so here I am."

Monir looked around, hoping someone else would show up, or that Eli would appear and reveal that it was all a practical joke.

"Let's go, Monir. I am not here to hurt you," Nadia said in her Russian accent.

Monir was unconvinced. Her voice alone brought back bad memories from Cyprus. "I'm not going anywhere with you," he said. He knew he couldn't fight or outrun Nadia. His feet felt stuck to the floor.

"Haunted by the past, Monir? I know the feeling. Here's a tidbit from your recent past," she said. "2013 Penfolds Grange Hermitage. Ever had it? It's delicious."

Monir recognized the wine he and Tan had been drinking. The bottle had been knocked over and smashed during the shooting; there was no way she could have known what it was. "You…that was you?" he managed to get out.

Nadia bowed slightly. "You're welcome. Now, let's go. It's getting late."

She walked out of the terminal. Monir hesitantly followed Nadia to a waiting taxi. "Malacca Hotel," she said.

"That's my hotel," said Monir.

"That's why we're going there. I'll drop you off." Her mouth curled into a smile that showed her teeth. "Eli asked me to make sure you got tucked into bed, safe and sound."

During the ride, Nadia took advantage of the driver's loud music to lean toward Monir and discuss the search for Tong, which Eli had finally told her about. She suggested that Monir talk to his Singaporean contact, assuming a government official would have access to airport surveillance.

"Not a good plan," he whispered as the driver bobbed his head in the front seat.

"Why not?" Nadia demanded.

"Because the next time I speak with Tan, he is expecting information regarding a deal we're working on. Any premature contact for favors like this can backfire. I can't do it. But I have a better idea."

"I'm listening."

"I have a friend who is connected here. She told me about a gathering tomorrow night that might help us find Tong."

"How? What type of gathering is this?"

"Religious, I think. Christian."

"Great, that's the last thing we need right now, religious nuts getting involved."

"Give it a chance. We can be discreet until we feel out the place. But we have nothing to lose by trying."

"Fine. You didn't say how they can help."

Monir willed himself not to let Nadia get to him. "You'll see tomorrow. I'm tired."

They rode the rest of the way in silence. Monir got out at the hotel. Nadia continued in the cab to Itai and Jael's safe house. Taking the elevator to his room, Monir wondered if Eli was trying to punish him by sending Nadia to protect him. If he and Nadia did have to spend the next few days together, it would be a wonder if both of them survived it.

Across the road from the hotel, Kong Li and three of his men watched Monir enter the building. They had followed the cab from the airport in two cars and were now parked diagonal to the hotel's entrance.

"Shouldn't we see where the woman goes, Kong Li?" someone asked. "Young is probably turning in for the night."

They had seen Nadia at Changi, when she'd met Monir at arrivals. Kong Li had felt mildly uncomfortable about her from the moment he'd laid eyes on her—she was too confident and calculated in her movements, not to mention muscular, to be a livery driver. But Monir was his priority.

"No. I'm not letting Young out of my sight. If the woman is anyone important, she'll turn up again."

"Should we all stay here?"

"We'll work in shifts. I'll stay with one of you. The other two join our people who are tracking those American spies at Drop. I want reports about their every move. If they're here for Tong and we stay on top of them, it's like they're working for us. If our luck changes, they may lead us right to him."

*   *   *

Nadia was back at the safe house, where she'd spent most of her time since the shooting. Lately it felt as though all she did was find ways to keep herself from getting too bored. Monir's gathering wasn't until the next night, so she once again had some time to fill.

She hopped on the treadmill, set a six-minute-mile pace, and ran. While she ran, she processed everything. The current operation. Her recent mission at Republic Plaza. Her encounter two months back at a restaurant in Paris. The disastrous turn of events in Cyprus six months earlier. The former Russian colleagues who had betrayed her. The family she missed. And Monir Young, who she now was assigned to protect.

Somehow Monir seemed to keep getting in her way. Somehow the Israeli spies who had saved Monir from her in Cyprus were the people Nadia was working for. Somehow Monir and Eli could do as they pleased and demand that Nadia risk her life for them.

And the spy was showing that he wasn't the kindhearted old man he passed himself off as. When Eli had called to tell her to pick up Monir at the airport, his voice had sounded almost gleeful. Nadia had protested, reminding Eli of her history with Monir, but Eli had reminded her that Farrouk Ahmadi's brothers were after her, and that Eli was her best chance of surviving to see her nieces again. The katsa was starting to enjoy his power over her too much for Nadia's liking.

She urged her legs to move even faster.

*   *   *

Aileen's second day of work started by meeting with Siena and Priyansh, who, she discovered, was working on the localization project with her.

"Who knew?" Priyansh said. "That's what the silos do to you—for all we know, other ninjas could be part of the project."

"It's for the best. Whatever a ninja is doing, it's on a need-to-know basis," said Siena. "First things first. Aileen, welcome. You and Priyansh will be leading the localization effort together. Did you catch up on the documentation?"

"Yep, and there was a lot of it," Aileen said. "I was surprised how detailed the instructions are. How do we know so much about what Frontfacer would need to look like in China?"

"China told us," Siena said simply. "We don't publicize that fact, but yes, we know what we'd need to look like in China—in theory, at least. The government's tech officials change their minds not infrequently, so keeping up to date is the challenge. Adrian thinks they like toying with him. If and when his efforts to win them over succeed, he wants to be ready to launch as soon as possible."

"Will we do anything they say?" Aileen asked. "I'm still getting all the details into my head, but we're giving the government tools to control what people see on Frontfacer?"

"I was a little hesitant too when I started here," Priyansh said. "Wasn't it just censorship? Wasn't I helping a government decide what its people can read? Was I OK with that?"

"And you are?" Aileen asked. "OK with it, I mean."

"It's more nuanced than that. What sounds worse to you: a social network connecting tens of millions of people but outlawing certain topics? Or those tens of millions of people not having the social network at all?" Priyansh rubbed the back of his neck. "Honestly, between those options, I think connecting people is the better one."

"Think of it as *giving* people something, Aileen, not taking something away from them," Siena added.

"I guess that makes sense. Once we have the localization updated to the current requirements, what do we do?"

"Test and fine-tune, test and fine-tune," Priyansh said. "It has to be seamless."

"Correct. If ever there are something that Adrian demands perfection for, it's this," Siena said. "When it comes to China, there's no such thing as a minimum viable product. For now, work on the current requirements. I'll assign you more when the time comes."

One of the less obvious perks about Frontfacer, Aileen was discovering, was that everyone was constantly looking at one screen or another—a phone, a laptop, a tablet, a wall-mounted monitor, a television. She could walk around staring at her phone, as she did leaving the meeting, and no one gave her any notice.

It had been over twelve hours since Aileen had last heard from the unknown number.

She decided to try texting it: *Hello? Anyone there?*

But she got no reply. Whoever was on the other end wasn't talking back.

\* \* \*

The next evening, Monir and Nadia met Aileen's friend Mae Mae at the Tiong Bahru Market on Seng Poh Road. The older woman had arrived a few minutes early by cab. So had Nadia, though the two did not speak to each other until Monir was there. He had taken the MRT and walked to the market after asking a station attendant for directions.

"Hi, Mae Mae, it's nice to meet you. I'm Monir, and this," he indicated Nadia, "is my Russian bodyguard."

"It's so nice to meet you, Monir," said Mae Mae, eyeing Nadia. "Would you like to grab a bite before we head to the meeting? It's just down the street from here." She was at least twenty years older than Monir and Nadia. Her voice was sweet and gentle, but her eyes conveyed that she was a woman to be taken seriously. Monir felt much safer around her than around the trained assassin who was accompanying them.

"No, thank you," said Monir. "I had some fish ball noodles earlier." Nadia shook her head but said nothing.

Mae Mae laughed. "You're becoming quite the Singaporean, Monir, eating fish noodles and all." She told them about the neighborhood as they walked toward the home where the gathering was taking place. "More than eighty per cent of Singapore's population lives in flats developed and run by our government."

"I did know about the government housing here, but not how extensive it is," Monir said.

"One of our governing party's greatest challenges when LKY came to power was to solve Singapore's housing problem. Since the 1960s, the Housing and Development Board has overseen the construction and governance of more than one million public housing units. They are essentially self-contained small towns, with schools, markets, recreational facilities, and even malls. It has worked well for us."

"All the buildings around us are those kinds of units?"

"Yes. Many of the flats in this neighborhood are only two to four stories high, because the Tiong Bahru district has the oldest HBD housing in Singapore. These homes may look modest in comparison to some of the newer luxury condos, but their value is through the roof." Mae Mae pointed to the left. "There's the place we are going."

They ascended two flights of stairs in an outdoor concrete stairwell and reached a landing with many pairs of shoes neatly laid on either side of the door. Monir looked to Mae Mae for direction.

"Take off your shoes. Don't worry, no one will bother them."

A young man opened the door, and the three new arrivals heard the sound of talking inside. Mae Mae led Monir and Nadia into the flat, where they were introduced to the hosts, a pleasant middle-aged couple whose names Monir missed.

"Everyone calls them Father N and Mother N," the young man who'd opened the door whispered to Monir.

Monir nodded, and he and Nadia took two seats in the last row of chairs in the living room. Moments later, Father N invited them to sit in one of the loveseats along the wall. "More comfortable here—in front of the air," he said, pointing to a neon blue fan. Monir thanked him and switched seats. Nadia stayed where she was. Mae Mae sat across from Monir, next to a young man she seemed to know well. Watching them interact, Monir wondered if they were related.

The meeting lasted about an hour. First there was singing, led by a young woman with a beautiful voice and a man playing the guitar. Then came a few announcements from Mother N, followed by Father N introducing the guest speaker. He was a traveling minister of sorts, originally from Yemen but now living in Sweden. He read a few portions from the Bible and told several stories from his work. Monir found it all interesting, yet very different from the last religious service he had attended: a Sunday morning gathering at a local Greek Orthodox parish in the mountains of Cyprus, with Stalo. Monir didn't consider himself a religious person by any stretch, but he couldn't argue with the Christian precept of helping other people.

While the speaker continued his presentation, Monir's thoughts drifted from the Cyprus church to his wife, and then back to the faces in the room. He was amazed at how many people fit into the relatively small flat; he'd heard that Asians were much more comfortable in close quarters than Westerners, and now he was seeing it for himself.

Refreshments were served after the speaker's talk. With Father and Mother N directing the process, Monir met almost everyone in the room. He was surprised by the crowd's diversity. It was a virtual cross-section of Singaporean society: business owners, bankers, an executive from a prominent Japanese company, an architect, a couple of accountants, some church pastors, students, engineers, office clerks, and a retired military general. Regardless of their socioeconomic differences, everyone got along as though they were longtime friends.

Monir had just finished talking to one of the bankers about Singapore's financial system when Mae Mae walked up with the young man she had been sitting next to.

"Monir, Aileen asked that I introduce you two."

"Dominic," said the young man, extending his hand. "Pleasure to meet you."

Monir shook Dominic's hand. "The pleasure is all mine."

Mae Mae suggested they talk on the doorstep, away from the people and noise. Once they were outside, Mae Mae looked at Monir. "Aileen said you would have something to give Dominic, is that correct?"

"Ah, yes." Monir pulled the thumb drive from his pocket. "This is what all the fuss is about."

Dominic looked at the drive, turning it over in his hand. "Any idea what's on it? Aileen said something about passwords."

"She told me it's encrypted. I was hoping you could figure out what it is."

"I'll do my best," Dominic said. "My computer skills haven't let me down yet."

"Dominic, don't you live nearby? Can we look at the drive there?" Mae Mae asked.

"Sure thing, if you don't mind squeezing into my flat."

Nadia was halfway down the stairwell. "I'll flag a cab."

# 18
# THE CARGO

After spending some time with the thumb drive, Dominic had figured out what they were dealing with. The drive was called "The Cargo." Whatever was on it had been hidden in the password-protected folder. The instructions in the other folder were deceptively simple: "Follow the clues. Enter the passwords. No second chances." Unlocking the drive, Dominic explained, would require an unknown number of passwords. The trick was in the last part of the instructions, "No second chances." Tong's security system for the drive was that they had one try to enter each password. A wrong password would make the drive automatically erase itself.

"Who did you say this guy is again?" Nadia asked.

"A better programmer than I am, for one thing," Dominic said. "Without his system in place, someone could try millions of passwords at random until they find the one that works. This way, you have to follow his clues, wherever it is they end up leading."

"Wonderful," she said flatly.

"What's the first clue?" Monir asked, leaning toward Dominic's computer. "Fruit from the ship?"

"Fruit? Ship?" Mae Mae said. "What could it mean?"

Monir thought for a second. "Aileen met Tong on a ship. That's where he gave her the drive. That seems like a pretty good place to start, unless anyone has a better idea."

"I'll text her right now. Oh, but what time is it in California?" Dominic said.

They all looked at each other, trying to calculate the time difference. The room was silent. Mae Mae was counting on her fingers. Monir cleared his throat.

"I can find a time zone website," Dominic offered.

"It's 4:30 in the morning," Nadia said. "She's probably asleep."

"I'll text her anyway. Hopefully we'll hear back in a few hours," Dominic said, tapping on his phone.

"But why the runaround?" asked Mae Mae, sitting down on the couch. "Why not lead us straight to the last location?"

"That I don't know," said Dominic.

"It's obvious," Nadia said. "Tong doesn't just want us to get the clue. He wants us visible, out in the world, so others who are looking for him can follow along."

Monir frowned. "How can you be so sure?"

"My training, for one," Nadia replied. "Whoever this Tong is, he knows a little about tradecraft." She looked out through the crack in the curtain and nodded in the direction of some parked cars below. "Also, that construction van down there. I've been watching them for half an hour now. Two large men, staying put and barely talking to each other. They're not here to fix anyone's sink at this time of night."

Mae Mae shivered. "There are men parked out there? It's like a gangster movie. Do you think they're dangerous?"

Nadia looked at Mae Mae. "Yes."

"OK, everyone, don't panic," Monir said. "Dominic, text Aileen. Then let's all try to relax for a little bit. It sounds like things are about to get busy."

They spent the next few hours waiting. Mae Mae folded her arms across her chest and fell asleep on the couch. Dominic put his headphones on and busied himself with something on his computer. Monir catnapped in between rounds of making tea. "You really need to get some coffee," he told Dominic. Nadia kept watch out the window.

Finally, close to midnight, Dominic's phone buzzed. He read Aileen's reply to the others: *Not sure what the clue means, but I remember him saying something about "king of the fruits."*

"King of the fruits?" Monir said.

"Durian!" said Mae Mae. "King of the fruits is a nickname for durians. The password must be 'durians.'"

"Durian or durians?" Dominic asked. "Singular or plural? We only get one try at this."

"The clue says 'king,'" Nadia said from the window. "Singular. The password is durian."

"I think she's right," said Monir. "Does everyone agree?"

They all nodded.

"Here goes nothing." Dominic typed the password and hit Enter. For a few seconds nothing happened. Then the password hint vanished and was replaced by another: "Give a rolled $100 to the Shunfu butcher."

"It's a good thing we were able to ask Aileen about the first clue," said Mae Mae.

"Yes, clearly she's linked to this…this scavenger hunt. Tong designed it that way. Without Aileen, we would never have gotten past the first step," said Dominic. "I'll let her know it worked."

"Do any of you know what the next clue means?" Monir asked. "I'm—I almost just said clueless."

"It must be referring to Shunfu Market, but it's closed now," said Mae Mae. "We can go tomorrow."

"Make sure we have a $100 bill to take with us," Nadia said. "The clue says we need to give it rolled to the butcher."

"Oh, I'm excited!" said Mae Mae. "This is the most fun I've had in ages."

Monir couldn't help but smile. "Just remember, this is serious. Some very bad people are after us. They've already tried to kill me once. I don't want anything to happen to you all, but I also don't know what the next few days will bring."

"No one will get hurt while I am here," said Nadia. "You should sleep. It's late."

"Yes, come on, everyone. Dominic, do you mind if we sleep here tonight?" Mae Mae asked.

"Of course. There are blankets and pillows in the closet." Dominic stretched and yawned. "Well, goodnight. Tomorrow we continue the hunt."

\*     \*     \*

Aileen was getting ready for work when her phone buzzed. Thinking it might be Dominic again, she checked it right away.

*Good morning, Aileen.*

*Valencik has a password that I need. Could be any length, any string of characters. It's written down somewhere in his office.*

*That's all I know. Find an excuse to go talk to him.*

*Please.*

"At least you're polite," Aileen said to her phone. She texted back: *Password to what? How do you know all this?*

*I know. To a Frontfacer system. Tell you more soon. Find the password.*

"Adrian's office? He claims he's always available to us. Time to put that to the test."

Aileen started typing an e-mail on her phone: *Hi Adrian, do you have time to chat today? Couple questions about my project. I can come by your office when you're free. Thanks in advance.*

She sent the e-mail and got dressed. When she grabbed her phone to leave her hotel room, she saw a reply on the screen.

*Aileen. Yes. Come by this afternoon. My door is always open. Adrian.*

* * *

Mae Mae woke up shortly after 7:00. Very quietly, so as not to wake the others, she made tea, finished a shopping list she had started the night before, and read a few pages from her Bible. Then, at 7:45, she woke up the men. Monir was snoring in an armchair across the room. By all indications, Dominic was also asleep. He was breathing heavily, his forehead resting on his folded arms on the desk. Nadia had awoken without Mae Mae noticing and was back to keeping watch at the window.

"We have to get going," Mae Mae said. "The markets open at 8:00."

The plan was to go on a lengthy shopping trip that would eventually end up at the butcher shop in Shunfu Market. With any luck, anyone following them would assume they were simply shopping, and hopefully would get too bored to watch them closely. Once they were at the butcher shop, they would hand over the rolled $100 and see what happened next.

"Why do we trust this butcher?" Monir asked.

"We don't have a choice," said Dominic. "That's where the clue says. We have to assume Tong knew what he was doing."

"If anything happens, I'm sure Ms. Nadia can protect us," Mae Mae said, smiling at the other woman. Nadia stared at her.

"So these are Tong's friends, or what?" asked Monir.

Dominic was shutting down the computer. "Not sure on that. All we know is that Tong trusts them to give us the second clue. It might look suspicious if I carry my laptop, but we shouldn't leave the drive here." He pulled it out of his computer. "I'll carry it, if no one objects."

* * *

When the clock finally said mid-afternoon, Aileen told Priyansh she was going to the cafeteria and nearly ran to the elevator. Walking across the Frontfacer campus, she thought about what to say to Valencik. Somehow she had to find a password in his office. She didn't know where it would be or what it would look like. All she knew was it would be written down somehow—assuming the person directing her knew what they were talking about.

Opening the door to Valencik's building, she saw Siena sitting at her desk.

"Go on in, Aileen, he's expecting you," Siena said.

Inside the office, Valencik was sitting at his desk reading a book. He pointed to one of the chairs.

"Hi, Aileen. How are you? This is your, what, third day here? How's it going? Any regrets about taking the job?"

"Hey, Adrian, thanks for seeing me. No, no regrets, but I feel…strange about my project. I was hoping you could help me see the bigger picture."

"Ah." He laid the book on the desk and stood up, slowly pacing back and forth. "Tell me more."

"It's the localization stuff. Priyansh and Siena have been talking me through it, but I still feel weird about it. What am I not seeing?"

"You know, Priyansh had some doubts when he started."

"He told me that, yeah. But not anymore."

"No, not anymore. Other people have felt the same. We had two ninjas leave Frontfacer shortly before you arrived. That's why your job was available, actually."

"I didn't know that. They left about the localization?"

Valencik waved his hand, irritated. "Oh, who knows? Those two never really fit in here. But I think you can fit in, Aileen. We always try to hire for fit, and I had a good feeling about you from the minute I met you."

"Thanks, I want to fit in. That's why I asked to talk to you."

"I'm pleased to hear that. If you want to fit in, it isn't difficult." He pointed to the Frontfacer motto on the wall. "This either is or isn't your guiding principle. If it is, you'll be fine. If it isn't, you're better off working elsewhere."

As Valencik talked, Aileen was sneaking looks around the office in all directions. She couldn't see anything written down anywhere. The office seemed entirely paperless.

"I believe you, Adrian. But how do censorship tools help us," she eyed the motto, "mess up the present and create the future?"

Valencik stopped. "That's a great question, but you're thinking about it all wrong, I can tell. How can I tell? Because of that word you used to describe the tools."

"The government deciding what people can read isn't censorship?"

"It's a gray area, isn't it? Sure, an autocratic authority telling people they can't access certain kinds of information may cross the line, but that isn't what's happening." He started pacing again.

"Then what *is* happening?"

"There's so, so much stuff online. There's a fire hose of content, way too much to read, way too much to consider. It's overwhelming. You can't read it all. One of the trends in the media industry is curation, packaging all that content into consumable chunks. What people need isn't *more* information; it's the *right* information. That's what we're helping with."

"Curation as a social network."

"Exactly. Frontfacer can be the place where people get the right information, the content they really need."

Listening to Valencik, Aileen couldn't help but be impressed by how thoroughly he seemed convinced of what he was saying. She took another look around the office, but there was no sign of anything that might be a password. "You've given me a lot to think about, Adrian. Thanks."

"Anytime, Aileen. Like I said, my door is always open. Unless there's anything else, I'm speaking at an event in San Francisco tonight, and I need to rehearse my speech."

On the walk back across campus, Aileen's phone buzzed.

*Valencik is speaking in San Francisco tonight. Siena will be with him. The office will be open. Get the password then.*

She texted back: *I don't know what it is yet. How do you know the office will be open?*

As usual, the reply was almost instant. *Then tonight you'll have plenty of time to look around. I know. Trust me. Tong is counting on you.*

\* \* \*

They exited Dominic's flat just before eight and walked out to the street to look for a cab. One drove by a few minutes later. They all got in and Mae Mae leaned toward the driver. "Tekka Wet Market, please."

The driver nodded, started his meter, and began the drive south to Little India.

"Did you tell the driver to head to a wet market?" asked Monir.

"Oh, yes. We call it 'wet' because the middle of the market floor is where all the fish and meat are displayed, on top of ice. Fruits and vegetables are arranged on the outer perimeter of the market. As the ice from the middle melts, water washes onto the floors. Hence, wet market."

Dominic was looking behind them, but Nadia made him face forward. "If we are being followed, we should not let our pursuers know we are onto them." The cab took the ramp onto the CTE, and the construction van did the same, staying a few cars behind.

Mae Mae's shopping trip lasted three and a half hours. She followed her list carefully, buying vegetables and fish at Tekka Wet Market and spices at a nearby street stand. Dominic purchased portable speakers at an electronics store in Little India and then stopped at an ATM to replenish his cash, making sure to get a $100 bill. Nadia bought some lemon drops. Monir bought a bag of coffee. They took another cab to Orchard Road, where Dominic made everyone stop for a snack at Noodle Place Restaurant. Mae Mae went into The Face Shop for some eye cream while the two men walked to AIBI, a fitness store at Plaza Singapura. The construction van had easily kept up with the shoppers. Its driver watched them reconvene outside the plaza, carrying an ever-increasing number of small bags.

Another cab ride took them to the Shunfu Market hawker center, located in the center of Singapore, east of the MacRitchie Reservoir and nature trail.

They entered Yung Foo Loi's butcher shop just after 11:30. The butcher was busy cutting pork in the back. His daughter was assisting. His wife greeted the group at the counter.

Mae Mae placed an order for pork loin, which Tee Min was happy to fill for her. Foo Loi and his daughter waved from the back. While the group waited, Tee Min told them how busy the shop was with Chinese New Year preparations—everyone was buying lots of pork—and that their daughter, a medical student in Sydney, had flown in for the weekend.

A few minutes later, Tee Min handed Mae Mae the bag of pork. Mae Mae passed the rolled $100 to her and waited. Looking at the bill, Tee Min smiled quickly at Mae Mae and counted out her change from the register. "Thank you for your business. Please come again," she said. Then, leaning forward, she whispered, "Merlion. Merlion." She stood upright again. "Have a wonderful day." She closed the register and walked to the back to assist her family.

Within minutes, Mae Mae, Dominic, Monir, and Nadia were in a cab heading back to Dominic's flat. Piled in the back were all the bags with the goods from their shopping. The cab was quiet as they drove, everyone silently wishing it would go faster.

*     *     *

Nicholas Tong was enjoying the day's pristine sky from his bedroom window on the second floor. He descended the flight of stairs, walked to the kitchen, opened a door, and stepped out onto the wooden deck. The perfect Singaporean afternoon greeted him. Warm but not too hot. Zero humidity. No wind. And above him, a cloudless sky that allowed the sun to fall across the impeccably manicured lawn and fruit trees in the backyard.

Tong went down a few steps and started to stroll around the walled-in garden. His eyes were on the flowers and shrubs. His mind was elsewhere.

Just minutes earlier, he had received a call from the butcher shop at Shunfu Market, where he had been a loyal customer for more than a decade. Tee Min had told him that a group of four customers had paid for their order with a rolled $100 bill. Tong asked her to describe them. The Singaporeans and the American made sense—it must be Dominic and someone else from the Tiong Bahru group, and Monir Young. But who was the other woman? At least the second password was in their possession.

So far, Tong's plan was unfolding exactly as he'd intended. As capable as the "scavengers" were in finding the clues, they were certainly being followed, which Tong was counting on. They would be safe enough, since all the clues were in public places, and their movements around the city would eventually attract the attention of a few other groups...or so Tong hoped. For the plan to work, both of its parts had to succeed: Find the clues to unlock the second folder. And be found—and followed—by everyone who wanted to know what the folder contained.

# 19

## CLUES AND LEADS

After getting back from the butcher shop, Dominic plugged the thumb drive into his computer and typed "merlion" as the next password.

"I almost forgot to ask, what is a merlion?" Monir said.

"It is a mythical creature that is half lion and half fish," said Mae Mae. "The merlion is one of our national symbols, seen all over Singapore."

"We walked by two merlion statues at the market," said Nadia, again looking out the window. The construction van was back, parked farther up the street this time. Now she was sure they were being followed.

Dominic hit Enter and the password hint vanished and was replaced with another: "The birds washing in the orchid fountain."

"The orchid fountain," Monir said, looking at Mae Mae and Dominic. "There must be hundreds of gardens in Singapore. How do we know which one Tong meant?"

"And what if this garden has different birds than when Tong wrote the clue?" Nadia said, still looking out the window.

Dominic looked at Mae Mae. "What would you guess? Tong was Singaporean, like us. What garden would he have meant?"

Mae Mae sat down to think. "You are right that there are many gardens in Singapore, Monir. But the first two clues have been words that have great significance for us Singaporeans. If Tong designed all the passwords that way, then there's only one place this clue could mean: the Botanic Gardens."

"Let's go," said Nadia, starting for the door.

"Um," Dominic said, a sheepish look on his face, "I hate to be a bother, but I have to do some work. I told my boss I was working from home today, but there are a few things I need to get done before the day is over."

"We do not have time for your job," Nadia said. "Can't you call in sick?"

"With apologies to Mr. Tong, I had this deadline before he sent us on his scavenger hunt," Dominic said. "It will only take a few hours, but I have to do it."

Monir was looking at the Gardens' website on his phone. "It'll be closed by then. Should we go without Dominic? Or can the hunt wait until tomorrow?"

"We stick together. If those men in the van see us splitting up, they may try to do something," said Nadia. "Tomorrow morning. We'll go right away."

"I don't mind waiting," said Mae Mae. "I'm tired out from all this excitement. Going tomorrow morning is OK with me." She put her feet up on the couch.

"If we're sleeping here again, I need some fresh clothes from my hotel," said Monir. "We could stop by your flat, too, Mae Mae. I'm guessing even Nadia wouldn't mind taking a shower. Maybe after Dominic is done working, we can all split a cab to stay together." He yawned. "But first I'm going to make some coffee."

The group spent the rest of the afternoon relaxing and talking. While Dominic worked, Mae Mae and Monir chatted on the couch about Singapore, Cyprus, and their families. The older woman was delighted to hear that Monir was newly married, and demanded to see pictures of Stalo. When Nadia was sure they were all occupied, she walked to the bathroom, closed the door, and called Eli.

"Hello, Nadia. What's going on there?"

"Tong is using a thumb drive to send us on some sort of scavenger hunt around Singapore. Monir got the drive from a woman in California. There are a series of clues to the passwords that unlock it."

Eli was silent, thinking. "So, Aileen had a thumb drive from Tong. That explains why Collins didn't find Tong's evidence on the submarine. And Monir didn't see fit to mention any of this to me. That's disappointing."

"What's on the drive that is so important?"

She heard Eli chuckle softly. "I don't know yet, but the slippery Mr. Tong convinced us and the CIA that the contents are worth helping him escape from China. Now we have the drive, but no Tong."

"I see. What do you want me to do?"

"Follow the clues. Monir is a smart man; I trust him and you to figure this out. Keep your phone on. Report in regularly. Is there anything else, Nadia?"

"We are being followed by two men in a van. So far, they're only watching us. They could be Chinese."

"I'll catch a plane to Singapore as soon as I can. If you need backup, call Jael and Itai. It sounds as though quite a few people want to know what's on that drive—including me."

\* \* \*

Aileen waited until nearly midnight to take a cab from her hotel to Frontfacer. Employees were known to work all hours, so it wouldn't seem unusual for her to show up so late. She asked to be dropped off at the edge of campus, and then walked the long way around to Valencik's office.

The building was unlocked, as the text message had said it would be. Aileen didn't even need to swipe her Frontfacer badge to get in. She moved quietly through the darkened building, wary of running into anyone. If someone saw her, she didn't know what she would say as her excuse for being there.

The door to Valencik's office was also unlocked, so Aileen ducked inside. Using her phone's flashlight, she illuminated the room, searching for whatever she hadn't noticed earlier. The motto, the chair, the couch, the desk, the books. She went to each piece of furniture, took the cushions off, felt for a loose piece of wood that might conceal a hidden compartment. But all the furniture seemed normal. The desk was only a thick, flat piece of glass on curved metal legs; there was nowhere to hide anything on it. She glanced at the motto on the wall, noting that it was a long string of letters.

*Could it be that obvious?* Aileen thought. *Valencik isn't stupid enough to hide the password in plain sight, is he?*

She decided he wasn't. She glanced at the books. One of them might easily contain a password, possibly in code. She turned them over to read the spines. The titles were about innovation, company founders, emotional intelligence, cross-culture leadership, managing large-scale change. She picked up the book Valencik had been reading earlier. A business school professor—a famous one, apparently—stared from the back cover.

Aileen ran her hands over the cover, feeling the embossed letters with her fingertips. She noticed that one corner of the cover felt slightly thicker. Taking the cover off, she turned it inside out and saw a folded Post-It note taped securely to the back. She pulled the note off and opened it. On the note was a long string of letters:

fUcKuP7h3pr3S3N7cr3@T3th3Fu7uR3

"This has to be it!" she whispered. She took a picture of the note with her phone. Then she refolded the note and tried to tape it back onto the cover, but the tape had lost some of its stickiness. She pressed the note firmly into place and wrapped the cover around the book. Good enough—the note wasn't going anywhere. She piled the books on the desk again and crept out of the office, closing the door behind her.

\*   \*   \*

It was a perfect day for a visit to the Botanic Gardens. The forecast called for lots of sun and ideal temperatures. Refreshed after sleeping and eating the breakfast Mae Mae had prepared, the group left Dominic's flat, again with the young man carrying the thumb drive.

Their cab driver started to make his way toward the Botanic Gardens entrance off Tyersall Avenue. The two men from the construction van had switched to a Nissan. They waited for the cab to take the first turn before following, again keeping pace a few cars behind. Once the cab dropped off the group at the Botanic Gardens, the Nissan's driver pulled into the car park. The man in the passenger seat took out his phone and sent a text: *Kong Li, they are at the Botanic Gardens. We are following them to see where they go.*

Ever the world traveler, Monir tried to take in as much of the Gardens as possible while the rest of the team walked to the National Orchid Garden, northwest of the main entrance. Monir noted the beautiful walkways, lined with birds of paradise on either side, and the majestic Tembusu trees on the spacious lawns beyond. The rest of the group was paying no attention to the scenery. The Singaporeans had seen the Gardens plenty of times, and Nadia was busy sizing up the people around them.

They presented their tickets and entered the National Orchid Garden. Before leaving the house, they had discussed the possibility that, as with the butcher, a specific person might have the next password. They looked over their stamped tickets carefully as they walked toward the fountain.

"Anything?" Nadia asked, turning to Mae Mae and Dominic.

"I don't know," said Mae Mae as she took one more look at her ticket. Dominic was quiet.

Monir was walking a few steps ahead and reached the fountain first. He looked left and right, noting the crowd of tourists taking selfies in front of the fountain. In the upper part of the fountain were a dozen tall, thin birds with stick legs. Monir turned to the others. "The birds washing in the fountain—that has to be them. What are they, flamingos?"

"Cranes," corrected Mae Mae. "Those are cranes. We often say that the crane is Singapore's national bird, because of all the construction cranes in our city."

"Could the password be that simple?" Nadia asked.

Dominic shrugged. "The other clues haven't been especially hard—they just required someone to be in the right location. Tong *does* want us to unlock the drive eventually."

"Please do not tell me we came all this way for ten minutes of walking," Nadia said.

"Hey, we follow the clues, that's the game," said Monir. "It's still early enough that we might be able to get through another clue today if we hurry. Unless Dominic has to work."

Dominic looked down, blushing. "I called in sick. Since I finished my project yesterday, my boss said it was OK."

"Outstanding. Great tradecraft, Dominic," Monir joked, slapping him on the back.

"Should we pick up lunch on the way home?" Mae Mae asked.

Nadia was walking back toward the entrance. "Maybe we can get some," she closed her eyes and shuddered, "fish ball noodles."

Back at the fountain, Kong Li's men were looking around wildly, trying to figure out what the group had found.

One looked at the other. "All I see is orchids and birds."

The other grabbed his phone and called Kong Li. "Whatever they found here, they're leaving. We don't know what they saw. It's just a bunch of nature."

"Stay with them," Li said. "I don't know what they're doing, but if we follow them long enough, we will find out. I'm coming to join you soon."

\*   \*   \*

Jun was at her desk, once again going through everything they'd found about the shooter. Until the woman surfaced, there wasn't a lot to do but be ready and let her people do their jobs. Jun's phone rang; caller ID was blocked. Her mind started racing, wondering if it was the call she had been expecting. She waited one more ring to compose herself, and then answered. "Jun Ai Boon here."

"Officer Ai Boon, this John Harden from the CIA. Did Director Low tell you about our offer to collaborate on your investigation?"

"Yes, Mr. Harden, he did. I appreciate your help." Jun was up and pacing the floor.

"We have a lead on your suspect, Officer Ai Boon. Our facial recognition software spotted her at the National Orchid Garden this morning. She had three people with her, one we know."

"You are already tapped into our security cameras? I thought we were going to work together?"

"Jun—that's your first name, right? May I call you Jun? We don't have time to do this dance. The bottom line is that your government accepted our offer to help. Your shooting suspect was at the Botanic Gardens. That's all you need to know."

"Who is she? And who is the man you already know? Have you identified the others?"

"Woah, slow down, Jun. The shooter's name is Nadia Dryovskaya. She's a Russian operative, SVR. Heavily implicated in some bad things that went down in Cyprus six months back. Honestly, we are very surprised to see her on your turf, especially next to Monir Young, who was with her. But that's a story for another time."

"Monir Young? He was with one of our officials at the shooting, most likely the target of the assassins who were killed."

"That's correct. And the fact that he and Nadia were together further confirms that Nadia was the shooter. She seems to be protecting Monir. But again, that's not your concern."

"What of the others?"

"A young man and an older woman. They haven't shown up in our system yet. They're Singaporeans—your databases should be better at identifying them. They don't seem to have criminal histories, not internationally, anyway."

Jun was still pacing, processing everything Harden was telling her. "What would you like us to do, Mr. Harden?"

"Check your e-mail. I'll forward everything we have. Then you can work on identifying the Singaporeans."

"I will, thank you, sir."

"Call me John. Oh, and one more thing. The security feed from the ticket booths showed two men entering just after Nadia's bunch and exiting just after they left. We're looking into them, as well. Check it out on your end."

\*   \*   \*

Dominic entered "cranes" as the next password as soon as they got back to his flat. For the third time, the password hint vanished and was replaced by another: "The high travel seen from Marina Bay Sands."

Nadia groaned. "How many of these can there be?"

"I confess the excitement is wearing off somewhat," Mae Mae said. "I do hope we're nearing the end of the clues."

Monir looked at his watch. "Is everyone OK with going after this clue today? We have plenty of daylight left." They all murmured in agreement.

"Marina Bay Sands is the fanciest hotel in Singapore," Dominic explained to Monir and Nadia. "It's pretty amazing, to be honest. But the high travel could be anything—the elevated infinity pool, the SkyPark, the observation deck. I guess we have to go look."

"But let's finish our fish ball noodles first," Mae Mae insisted. "We need our strength."

As the others ate, Nadia was back at the window. "We have company down there," she said after a few minutes. "The two men from the construction van are now in a car. The police are nearby too. I counted three cruisers. One female officer looked this way while driving by."

"The police? Why would they be here?" Mae Mae wondered. "Maybe they're here for those awful men."

Monir caught Nadia's eye but didn't say anything. He nodded toward the bedroom, motioning for her to follow him. Once they were alone, Monir spoke. "Are the police here for you?"

"It seems likely," she said. "You all would be better off without me. I can get away while there's still time."

"Stay with us. We can help you," Monir said.

Nadia raised an eyebrow.

"No, really," he said. "Put on a disguise or something, and blend in with us. Maybe they'll think we're a group of tourists."

"As touching as your offer of 'help' is, I think I will be all right on my own."

"Look, Nadia, we're going out anyway. At least stay with us until we get away from this neighborhood. We can distract the police if it comes to that. They aren't looking for the rest of us."

Nadia gave in. "You make a good point. But we need to go now." She started back toward the living room, and then stopped. "Thank you, Monir."

"Don't mention it," he said. "Really. Please don't."

\*   \*   \*

Everything had clicked for Jun from the moment she had arrived at the CID analysis lab. Her technicians, working in conjunction with their CIA counterparts at Langley, quickly identified the Singaporeans from the Gardens as Mae Mae Chong and Dominic Sim. Next came their past and present addresses, occupations, tax records, and phone and travel logs. Using footage from the Gardens, Jun and her colleagues traced Monir's group to a cab, enlarged a still shot of its license plate, and followed the cab's route with feeds from cameras on the main roads. It didn't take long to figure out they were going to Dominic's flat, on a road perpendicular to the northern end of Mt. Elizabeth Hospital.

Jun ran her findings by her supervisor, assembled a team of patrolmen in two cruisers and an unmarked car, and set off for Dominic's neighborhood. Identifying the other two men at the

Gardens would have to wait; Jun's focus was on finding and apprehending the sniper suspect. So neither Jun nor the officers accompanying her were aware that those same two men were currently sitting in a sedan up the street from Dominic's flat.

*     *     *

"Here is the plan," Nadia said as Mae Mae and Dominic hurried to finish their food. "We escape over the rooftops. The buildings next to this one are approximately the same height, so we shouldn't have too much trouble. And we have been under surveillance at the flat from the beginning, so try to avoid any locations that have cameras."

"The rooftops? I'll do my best, but I hope I don't slow you down," Mae Mae said.

Monir squeezed her hand reassuringly. "Is everyone ready? Dominic, this time you should bring your laptop. With the police and those other guys after us, who knows what could happen."

While the others gathered their things, Nadia sent a text to Jael and Itai: *Need backup now.* She sent them Dominic's address and hoped they would see it in time.

The four of them climbed the stairwell to the roof. Nadia easily broke through the door at the top, then led the way to the building east of Dominic's. They were pleased to discover that the gap between buildings was small enough for a short jump. Once she reached the edge of the easternmost building, Nadia stopped. There were no more buildings—just a sheer fifty-meter drop to a sidewalk below. Going north would be impossible, since it required a sizable leap that Mae Mae was convinced she could not attempt. Dominic, too, was uneasy about it, weighed down by the duffel bag carrying his laptop and some other gear.

Nadia suggested they take the fire escape from the side of the building. Dominic agreed. "The sidewalk leads to Nutmeg Road. It's just a block to Orchard Road from there. We can grab a cab on Orchard and disappear."

Nadia and Monir navigated the green steel stairs first, descending quickly. Mae Mae went next and took a bit longer. Dominic, who had wound up last due to his heavy bag, was inching down from the roof to the stairwell when Nadia heard footsteps coming up the road. At least two men, she thought.

"Hurry up, Dominic! Someone's coming," she hissed.

Watching the flat, the two men in the sedan had assumed it would be another night of nothing but sitting in the car. One of them slowly scanned across the roofs on the street, searching for anything to entertain him. Then he saw movement. He pointed upward. "There—see that?"

His partner leaned over for a better view. "Yep, that's them."

They were out of the car in seconds, running in the direction their four targets had been moving. Rounding the last building, they saw a young man with a bag across his back descending the fire escape. They ducked around the corner and called their boss. "Kong Li, they are moving. They left the flat on the roof."

"Follow them—do not lose them! But avoid contact. We have to let them lead us to Tong. I'm almost there."

From his car, Jun's patrolman noticed the two suspicious-looking men running down the street. He got out of his car and jogged after them, curious. Ducking behind some bushes, he spotted Nadia, Monir, and the others, recognizing Nadia from the pictures Jun had circulated. He immediately grabbed his radio and called for backup. "I am on foot, pursuing the sniper suspect. Two unknown men are also after her."

Soon the patrolman was joined by a colleague from Jun's team. Moving carefully, they followed the two men who were following Nadia, but soon realized they were too far away to pursue the suspect. They ran back to their vehicle, radioing the situation to Jun. "Suspect is on the move, heading your way on Nutmeg."

"On it," she replied. "Get over here, quick! One of you stay on Nutmeg, the other head to the small park at Mt. Elizabeth Hospital. We have to stop them before they get to Orchard Road!"

Monir and the others were almost at the end of the road when Nadia looked behind her and saw the two men closing in. Had she been alone, Nadia could have evaded or confronted them. Monir was in decent shape, so he may have been able to outrun them. But Dominic and Mae Mae had reached their limit soon after they hit the sidewalk. Both of them were breathing heavily, barely keeping up with Nadia and Monir. Nadia turned around and ran back to Dominic and Mae Mae. There was no choice but to face the two pursuers head-on. She crouched into a fighting stance.

The bushes behind Nadia rustled. Turning, she saw Itai and Jael emerge from an alley. They barely made eye contact with Nadia, facing the two approaching men.

Nadia had heard of Israeli agents being trained in krav maga, a brutally effective form of martial arts developed for the Israeli Defense Forces. From the look of it, Itai and Jael were well acquainted with the discipline.

"Keep running!" Nadia yelled to Monir and the others. "They'll handle those guys."

"This way," Dominic sputtered between breaths. "I know a shortcut through the hospital gardens. It'll put us on Mt. Elizabeth Link and onto Bideford Road."

Jun had arrived at the end of the sidewalk just as her suspects were turning into a garden to their left. Up ahead, three men and a woman were fighting in hand-to-hand combat. "Police! Everyone freeze!" she yelled, jumping out of her car and sprinting forward. She knew she had to stay on the suspect, but hoped her authoritative voice would have an effect on the fighters. It didn't. The sharp kicks and punches continued, the two Chinese men groaning and yelping in pain. The police car from up the road skidded to a stop behind Jun's cruiser.

"Get them!" Jun yelled to the arriving officers, pointing at the fighters. "I'm going after the suspect."

The two Chinese men were on the ground, barely moving. Itai looked at Jael. They ducked back into the bushes and ran down the alley they'd come from.

On Bideford Road, Mae Mae hailed a cab frantically and they all dove in. "Marina Bay Sands, as fast as you can!" Mae Mae said to the cab driver. They took off just in time to avoid Jun, who had nearly caught up to them running down Mt. Elizabeth Link.

"Damn it!" she yelled. Looking back, she saw her officers were still occupied with the two men. Meanwhile, the cab was disappearing down Bideford Road. Jun walked to her car, seething.

"Your orders, Officer Ai Boon?" said the patrolman.

"Back to HQ. Let the cameras find them," Jun said, catching her breath. "Note the time, and let's hope there weren't too many cabs going down Bideford just now."

Kong Li and two more men drove up just in time to see the men from the construction van being loaded into the back of a police car. He continued past without stopping, not wanting the police to notice him. So, Young had gotten away and his men were in police custody. Neither of those setbacks was serious. He had more men, and he would bring them all into the chase for Tong.

\*   \*   \*

Almost an entire workday had passed since Aileen had found the password in Valencik's office, but she hadn't heard from the text-message informant. She'd texted the number after getting back to the hotel from Valencik's office, saying she'd found what she thought was the password but wanted some answers before sending it. That had been about fifteen hours ago. Still no response. Aileen was nervous. The only reason she'd gone along with the unknown person was that he or she knew Tong. Was the person abandoning her? Had something happened to the person? Was something about to happen to Aileen? She kept working on her project, trying not to let her anxiety show.

\*   \*   \*

"Marina Bay Sands!" exclaimed a technician, jabbing at his screen. "See here? A camera at the junction of Bideford and Orchard picked up the cab turning left. It has to be her, given the time the suspect escaped and the direction she went."

"You *know* she went to Marina Bay Sands?" Jun asked.

"Thankfully, the cab stayed on main roads. We find it here, here, and there." The technician pointing at three locations, going west to east, on the map before them. "Then it turns from Raffles Avenue onto Stamford and crosses over the reservoir to the hotel."

The technician turned around to get a reaction from Jun. She had already left and was shouting orders into her radio.

# 20
# FLYER

Mae Mae and Dominic were still in shock, breathing heavily and wiping sweat from their foreheads. Nadia seemed calm, but glanced behind the cab every time it turned. There was only one way to explain what had just happened: the Singaporean police were onto her, perhaps with help from other agencies. And something about Eli telling her to keep her phone on didn't feel right. Could they be tracking her with it? She looked back one more time. No sign of being followed. Good. She sent a text to Itai: *Thx for the help*. Then she took the battery out of her phone.

Monir was absorbed in his own thoughts. The events of the last half hour had felt disturbingly similar to the danger he'd been in six months earlier in Cyprus. Nadia had been involved both times—but in Cyprus she had tried to kill him, and now she was tasked with keeping him alive. He had a few choice words in mind for Eli once this was all over.

No one spoke for a while, due more to adrenaline than to being discreet around the cab driver. When Dominic finally broke the silence, he used a makeshift code to disguise his meaning.

"We have to consider the increased *interest* for the flat, the fact that there were more *buyers* today than yesterday. It's best that we stay away for a while. Because of the heavier *publicity*, we should decide on our next move before meeting the realtor at the hotel."

Nadia flashed him a small smile, pleased at his caution. "I agree. There has been more *media coverage* on the property—that's what we have to watch out for. We should expect the coverage to be present at Marina Bay Sands, too. But I think I can steer us away from it. I'll explain when we get there."

It was her way of letting everyone know she was taking the lead. No one objected. Dominic and Mae Mae knew nothing about Nadia's past, but they recognized that she had been unusually capable in everything that had happened. Monir, in spite of his many unanswered questions about Nadia, nodded in agreement. She was faster, stronger, and a better fighter than he was; denying it was pointless.

Nadia directed the taxi to stop along the curb, fifty meters from the hotel's entrance. Video surveillance would be more focused near the front doors, so this spot let them evade detection for now. She stepped over a row of marigolds and walked to a clearing in a small garden to the left of the hotel's entrance. Gathering everyone between two large fan palms, she asked, "Dominic, can you get internet access here?"

"I can hotspot off my phone. What do you need?"

"Schematics of the hotel's fire escapes. We need a stairwell for after we find the clue on the observation deck."

"On it. I won't be able to tap into security protocols, but the hotel's basic layout is likely available online." He sat down and got to work, balancing his laptop on his knees.

Mae Mae sat down next to him to watch. "Oh, look!" She pointed at something, delighted. Monir turned and had to smile. On the far side of the bay was an enormous statue of a merlion.

\*    \*    \*

Eli's flight touched down in Singapore, and he made his way through immigration and out to the arrivals hall. He called Itai.

"What's going on? How is the stakeout holding up?"

"Things could be better."

"Why?"

"It's best that I tell you in person."

"We don't have time—tell me now!"

A Mercedes-Benz idling at the curb flashed its lights. Jael got out and stood by the door, waiting for Eli. She bowed her head slightly as he entered the vehicle.

"Shalom, sir," said Itai. "Is Gina with you?"

Eli bowed his head in reply, thanking them for the ride. "Itai. Jael. No, Gina is handling a task elsewhere."

Itai briefed Eli on what had happened at Dominic's flat. "Nadia called us in to help her and her friends get away. It wasn't a problem, but the Singapore police are getting closer to her, and now they are aware of Jael and me. How much do you trust her?"

"Nadia? I trust her to get the job done. She knows the stakes."

"She texted to thank us for saving them, but she hasn't been responding since. We don't know where she is."

"Don't worry about Nadia. She's going nowhere. If the Singapore police are onto her, she needs us more than ever. We have more pressing things to consider—Tong, for instance. Where the hell is he?"

Jael scowled, her eyes on the road. "Sir, I believe you need to talk with our American friends."

\*     \*     \*

Aileen was in bed in her hotel room, willing her phone to buzz. It had been nearly twenty-four hours since she'd left Valencik's office, and still she'd heard nothing from the unknown number.

She was starting to feel terrified that Valencik would find out what she'd done, even though she didn't really know what that was. Other than the picture she'd taken of the character string, there was no evidence she'd been in Valencik's office. Aileen could delete the picture, go to work tomorrow, and pretend it all never happened. Valencik didn't have cameras in his office, did he? Her anxiety climbing, Aileen texted the number again: *Where are you?? I'm freaking out over here. What is this password??*

\*　　\*　　\*

"The high travel seen from Marina Bay Sands." Monir repeated the clue as they walked into the lobby of the hotel. Dominic and Mae Mae exchanged a knowing look. They had a good idea of what the next password was, but knew they needed to be sure.

"During the SG50 celebrations—the fiftieth anniversary of our nation—I stood at the very spot these directions are calling us to, marveling at the magnificence of Marina Bay and all that surrounds it," said Dominic.

"I was there, too, on that day, said Mae Mae, "but on the lower side of the deck. I love to look at the Fullerton Hotel from there."

Monir bought tickets for the observation deck and the group waited for an elevator. Nadia had coached everyone not to look directly at the lobby security cameras. "Act normal," she said. "Do not let them know that we know they are watching."

On the observation deck, Dominic walked briskly to the edge and beamed. "Yup, exactly what I thought."

"Me too. What's higher travel than that?" said Mae Mae, pointing at the huge Ferris wheel across the water.

"The Singapore Flyer?" asked Monir. "The one that looks like the London Eye?"

"'Flyer' must be the next password!" Mae Mae said. "To be truthful, I thought it might be before we left Dominic's flat, but we had to be sure, didn't we?"

"Once we get away from all these people, I'll type it in," Dominic said.

They stared out at the Ferris wheel, which was lit up in blue and purple. Even Nadia seemed struck by the view. The sun had just set behind a cluster of high-rise condominiums. A golden glow was painted across the lower parts of scattered clouds. In the distance to the east, Monir could just make out a plane taking off. It reminded him of home, and how much he'd been away from it lately. He wished Stalo could be in Singapore with him to see how the city looked right now. He pushed his feelings aside, focusing on their task. "Mae Mae, Dominic, is there a safe place nearby for us to put the password in? The hotel is a little too public."

Far below them, half a dozen CID cruisers were nearing the hotel. Nadia had already started moving along the eastern wall of the observation deck to avoid cameras.

"We can figure that out once we get out of here. Come on, the emergency exit is this way."

\*　　\*　　\*

Kong Li called Zhang Wei to give him an update. He explained what had happened with the Singapore police.

"Not good, Kong Li, not good. At this rate, I will need to begin interviewing new henchmen any day now."

"Forgive me, Mr. Wei, I was not finished. We lost the trail of Monir Young, but I have another lead that may prove even better."

"Better than the man who is being directed around Singapore by Tong himself? I am intrigued, Kong Li."

Li told Wei about the Americans he'd been following, explaining that they, too, were after Tong and surely had resources that Monir didn't. "In addition, common sense suggests they are following Young while he follows Tong. So I am following all of them at once."

"Kong Li, if you had common sense, we would have found Tong days ago. But these Americans interest me. Yes, see where they go. Perhaps you may salvage the Tong debacle yet."

"I will, Mr. Wei, thank you."

"Kong Li, before you go, I have something I wish to show you. Hang up and FaceTime my assistant's phone."

Li was curious what Wei was talking about. He did as instructed and soon was looking at Wei's office.

"Ah, Kong Li, welcome," Wei said. He rose from his desk and walked toward the phone, which his assistant held at eye level. "Your small opportunity with these Americans notwithstanding, you have been a razor's edge away from complete failure more than once while working for me. I wish to show you what will happen if the razor ever finds you."

Li wondered if he was about to see Wei's famous temper in action. He watched as Wei spoke Cantonese to someone off-screen. A man shuffled into view, dressed in a shabby suit, his head bowed as he stared at the floor.

"Kong Li, this is another employee of mine, one who, like you, has not honored his side of our relationship," Wei said, his voice totally calm. He spoke to the man in the suit. "Tell Kong Li what you did."

Head still bowed, he spoke in short gasps. "I failed Mr. Wei."

"Yes, you did. I gave you several chances, did I not?"

"You did, Mr. Wei. Very generous. Thank you." The man sounded as though he was about to cry.

"You are welcome. You know what must happen now," Wei said gently. Li braced himself for whatever he was about to see. Wei spoke off-screen again, and a woman walked into view carrying a laptop.

"Do it," Wei said to the man in the suit. Now the man did burst into tears. Wei walked to his desk and found a tissue. He handed it to the man in the suit, who blew his nose.

"Thank you, Mr. Wei," he said.

"Do it," Wei said.

Sniffling, the man walked to the laptop, stared at it for several seconds, and tapped one key.

Li frowned. This was Wei's temper? "I don't understand. What was that?"

"Tell Kong Li what you did," Wei said to the man.

"Mr. Wei prefers to punish me digitally. He created a program to do it. He was gracious to let me run the program for him."

"A cyberlashing, I call it," Wei said proudly. He looked to the side. "The name is a work in progress."

"What is a...cyberlashing?" Li asked.

"Tell him," Wei said to the man.

"Mr. Wei has erased my bank accounts," the man said, his eyes closed tightly. "Deleted ownership records of my house. And submitted paperwork to legally change my son's name to 'Zhang.'"

Li's eyes grew wide. "You can do all that with one click?"

"Technically, no," Wei admitted. "It is more complicated than that. But the program starts those processes. And I did not erase his bank account. I left one yuan in it. That seemed more humiliating to me."

Li was too shocked to speak. If Wei could do the same to him... "Mr. Wei, I—"

"Kong Li, I know your methods," Wei said. "You speak the language of violence, but it is the language of the past. "This," he motioned to the laptop, "is the language of the future, and it is the language I speak." Wei walked toward the phone until his face filled the entire screen. "Now go find Nicholas Tong."

\*   \*   \*

Eli was on the phone with Jeff Collins, rapidly catching the CIA agent up on everything Jael and Itai had told him.

Collins let the news sink in before responding. "Let me make sure I have this right. Not only is Tong nowhere to be found since we flew him back to Singapore, but he's also conducting a treasure hunt for his thumb drive—and we still don't know what's on it. Nadia, Monir, and a couple Singaporeans are on the run, and the police and some Chinese gangsters are closing in on them. Eli, is it just me, or has this situation spiraled out of control?"

"Oh, I don't know, Jeff. Nadia is quite capable, and Monir…well, Monir never fails to surprise me. I don't think it's too late for this to work out the way we'd like, as long as Tong is still breathing. Nadia's group is following his instructions, so you and I should stay behind them and make sure nothing blows up in their faces. Earlier today they picked up tails and narrowly escaped the CID. My agents had to get involved to bail them out." Eli tried to ask his next question as casually as possible. "Do you know where they may have gone from there?"

Collins thought he must have misheard. "This is delicious— *you're* asking *me* where your agent is? Just call her and ask, Eli. Or could it be that Ms. Dryovskaya not as loyal as you claim?"

"Her phone was damaged while escaping from the CID," Eli lied. "Come, Jeff. We have to work together on this. Remember, Nadia has the thumb drive."

Collins let out an exasperated breath. "Fine. CID tracked them to Marina Bay Sands but lost them shortly after their arrival. Officers are searching the hotel."

"Lost them? How?"

"We're not sure. The four entered the hotel from the front, bought tickets to the observation deck, and took the elevators to the fifty-seventh floor."

"I'm assuming you are getting all this from security cameras?"

"Yes, we've been helping CID with surveillance and analysis."

Eli wanted to ask why Collins hadn't mentioned that earlier, but he wasn't eager to start on the topic of sharing information. "Did they actually go out onto the observation deck?"

"Yes. CCTV shows them exiting the elevators, but not returning. That's where CID lost the trail."

"One of them is a spy, after all."

"A spy *you* recruited. And now can't find."

"This isn't the time for blame games, Jeff. We have to find them, and we have to know where they are going for the next clue. More important, we have to find Tong."

Collins sighed heavily. "Eli, as it happens, I'm on a flight to Singapore right now. I'll talk to Harden about using facial recognition in a larger radius around Marina Bay Sands. As for Tong, I don't think we have to worry about finding him."

"Why is that?"

"Because from the look of things, Tong will bring us to him when he's ready to be found."

\*     \*     \*

The buzzing of her phone woke Aileen, who had drifted off to a fitful sleep. She rolled over and grabbed her phone from the bedside table, thumbing it open. The screen was lit up with a text from a new number:

*Sorry for delay. Had to ditch phone. Communicating is tricky right now.*

As she read the text, a second one arrived from the new number, short and to the point:

*He knows. Valencik knows.*

*   *   *

Mae Mae suggested they go to Bishan Harmony Park. It was a sprawling area of lawns and gardens and several dog runs. She was certain there would be no cameras there, and Nadia's brief reconnaissance after the cab dropped them off proved her right. Nadia had been thinking about their next move during the cab ride, and once they arrived at the park, she laid out her plan: They had to stay away from anywhere equipped with cameras. Main roads, malls, banks—most of the city proper. They couldn't leave an electronic footprint. That meant no e-mail, no social media, no phone calls, no texts. Nadia made them take the batteries out of their phones to be thorough.

"But why?" Mae Mae asked. "The cameras I understand, but why our phones?"

Nadia tried to be patient. "It's standard procedure in a situation like this one, Mae Mae. Obviously, the Singapore police have the ability to track our location. I don't know exactly what their technological capabilities are, but the Americans are involved too, and they can sniff out an electronic scent anywhere in the world. This may not stop them, but it will slow them down." She smirked. "Besides, I want to find Tong before they do."

"I have to put the next clue in the computer. That should be OK, right?" Dominic asked.

"Hopefully," said Monir. "We don't seem to have a choice."

"Don't be on there too long," said Nadia.

Dominic opened his laptop and waited for it to boot up.

"Flyer!" Mae Mae exclaimed. "This one was too easy, Mr. Tong. You hid it in plain sight!"

Dominic plugged in the drive and typed in the password. He glanced around. "Ready?"

Mae Mae's words were echoing in Monir's ears. You hid it in plain sight. In plain sight. *Plain sight*. "Stop!" Monir shouted. "Flyer isn't the password!"

"What do you mean?" said Dominic, his finger hovering over the Enter key. "Of course it is."

Monir pointed to Mae Mae. "You're right, Mae Mae, it was too easy. 'Flyer' doesn't match the pattern of the other words. We've been dealing with words that are symbolic in Singapore. Durian, merlion, crane. Flyer is the name of a tourist attraction. No offense."

"You might be overthinking this, Monir," said Dominic.

"Then what is the password?" asked Mae Mae, annoyed that she'd been wrong.

Monir thought back to the observation deck. The view at sunset, Cyprus, Stalo, the plane taking off. *Plane sight*. "The high travel seen from Marina Bay Sands. What's the highest travel in Singapore?"

"Is there something taller than the Flyer?" Mae Mae asked.

"Airplanes," Nadia said.

"Yes! And does anyone know a symbolic Singapore word for air travel?"

"Changi?" Dominic asked. "But you can't see the airport from the observation deck."

"True, but it fits the pattern. It has to be the password."

"I don't know. I think flyer makes more sense," Mae Mae said.

"You yourself told me I'm becoming quite the Singaporean, Mae Mae. The password is Changi, I know it."

"It fits the pattern," Nadia agreed. "I vote we try it."

"We only get one chance, remember," Dominic said. "If Changi is wrong, the hunt is over."

"Just use Changi already," Mae Mae grumbled.

Dominic typed in the new password and hit Enter. They all held their breath. An eternity passed, and then a new password hint appeared onscreen: "The maid knows Singapore's place in the world. LKY residence, Summer 1965."

"Lee Kuan Yew residence?" said Dominic. "What the heck?"

"We do not have time for a history quiz," said Nadia.

Dominic turned to Mae Mae. "Where did LKY live then?"

"Oxley Road, of course," she replied confidently.

"Right. That's correct, but the clue specifies where he lived that summer. There must be something we're missing. We need to find someone who knows their Singapore history. But it has to be a person we can trust."

Monir pursed his lips. "I think I know who would have the answer. Just one call, Nadia?"

"Do it," she said. "We must assume that whoever is looking for us will be able to pinpoint our location. We should be ready to move once you make the call."

"I'll be fast." Monir had already turned on his phone and was dialing William Tan's number.

*   *   *

Jael parked the car at the safe house and they all went inside. Eli put his bag on the table and stretched. Jael had been silent for a while, but now she spoke.

"Sir, I agree with Itai that we must find Nadia. You may trust her, but I do not."

"Forgive me, Jael, but I'm feeling jet lagged. If Nadia doesn't want to be found, then I'm not sure what we can do at the moment. Collins may turn up something soon. Or we can try to track her phone."

"We cannot wait for Nadia to feel like getting in touch with us, sir. We must make her come back. She must know who's in charge."

He yawned. "Who is in charge, Jael? I was, the last time I checked. Unless either of you knows how to make Nadia do something she doesn't want to do, I'm going to take a shower."

"It's just that…our team, sir, we've always operated on trust. Closer even than family. Nadia does not understand or respect that."

*Closer than family.* A slow smile spread across Eli's face. "Jael, you have just given me an idea."

# 21
# THE COTTAGE

"Monir, I'm pleased to hear from you," said William Tan, "though I hoped you would be calling about the lithium. But I'm intrigued by the topic you brought up. Why are you asking about Lee Kuan Yew and 1965?"

"I promise to explain soon, William, but unfortunately I'm in a hurry. Is there anything you can tell me?"

Tan knew a lot about the early history of Singapore and its first leader, and he was happy to share his knowledge on the subject. "I'm pleased to say that I have long been a student of our country's beginnings. Just north of Changi Airport is Changi Luxury Estates, a very prestigious resort. On the resort premises is a preserved estate, formerly known as Changi Cottage. At the time LKY became prime minister, the cottage was government property, enclosed within the confines of Changi Air Base."

Monir looked at the others, who were sitting on a bench nearby, and gave them a thumbs up. "I see."

"Shortly after the break from Malaysia, Mr. Lee's life was threatened. For his safety, he and his family were moved to Changi Cottage, where they lived for several months while security was increased at his home on Oxley Road."

William continued speaking for several minutes, telling Monir much more than he'd ever wanted to know about the construction of the cottage and its history before being inhabited by the prime minister. Monir glanced at Nadia, who was pointing to her watch. He mouthed *I'm sorry* and tried to politely hurry William along.

"Thank you, William, that's very helpful. How is the estate used today? Is it part of the resort? Can people rent it?"

"My understanding is that the cottage, though seemingly part of the resort complex, has remained a secure government building, under the supervision of one of the ministries of our government. It was all part of the deal when the property was sold. I don't know which ministry, but if I were to guess, I'd say the Ministry of Foreign Affairs. I've heard that our government uses the facility to house foreign delegations on state visits."

"Do you happen to know the address? I'm just curious. I may try to see it sometime soon."

"No, I haven't been to the cottage in years. If it would help, I can look up the address and text it to you."

"Would you mind, William? We would appreciate it. I have to go, but I promise to call soon about the lithium."

"Did you say 'we'? Who else is with you?"

Monir immediately regretted the slip. "Long story. I'll explain later. Thank you, William. Goodbye."

He hung up and turned to the others. "I guess now we wait for the address."

"What do we do until then?" Dominic asked. "It's getting late. Should we find a place to spend the night?"

"While we figure that out, Monir, remove the battery from your phone," Nadia said.

"Oh, right." As Monir turned his phone over, it buzzed in his hand. He stopped and looked at the screen, then at Nadia. "I think this is for you."

Nadia took his phone and read the text that had just arrived: *Nadia, it's Eli. Texting Monir too in case your phone is off. Something happened to your niece. If you see this, come to the safe house. Urgent.*

"Is everything all right?" Mae Mae asked, noting the ashen look on Nadia's face.

Nadia was trying to decide if the deliberately vague text could be true. Would Eli lie about something like that? She wasn't sure, but either way they needed somewhere to sleep. "Everything is fine. I know where we can go."

"Are you sure?" Monir asked, knowing what she was thinking.

"There will not be surveillance there. We will be safe. Let's go."

\*     \*     \*

Jun was reviewing footage and interviews from the hotel, trying to figure out where her suspect was and where she might be going next. Jun considered the possibility that the shooter and her friends may have ducked into a hotel room, but she quickly dismissed the idea. The group was going from place to place, searching for something, so they would keep moving. But how did they get away? She had flooded the property with police, who had searched everywhere from the car park to the observation deck. Jun started dialing John Harden. She didn't like depending so heavily on the CIA, but if they were going to offer assistance, Jun might as well make the most of it. She was getting desperate.

\*     \*     \*

Eli sat down in a chair facing the group. He spoke slowly and deliberately. "I'm aware that some of you want answers, maybe even explanations. Those will come with time. All I can say is that we are in the middle of a crisis." He looked at Nadia. "And sometimes we have to do whatever it takes. For now, what you need is instructions."

A few minutes earlier, Nadia had stormed into the safe house and demanded to know what had happened to her niece. When Eli had calmly confirmed her suspicion that the text was a ruse, she'd given him a look of pure hatred and spat on the floor. She hadn't said a word since. Monir sat next to her on the couch, surprised to realize he felt bad for her. Whatever Monir and Nadia's relationship was, Eli's trick had crossed a line.

Itai and Jael smirked at each other. Their katsa was doing what he did best: diffusing tension, calming fears, and taking charge. He hadn't come halfway around the world to be pushed around by a Russian turncoat. No, Eli would take charge. He would control the environment, he would set the tone, he would prevail.

"You are safe here," Eli said. "Tonight you will rest, and tomorrow you will find the next password. I will tell you exactly what to do. With any luck, Tong's trail of breadcrumbs will soon be at an end. Now, what have you been up to for the last few days? Don't leave anything out."

Dominic and Mae Mae began recounting the events since the faith group meeting. Eli, who had introduced himself to the Singaporeans as a foreign investigator helping the police, listened carefully. He asked a few questions for clarification, and then he laid out his plan.

Given the attention that Monir and the others were attracting from the police and the Chinese gangsters, Eli wanted Itai and Jael to discreetly accompany them for the rest of the hunt. "There's no telling what you will find at the remaining clues. A cab will drop you off near the gate of Changi Cottage. Present yourself as tourists, and ask if you may see the cottage. Say you are interested in Singaporean history. Invent a reason to talk to the maid. We will be monitoring from nearby. Once inside the cottage, Nadia, we will depend on your operational experience for reconnaissance of the interior and points of entry by potential intruders. The rest of you must follow her directions. We should assume the police and gangsters won't be far behind you. Any questions?"

\*   \*   \*

Collins was eating dinner on the plane to Singapore when his phone rang. He put down his fork and picked up his phone.

"Jeff, I gave some consideration to your pep talk the other day," said Eli. "You know, the one about us working together." Eli's tone was playful, but Jeff knew the Israeli was rarely anything but serious.

"Glad to hear it, Eli. And?"

"And I'd like to give you a heads-up about something that is taking place tomorrow morning."

Collins grabbed a pen and the napkin his drink was sitting on. "Shoot." He wrote a few words while Eli talked, and then thanked Eli and hung up. He reread his note while dialing Harden, whispering the words to himself before the deputy director picked up. *Changi Cottage. 853 Loyang Lane.*

"What are we doing about it?" asked Harden after Collins explained his conversation with Eli.

"I'll send some of our guys over there to check it out tonight. We'll return in the morning to see what happens."

"What about the Singaporeans? Do we let CID know?"

"Not unless you want them to beat us to whatever Tong is leading up to. Leave them out of it."

Harden sighed. "I don't like it, but I'll trust you on this one."

"Thanks. I'll keep you posted once I land in Singapore."

\*   \*   \*

The cyberlashing had changed things for Kong Li. He'd known Zhang Wei was influential, but he hadn't truly been worried about Wei's threats. Li was an experienced gangster; he'd hurt—and killed—plenty of people. When it came down to it, what could a man who sat behind a desk for a living do to him?

Now that he'd seen the answer to that question, Li called all his men together and told them their new objective: Find Monir Young and his friends, and "encourage" them until they give up their information on Tong's whereabouts. If there was one thing Li knew, it was that everyone talks sooner or later. Cyberlashings might be the way of the future, but for the time being, Li was bent on doing what he did best: exercising brutal, old-fashioned force.

\* \* \*

Later in the evening, Eli was entertaining Dominic and Mae Mae with stories of the many kinds of fish he'd caught in his travels around the world. Jael had opened a bottle of wine and was passing around paper cups. Monir saw Nadia standing alone at the window, looking out into the night. He went to join her.

Speaking quietly, he said, "I'm sorry about Eli's text. That was cruel."

"It's nothing," she said. "Forget it."

He looked out the window with her. "So you have nieces? Are they in Russia?"

"Monir, why are you asking? I know you don't care."

He sighed. "Nadia, can you stop it for one minute? I'm trying to be nice to you, though God knows why."

Neither spoke for a while. Behind them, Eli's arms were spread wide, showing Dominic the size of one of his greatest catches.

"I...am sorry, Monir," said Nadia. "It is nice of you to ask. Yes, my sister in Russia has children. Very sweet girls. They are...I don't know how old they are now. I have not seen them in some time."

"Why not?"

"You mean other than being busy trying to kill you?" Nadia laughed to herself. "Sorry. I couldn't resist."

"Hilarious," Monir said.

"It is a long story, but I am not welcome in Russia. I have not been able to go home for a while."

"Huh. You know, I'm something of an exile myself. I left New Jersey and the U.S. when I was much younger. I, too, haven't seen my family in a long time."

Nadia turned to look at him. "You're from New Jersey? I have family in Brighton Beach." She turned back to the window. "Where is your family now?"

"I'm not sure. Well, I don't know where my parents are. My new family, my wife, is in Cyprus."

"I heard you married the Cyprus woman. How is married life?"

"It's really nice, actually. Once this is over, I'm looking forward to getting back to her."

"Yes, that will be good for you," Nadia said. "I admit I am jealous."

Monir looked down at his paper cup of wine. He swirled it gently and raised it in a toast. "Hey, Nadia, here's to being exiles. I hope you're able to go home soon."

"Thank you, Monir," Nadia said. "To being exiles."

They drank together.

"You know, I'm starting to be glad I didn't kill you."

"OK, I think that's enough bonding for tonight." Putting his hand in his pocket, Monir felt his phone. "I just remembered, I never checked for the address. I know Itai already found it, but remind me to thank William again when this is all over."

Nadia took another sip of wine. "I have a feeling this will all be over very soon."

\*   \*   \*

Li's men caught their break at Drop. One of the American agents answered a call, talked to someone, and rushed out of the bar with his partner, leaving their drinks unfinished. Li's men followed the Americans to a street called Loyang Lane. Keeping a safe distance, they observed the Americans with binoculars, narrating the scene for Li over the phone.

"They're stopping outside a property that is mostly hidden behind a tall hedge. Can't see it from here. A house, I would say, or a cottage. One of them is getting out and looking around. He is trying to see what's behind the fence. Still looking. Still looking. He sees something, but I don't know what. He's returning to the car. Now he's on the phone."

"Are they going into the cottage?"

"No. They're pulling away right now."

"Go confirm what is behind the fence. Move the car out of the way, and keep your eyes on the property. The Americans may have been doing reconnaissance. Something could be happening at that location. If you see anything else, call me immediately."

\*   \*   \*

The next morning, Monir and the others took a cab and directed their driver to an address a few blocks away from Changi Cottage. Everything seemed in order in the neighborhood. There was barely any traffic on the street, and no sign of pursuers.

The cottage was not visible from the road. A tall bougainvillea hedge, replete with burgundy blossoms, completely hid it from view beyond the wrought iron gate.

Once out of the cab, Monir spoke first. "Nadia, are you satisfied with the way things look?"

"Yes, the streets appear clean. Remember, we are tourists who are interested in the cottage as a historical site. Stay calm and we will be fine."

To everyone's surprise, their plan became obsolete almost immediately. The gate cracked open as they approached it. A woman's voice crackled through a small speaker on the side.

"Please come in. Your host says do not be afraid. Welcome to Changi Cottage."

They all spoke the same word in surprise: "Host?"

\* \* \*

Aileen had almost called in sick to work that day, but doing so would have seemed more suspicious than showing up, no matter what Valencik knew or didn't know. She'd barely been able to get any work done, head swiveling constantly, watching for any sign of Valencik. She hadn't seen Siena all day either. And she'd been enduring another period of silence from the texter's new number, though she'd sent half a dozen frantic requests to clarify what was going on. "Communicating is tricky right now"? What did that mean? Who was this person, and why had they suddenly been impossible to contact?

Aileen was attempting to look productive, eyes locked on her laptop, when her heart nearly stopped. Valencik was walking toward her from across the office. He paused by her desk.

"Hey, Aileen, do you have five minutes? We need to talk."

216

Aileen balled her hands into fists under her desk, trying to stay calm. "Sure, Adrian, what's up?"

"Mmm, I'd rather talk in private. I'll grab a conference room. Meet me in there when you're ready."

Aileen quickly stashed her phone in her desk, locked the drawer, and walked after Valencik.

*   *   *

From their hiding place, Li's men watched Nadia, Monir, Mae Mae, and Dominic walk toward the cottage. They seemed to be speaking to someone over an intercom. One of the men dialed Li.

"It's them. All four of them are here," he said.

"Good," said Li. "We have to move quickly, before the Americans show up, or anyone else. I'm coming there right now. Call the others and tell them to meet at your position. Once we're all there, we make our move."

Nadia pushed the gate open and led the way up the winding brick sidewalk toward the front steps. Mae Mae and Dominic followed. The place was a small paradise, fortified by bougainvillea flowers. Fruit-bearing trees stood at various places on the beautiful lawn.

Nadia reached the door first and knocked. A young woman wearing a head covering and an apron opened the door. She greeted them, invited them inside, and closed the front door.

From the landing above, a man looked down at the group. "I am so pleased you made it!" he said. "I have been wondering whether I made the Changi clue clear enough."

# 22
## REVELATIONS

Valencik was already leaning back in a chair when Aileen got to the conference room. "Thanks for taking the time, Aileen. Do you want anything? Water? Beer? Red Bull?"

"I'm fine, Adrian. What's this about?" Aileen didn't know how much he knew about the last few days. Was Valencik aware of what she'd been doing? She'd tried to be careful.

He motioned to the room's glass wall, beyond which a handful of employees were absorbed in a game of doubles Ping-Pong. "I love that they aren't afraid to waste time thirty feet away from their CEO. Marvelous."

Swiveling around, he answered Aileen's silent question. "You've been busy, Aileen. I like that. I like employees who take the initiative and follow their instincts."

"Um, thanks, Adrian. The last few days have been a whirlwind."

"Yes, I've heard. Here's the thing. It may seem as though you found something in my office, but it isn't what you think. You're doing great work so far, Aileen, but you're still new at Frontfacer. I asked you to meet because I want us to be on the same page if we're going to keep working together."

*He's heard? Heard what, from who?* "I'm not totally sure what we're talking about, Adrian."

Valencik nodded slowly. "You still don't understand what you took from my office, do you? OK. I'll tell you."

\*   \*   \*

Nicholas Tong led the group down a long hallway to a sitting room in the rear of the cottage. The young woman closed the door and asked everyone to sit.

Tong remained standing. "I am assuming that various groups have been aware of your movements and are tracking you."

"You'll have to be more specific," said Monir. "The police? Those gangsters? The CIA? Eli and his sidekicks?"

"I am no one's sidekick," said Nadia.

"I didn't mean you," said Monir.

"My, that is a lot of people. Excellent." Tong turned to the young woman. "Now that our friends have arrived, please make the call." She opened the door and stepped out into the hallway.

"She wouldn't be the maid here, would she?" Monir asked.

"You're a clever man, Monir. I set up the thumb drive so that Aileen and anyone she trusted would be able to follow the clues and unlock it if my escape plan failed and something happened to me. Or if Eli and the CIA turned out to be less than reliable. I was not sure I could trust them."

"With what? We still don't know what this is all about."

"You're right, Monir. It's time that you, all of you, learned what's really going on."

\*   \*   \*

Valencik folded his hands on the table and put on the voice he used for television.

"The world is changing, Aileen, and companies have to change with it. We can't depend on the strategies we've used in the past to carry us forward. If we don't keep up with the times, our competitors will. I told you when I hired you, I have both eyes on the future. I'm not focused on what Frontfacer will look like next year, or even in five years. That's easy—and what's infinitely worse, it's boring. I'm thinking about what we'll look like twenty, thirty, fifty years from now."

"What are you saying, Adrian?"

"A few months ago, an unexpected opportunity came up. I acquired a new business partner. And I made a deal for the future of Frontfacer."

*   *   *

"A few months ago," Tong said, "I was working as an adviser for the Chinese government. I was charged with helping the country find ways to keep its technology sector strong, and to stay ahead of new developments in the global tech industry. I had free access to much information. It was my job to know things. One day, I stumbled across something so unbelievable that, well, I didn't believe it. It was a plan to reinvigorate China's economy through its tech industry. The problem was the method."

"What was it?" Mae Mae asked.

"You must mean the lithium," Monir said.

"Clever once again. Yes, it was a plan for China to replace Singapore as the buyer of the Cyprus lithium. The plan was engineered by a man named Zhang Wei, who has been trying to regain his former position of power in the government. He thought securing the lithium for his country was his way to do it."

"What does Adrian Valencik have to do with Wei?" Monir asked. "He wanted to bribe Cyprus to sell the lithium to China."

"Frontfacer has wanted access to China's internet for years. Wei used that to his advantage. He claimed that he and his allies in the Chinese government could finally get Frontfacer access to the country, but first Valencik had to help him with the lithium. Given that Cyprus's technology infrastructure is weak and Valencik's net worth is in the billions, a monetary gift to Cyprus seemed simple enough. But Wei saw a chance to gain even more influence over Frontfacer."

"How?" Nadia asked, her eyes narrowing.

"Wei added one more element to the deal: something very simple, yet very powerful."

\*　　\*　　\*

"A backdoor?" said Aileen. "You built China a backdoor into Frontfacer? Is this a sick joke, Adrian?"

"I don't see what's funny about it. Collaboration is the cost of doing global business. China already controls what its people read. The UK has become the most extreme surveillance state in the West. Who knows what the U.S. will look like in a few years? Frontfacer can't stay competitive if we aren't prepared to make some concessions. Because you can bet other companies are prepared to. The tide is turning, Aileen, and I intend to surf the wave." Valencik tapped his finger on the table. "Did that metaphor work? You know what I mean."

\*　　\*　　\*

"I don't understand," Mae Mae said. "What's a backdoor? A backdoor to what?"

"To Frontfacer," Nadia said. "The entire website. The entire social network."

"Nadia is correct. Essentially, Valencik created a method for Wei, or anyone with access, to observe anything happening on Frontfacer, anywhere in the world. Using the backdoor, you can read what people are posting, follow private conversations, monitor activity—the surveillance opportunities are endless. With a government like China's, the implications are truly frightening."

"But how can Frontfacer just *do* that?" Monir asked. "Who else knows about this?"

"The most likely scenario is simply that no one knows about the backdoor. When I ran from China, only Wei's team there and Valencik's team in California knew about the project. Wei was keeping it a secret until he had the lithium. With the backdoor and the lithium at his disposal, he would be in a position of considerable strength in the Chinese government."

\*   \*   \*

"Why did you go along with Wei?" said Aileen. "Even for a billion new users…Adrian, this is awful. What about people's privacy? Free speech? Human rights?"

"Everyone needs China, Aileen, and Zuckerberg was beating us to it. Have you seen that photo of him running in the Beijing smog and grinning his idiotic grin?" Valencik gritted his teeth. "I have it taped to the wall in my game room. I throw darts at it. We had to get into China first, and it wouldn't have happened without letting the Chinese government curate the Frontfacer experience."

"Curate? You mean control, censor, spy on?"

"Now you're being dramatic. Obviously we're having a difference of opinion over this, but whatever you think of me, I'm not stupid, or shortsighted. Once we have most of China using Frontfacer, I'll have the leverage to renegotiate the deal—network effects. The backdoor is a temporary solution, a stopgap. It'll be gone eventually."

Aileen slumped in her chair, grasping for a response. "Adrian, I don't even know what to say. You're delusional, and you have to know I'm going to tell everyone about the backdoor as soon as I leave this conference room."

"You aren't the first to say that, but I'm not delusional. Merely practical." Valencik looked at his watch. "On that note, I have to run in a minute. But speaking of practicality, I want to remind you of something you're forgetting: the nondisclosure agreement in your Frontfacer contract."

\* \* \*

"So what's on the thumb drive, Mr. Tong?" asked Dominic. "I assume it contains evidence of the backdoor?"

"Shall we unlock it together? You have one password remaining," said Tong. "Siew Ling, would you please give our friends your password?"

The maid returned from the hall, carrying a phone.

"Of course, Mr. Tong." She looked at each person in turn. "Singapore's place in the world. The password is 'little red dot,' a nickname for Singapore that refers to its depiction on maps as well as the great accomplishments of such a small nation."

"Bravo, Mr. Tong," said Mae Mae. "Your choices for the passwords have all been wonderful. Though I still think the previous one should have been 'flyer.'"

"Thank you, and I apologize for the confusion of that clue. You will not be surprised to hear I was in a great hurry when I organized the hunt for the clues to protect the thumb drive. My method was outlandish, I admit, but I have always loved crime and mystery novels, and I could not resist the opportunity to create a mystery of my own."

"Well, it worked. We made it here," said Dominic. He typed in the last password, hit the Enter key, and waited.

*   *   *

"You seriously think my NDA covers this?" Aileen asked. "Are you sure you aren't delusional?"

"Aileen, I'm not a gangster. I'm not going to threaten to break your legs. I run a technology company," said Valencik. "And I don't like to talk about money. It's crass, and there's no inherent value to money, it's just a means to an end. That said, we both know I'm a man of means, and you—actually, how much are we paying you?"

Aileen told him.

"Really? That's pretty good, even for Silicon Valley. Good for you. Look, the fact is, I'm a billionaire, and if you tell anyone about the backdoor, I will ruin your life. That's the long and short of it." Valencik stood up and pushed his chair toward the conference table. "I really have to run. Thanks again for taking the time, Aileen, and keep up the good work. Think about what I said. We'll talk soon."

Valencik left the conference room and walked off, giving the Ping-Pong players a thumbs up as he passed them.

Aileen sat in her chair, feeling too heavy to move and wondering what she was going to do next.

*   *   *

The group gathered around Dominic's computer to watch. On the screen, the last password disappeared and was replaced by icons for a folder and a program.

They all looked at Tong.

"The folder is evidence of Wei and Valencik's collaboration," he said. "The program is how you access the backdoor."

"We could open that program right now and see literally anything on Frontfacer?" asked Monir.

"Yes, but that is not what we will do," said Tong. "One of the commands available in the program can remotely connect to Frontfacer's systems and disable the backdoor. Valencik insisted on building the capability, in order to have multiple safeguards."

"What are we waiting for? Let's shut it down!" Dominic said.

"We cannot. Wei agreed to the disable option, but required that two passwords would be necessary to use it. That way, both sides would have to disable the backdoor together."

"Do you know these passwords?" asked Nadia.

"Wei has one of them," said Tong. "I know what it is. Valencik has the other. I believe Aileen is close to obtaining it, if she has not already. Once she does, I will close the backdoor before anyone else can use it."

"You're in contact with Aileen?" asked Monir. "This keeps getting stranger."

"No, with a group of hackers who call themselves Clandestine. One of them works at Frontfacer. With my help, she has been leading Aileen to Valencik's password over the last few days."

\*     \*     \*

Hearing the door to the conference room open, Aileen swiveled around.

"Hi, Aileen," said Siena. "I know you probably would prefer to sit there a while, but I need you to show me where you're keeping the password from Adrian's office. Nicholas Tong is waiting."

\*   \*   \*

"Unless there are any other questions, I would like to thank you all for keeping the thumb drive safe for me," said Tong, ejecting the thumb drive. "I was not sure I would escape from Wei's men."

"I have a question," said Monir. "Why Aileen?"

Tong smiled. "First, she is a fellow Singaporean. Second, I knew of her from her time in university, and I was confident that she had the skills my plan required. Third, she used to attend a faith gathering—the one that I understand you went to, Monir—hosted by dear friends of mine. They told me that Aileen is on a journey to figure out her beliefs, but they assured me her character is beyond question. I needed to give the drive to someone I could trust absolutely. Aileen was a logical choice."

"Mr. Tong," said Siew Ling, holding up the phone.

Tong clapped his hands. "Yes! Thank you, Siew Ling. I was so busy talking that I nearly forgot you made the call. Everyone, we should get ready. Soon we will have many new guests arriving."

"What guests?" asked Nadia. "Who did she call?"

"Unless I am mistaken, the police, the CIA, and possibly Eli's people should be here in minutes."

Kong Li and his men stepped out of their cars and surveyed the cottage, looking for points of access. Li decided to enter at the southwestern edge of the estate, where the natural bougainvillea wall met a tall wooden fence that lined the back. He told his men he would keep an eye on the street and neighbors while they broke branches near the bottom of the fence, where the hedge was thinnest. They would all crawl in from there.

# 23
# SHELLS AND KNIVES

Jun was poring over pictures that Harden had provided when her radio crackled and a voice said, "Officer Ai Boon, do you copy?"

"Ai Boon here."

"We received an anonymous call from a woman who says police assistance is needed immediately. She claims the sniper suspect is at 853 Loyang Lane. It's a place known as Changi Cottage."

"Changi Cottage? You have to be kidding me. That's all we need," Jun said. She grabbed her radio and ran for the door.

\*   \*   \*

Nadia walked around the cottage, noting the exits and windows and deciding what to do. If the police were on their way, she had to get out of there, or else she'd be arrested on sight. The police were unlikely to care that the restaurant shooting had been carried out on Eli's orders, but that didn't mean she wouldn't try to use the information in her favor if she had to. She guessed the Singaporean authorities would be very interested in what she knew about the foreign intelligence agencies operating inside their borders. If Nadia was going down, she was taking Eli with her.

"Mr. Tong!" shouted Siew Ling from across the cottage. "Three men are in the backyard. I believe they are carrying knives!"

Nadia ran to the closest window and saw three men slowly approaching the cottage. They were dressed like the Chinese men who had been following them for days. Cursing in Russian, Nadia went to the kitchen to look for anything she could use as a weapon.

"Everyone, get upstairs!" she shouted. "That isn't the police outside. Find somewhere to hide." Nadia gathered a couple of knives and other sharp kitchen tools and stuck them in her belt. She ran upstairs and pointed to Monir and Mae Mae. "You two, go to the windows at opposite ends of the cottage and keep watch. Monir, take the front, Mae Mae, take the back. If you see more people coming, tell me where."

"It must be Wei's men from China," Tong said. "They're here for me, but they will not hesitate to hurt others. Please be careful, all of you."

"What should I do?" Dominic asked, his voice shaking.

Nadia handed him a knife. "You, Tong, and Siew Ling go up to the attic. If those men get upstairs, I may need you to protect Tong. Try not to stab yourself."

Dominic took the blade and held it as far away from his body as he could. "I'll do my best."

Nadia ducked into the other rooms to look for anything that could be useful. She grabbed a handful of small decorative seashells and put them in her pocket. She also took two brass statues from a shelf in the hallway and handed them to Monir and Mae Mae, who struggled to lift hers.

"If anyone attacks you, hit them right here as hard as you can." Nadia pointed to her temple.

"Are you all right, Mae Mae?" Monir said.

The older woman gripped her statue and scowled. "Just let them try to get upstairs."

From below came the sound of glass shattering. Then hard pounding against a door and a splintering noise. Nadia vanished downstairs, hardly making a sound. Monir and Mae Mae exchanged worried looks. They really hoped Nadia knew what she was doing.

\*   \*   \*

Aileen stared at Siena. "You know Tong? You're the texter?"

Siena's mouth twisted into a tight smile. "Guilty as charged."

"But you work for Frontfacer. What am I not getting?"

Siena walked closer to Aileen. "I've been Adrian's assistant for a couple years. I was a developer here before that. The whole time, I've been a part of Clandestine—one of the more reasonable members, to be frank. I think Monir met some of the militant ones after he talked to Adrian."

"You're, I'm sorry, you're a hacker? You're working inside Frontfacer? Help me out."

"It's taken us years to get someone into a job like mine, a job with my kind of access inside a major tech company. Tong contacted Clandestine when he found out about the backdoor, but he didn't know if he could trust us with the details—for good reason, if you look at some of the things we've done in the past. Of course, when he described what he'd found, I knew what it was because I'd worked on the backdoor with Adrian."

"So you're not on Adrian's side?" Aileen asked.

"It's not that simple. I contacted Tong privately, without telling the rest of Clandestine. I told him who I was and offered to help him. He told me how he needed a password from Adrian to close the backdoor, but we both agreed I couldn't be the one to get it. I couldn't do anything that looked suspicious. My proximity to Adrian was too valuable to jeopardize."

"Which is where I came in," Aileen said, starting to fit the pieces together.

"Yes. Tong arranged for you to come to Frontfacer to get the password for us. If anything happened to him, I could lead you to the password, and you would already have the thumb drive. The plan was a bit convoluted, but we needed it to work, and it did."

"Why didn't you tell me about the backdoor from the start? That would have made things easier."

"Be honest, Aileen, what would you have done if I'd said there's a backdoor to Frontfacer? You'd have called every tech reporter in San Francisco. We had to ease you into it, keep you on a need-to-know basis. You're one of the ninjas, remember? Everything is on a need-to-know basis." Siena grinned. "Lame joke, sorry."

*    *    *

Kong Li and his men crept into the kitchen of the cottage. With knives drawn, they started to search the rooms on the lower level. Li used hand motions to silently direct them. Finding nothing downstairs but furniture, they moved to the front of the cottage and met at the stairwell. Li pointed his knife at the second level.

In the attic, Tong, Dominic, and Siew Ling were crouched behind boxes. Tong took a laptop from inside one of them and opened it, an e-mail system on the screen.

"What—" Dominic started to ask, but Tong immediately put his finger over his lips. He opened a text file, typed something, and showed it to Dominic: *Waiting for the second password. Will come through my secure email server. Expecting it soon.*

Dominic set down his own laptop and held his knife more tightly. They had to stay put and trust in Nadia's ability to keep the intruders occupied.

\* \* \*

Jun coordinated the police response while en route to Loyang Lane. Ten police cars and twenty officers were on their way to Changi Cottage, all arriving within minutes of one another. Jun's orders were to set up a perimeter two blocks out and wait. Her team at headquarters provided information from live satellite feed. Jun's radio crackled and someone told her that the satellite showed three men were entering the cottage from the back, and more were in front. Jun stepped on the accelerator, blowing through a red light.

\* \* \*

As soon as Li's men reached the top of the stairs, they heard something drop onto the wooden floor in the rear of the cottage. They flashed their lights in the direction of the noise and saw a seashell. They rushed into the room. Monir's attempt to strike the first intruder with his brass statue completely missed. The man knocked the statue out of Monir's hand and took him to the ground in one motion. The second man walked in and was struck in the back of the head by Mae Mae, but not hard enough to do any real damage. Soon she joined Monir on the floor. One of the men shouted a few words toward the stairs.

Although Monir's neck had a knife pressed against it, he was aware that Nadia was nowhere to be found. His captor's outburst in Chinese suggested that more people were downstairs. Where was Nadia?

In the attic, Tong nervously tapped his laptop, listening to the commotion below them.

"Siena, where are you?" he whispered. "You said she had the password." The sounds below stopped.

"Mr. Tong!" Siew Ling whispered.

"Dominic, this does not look good," Tong said. "Get ready to do as Nadia instructed."

\*   \*   \*

Siena pushed open the conference room's glass door. "I know you have more to ask me, Aileen, but we need to get that password to Tong. Come on."

Aileen got up and followed her to the ninjas' workspace. When Priyansh saw them approaching, he tugged his headphones off.

"Hey, Siena, can I talk to you? I'm having a problem with this one localization requirement. Not sure I understand what it's asking for. I use the word 'asking' very loosely in this case."

Aileen walked to her desk and unlocked the drawer, grabbing her phone from inside. Walking behind Priyansh, she stood in Siena's line of sight.

"Priyansh, can we talk about this later?" Siena asked. "I'm sorry, but I have to see Adrian about something. He's waiting."

"Oh, sure. He walked past here not long ago. He might still be around somewhere." Priyansh sat down and returned to his headphones.

Siena led Aileen toward the elevators, walking so fast that she was almost skipping.

"Tong set up a private e-mail server for him and me to use. That's how we've been communicating. He didn't trust texting," Siena whispered to Aileen.

"What about end-to-end encryption?" Aileen whispered back.

"He was worried that a phone would be too easy for someone to steal, and he was wary of his employers in China. He didn't want our entire project to depend on one little device."

The elevator doors slid open and they got in.

"I have access to the e-mail server on my laptop," Siena said, speaking normally. "It's on my desk in Adrian's building. That's where we're headed."

"He didn't trust texting, but he trusted an e-mail server?" Aileen asked. "Is it secure enough?"

"Is anything?" Siena replied. "Everyone has their own quirk. This is Tong's."

\*   \*   \*

A small seashell landed on the floor outside the sitting room. One of Li's men went to investigate. As he stepped into the hallway, a strong hand gripped his shoulder and spun him around, driving a carving knife into his throat. He made a gurgling sound and crashed to the floor. A few seconds later, someone from downstairs yelled something in Chinese that ended in a scream.

Monir watched his captor, who had a worried expression on his face. They heard more shouts, more dull thumps, and glass breaking.

"You guys didn't know what you're in for," Monir said. "Bet you wish you hadn't—"

His captor pressed the knife harder into Monir's neck, drawing a trickle of blood. "Quiet!"

No more sounds came from downstairs. The whole cottage was silent, waiting with held breath. Monir heard a soft footpad on the floor behind him. He tilted his head slightly and caught a flash of someone entering the room.

What followed took only seconds. Monir heard several violent grunts in a woman's voice as knees and elbows bashed into Monir's captor again and again. The man let out a muddled groan as the wind was knocked out of him, and then another as he crumpled to the floor. Monir lifted his head. Nadia was crouched over the man, her body tensed in a powerful fighting stance.

Nadia helped Monir and Mae Mae off the floor, moving quickly and fluidly. She held a finger to her lips to indicate the need for silence. Then she yelped loudly and threw her elbow into the wall. Footsteps pounded in the hallway and Li rushed into the room, his knife drawn. Spinning on her heel, Nadia kicked the knife out of Li's hand and raised an elbow to block his punch. She landed a roundhouse kick on Li's face, and while he stumbled backward she ran behind him and jumped on his back, wrapping her fingers around his neck. He slapped at her head with both hands, but the angle kept him from reaching her. Nadia pulled her elbow around Li's neck and yanked. He threw his hands toward her face, trying desperately to jab her in the eyes.

Monir and Mae Mae were crouched in the corner, nervously watching the fight. Monir's eyes darted around the room, looking for something to help with, but there was only Li's knife on the floor. He reached for it, but Li's foot flew backward and kicked it across the room. Nadia used her free hand to pull her elbow tighter around Li's neck while the man coughed and choked from the pressure, twisting and backing into walls to get rid of her.

The front door was kicked in with a loud crunch, and police poured inside. "Everybody freeze!" shouted a woman's voice.

\*　\*　\*

Aileen and Siena walked quickly across the Frontfacer campus.

"Your laptop is the only link to Tong's e-mail server, and you leave it lying around?" Aileen asked.

"I told you, it's paramount that I don't look suspicious. Who takes their laptop everywhere?" Siena replied. "Besides, it's heavy."

They arrived at Adrian's building and went inside, continuing to Siena's desk. She unlocked her desk drawer and took out her laptop. They were about to leave when Valencik walked out of his office.

"Hey, Aileen, Siena. What's up?" he said.

Aileen stared at Valencik, who not half an hour ago had told her about the backdoor, threatened to ruin her life, and seemed to say she still had a job at Frontfacer if she wanted it. She had no idea what to think of him.

"Hey, Adrian," Siena said. "We have a meeting with Priyansh in a few about localization. Aileen has some killer ideas we're going to discuss. Just needed my laptop. What are you up to?"

"That's great. Great to hear your head is in the right place, Aileen." Valencik showed them his book. "Reading a few pages before my own meeting. You should check out this business school professor, Siena, he really knows what he's talking about."

"Sure, put it on my desk after you're done. See you later."

"Have a good one, guys." Valencik went past them, reading as he walked.

Aileen waited to speak until he was gone. "That was creepy. It's like he forgot the conversation we had."

"He didn't forget," Siena said. "He thinks he has the upper hand, and he thinks you'll realize that. Come on, we can send the e-mail from a nap room."

\*   \*   \*

Ten police officers rushed into the lower level of the cottage, with the rest sprinting up the stairs toward the crashes they heard. They entered the sitting room, pointing weapons at Nadia and Li.

"I said freeze!" shouted Jun, aiming her gun at Nadia. The Russian let go of Li's neck and used her feet to kick him forward. She locked eyes with Jun, breathing heavily, and raised her arms in surrender. Li was bent over on the floor, holding his throat and coughing hoarsely. Monir and Mae Mae were sitting down, hands raised above their heads. One of the police officers checked the pulses of Li's men and looked at Jun, shaking his head.

"Handcuff all of them," Jun said. "Search the cottage for anyone else." Two officers cuffed Li first, then stepped behind Nadia and grabbed her wrists. Nadia was still glaring at Jun.

"Everybody chill out or we blow this place to kingdom come!" shouted Dominic at the entrance to the attic. The police officers flung themselves against the walls for cover and crept around the corner toward Dominic. Jun followed, inching forward, gun raised.

"Don't shoot, or we're all goners!" Dominic yelled. "I mean it!" he added.

"Is that Dominic Sim?" Jun called, peeking around the corner. Five neon green dots from the police's laser sights were centered on his chest.

"You know who I am?" Dominic asked, surprised. He looked back at Tong, who shrugged.

"Dominic, my name is Jun. I'm with the police. I know you must be scared, and you've had a long couple of days. But I am going to ask you a question, and I need you to think very carefully before you answer. Can you do that?"

"Uh, sure," Dominic said. He looked back at Tong again, who pointed to his laptop. Still nothing from Siena. They needed more time.

"Dominic, you know about the recent sniper shooting. I'm the lead officer in the investigation. That shooting is what started all of this, so we have no patience for false threats of violence. Do you understand?"

"Yes, I understand."

"Very good. Before I ask you the question, I'll tell you that if you do have a bomb or other explosive device, these officers are going to shoot you. Do you understand?"

The blood drained from Dominic's face.

"Dominic? Did you hear me?"

"Um…I, I heard you."

"Very good. OK, Dominic, I'm going to ask you the question. Are you sure, absolutely, totally sure, there is an explosive device in this house?"

"I…I…it…" Dominic looked back at Tong, who shook his head again.

"Dominic, I'm going to count to three. If you don't say anything by three, I will assume you *do* have an explosive in the house, and these officers are going to shoot you. One."

Dominic swallowed hard, his legs trembling.

"Two."

"There's no explosive!" he shouted. "I'm sorry! I'm sorry! I was only trying to—"

"Grab him," Jun said. Her officers sprinted forward, yanked Dominic from the attic entrance, pinned him down, and handcuffed him.

"Sorry I'm sorry I'm sorry I'm," he babbled, his face pushed against the floor.

The officers circled around the entrance to the attic. "Who else is up there?" Jun yelled.

\*   \*   \*

Aileen texted the picture of Valencik's password to Siena, who e-mailed it to herself, downloaded it, and saved it on her laptop.

"It takes a minute to connect to the e-mail server," Siena said. "Then we send the password to Tong and pray."

"There's one thing I don't get," Aileen said.

"Ask away. We can't make the server go any faster."

"Wait, two things. Why did you stop responding to me? And how did Adrian know I had his password? I think I was pretty careful. I didn't even take the thing out of his office. Was there a camera in there?"

Siena watched the cursor on her laptop spin in a colorful circle.

"How did Adrian know?" Aileen asked again.

The cursor stopped spinning and the server appeared on the screen. Siena looked up. "I told him."

\*    \*    \*

From downstairs, someone called, "Officer Ai Boon, these Americans are demanding to speak with you."

"Hi Jun, my name is Jeff Collins," said a voice. "John Harden sent us. He said to tell you not to do anything without talking to me first. Can we have a moment, please?"

"We're in the middle of a situation, Jeff. This isn't the time," yelled Jun.

"That's exactly why we've been sent—to help with your situation. Let me come up and I'll explain."

Jun ordered her men to escort Collins up the stairs. The other people with him would have to wait below. Jeff looked around as he walked up to the landing. Dominic was lying facedown on the floor. Monir and Mae Mae were sitting in the next room, handcuffs on. Half a dozen officers were focused on the attic entrance. Nadia and Li were handcuffed and being held at gunpoint. The bodies of Li's men were scattered around in various unnatural positions.

"You CID folks don't mess around," Collins said approvingly.

"State your business," Jun said.

"Relax, Jun. Relax. Everything will be all right." Collins walked toward the attic entrance.

"Get back here," Jun ordered.

Collins ignored her and called up to the attic. "Nicholas? Are you in there? It's Jeff Collins. You're a hard man to find."

"Hello, Jeff," Tong called back. "I suppose you finally caught up to me."

Collins flicked his thumb toward the attic. "You all want to bring Mr. Tong down here? He's harmless. You'll be fine."


Jael called Eli from a side road parallel to Loyang Lane. She and Itai had been instructed to keep a low profile at the cottage.

"Too much traffic in the area, Eli. First the Chinese, then the police, and now the Americans, it looks like. Your orders?"

"That's quite a crowd. I wonder if Tong is in there."

"Can't tell from here, sir."

"Come back to the safe house. We can't risk the Singapore police getting close to you two again. I'll deal with the Americans later. Monir, too."

"What about Nadia?"

"Don't worry about Nadia. That plan is already in motion."

*     *     *

"*You* told Adrian? Why?" Aileen asked, more confused than angry at Siena.

"Hold on one second." Siena attached the picture to an e-mail, typed "Valencik Password" in the subject line, typed in the destination address, and click Send. "That's it. The e-mail will take a few minutes to arrive, since it has to go through encryption on our end and decryption on Tong's end. He'll let me know when he's received it."

"Why?" Aileen asked again.

"I had to tell him something," Siena said. "This is going to sound bizarre, but Adrian has a sixth sense. He says meditation gives him a feel for the shape of a room's energy. He really trusts it. The day after his speech, he got to work and entered his office and instantly felt something was off. He made me walk through his office in a zigzag, feeling for where the energy was wrong. Eventually he settled on his book being what was off. From there, it didn't take long for him to decide that someone had been looking for the password. That was the reason for my radio silence—I had to be extra cautious while he was suspicious."

"But why did you say it was me?"

"It made sense that the intruder would be you, since you're new and asking lots of questions, and it gave me a chance to turn you in. Adrian felt good because he could address your concerns head-on, and I looked good because I was loyal to both the company and the team. I told him that I knew you were poking around but that I'd been loathe to rat out one of the ninjas."

"That is sort of insidiously clever. If Tong has the passwords to close the backdoor, is this it? Are we done? What do I do now?"

"For one thing, Adrian is right that you can't say a word about the backdoor. If news comes out about it anytime soon, he'll know it was you."

"So, quit? Go to another company? Keep my mouth shut?"

"Maybe. But you know," Siena said, "there are benefits to working at a company you disagree with. What better way to make a difference than from within?"

"Now you're saying stay at Frontfacer?"

"If you really want to keep an eye on technology and where it's going, this is the place to do it. Besides, people in Silicon Valley may job hop all the time, but you probably don't want your first job here to last a week."

"That does make some sense."

Siena got a sly smile. "I had an idea, actually. If you're interested—no pressure, but if you're interested—I could look into sponsoring you to join Clandestine."

"You want me to join your hacker group?"

"Why not? You're smart, and Frontfacer ninjas are a valuable commodity. You could help us protect the whole world from predatory technology and the people who use it."

"I'll think about it. I've only been here a few days. I don't even have a flat yet."

Siena laughed. "OK, think about it." She bent over her laptop. "Still no reply from Tong. That's strange."

*     *     *

Tong walked down the steps from the attic, his arms wrapped around his laptop. Collins took him firmly by the arm.

"Jun, on the authority of the United States, I'm taking responsibility for Nicholas Tong's laptop and thumb drive. You can have Tong, but his equipment is coming with me."

"No! This is *my* arrest and *my* investigation," Jun snapped.

"Only because of our benevolent assistance, Jun." Collins shouldered his way through the room, dragging Tong behind him. The other CIA agents were upstairs now and pried the laptop out of Tong's hands. The police officers were shifting their weight, looking to Jun for instructions.

Collins extended his arm toward them. "Easy, fellas. There's no fight here."

Jun's face was a shade of dark red. "I will call John Harden right now about this."

"Be my guest. John is the one who gave us our orders." Collins waved at his agents. "Let's go. Take it easy, Nicholas. Thanks for keeping the world safe. If we ever cross paths, don't screw me over again."

"But—" Jun said.

Loud thumps and a crash sounded from the other room. Jun whipped around and ran forward, feeling a breeze on her face. Monir and Mae Mae were still sitting quietly, but Li and two police officers were lying on the floor, unconscious. The window was open.

"The woman!" Jun shouted. "Find her!"

"So long, Jun," Collins called, walking downstairs. "I think your shooter went out the back."

Jun ran to the window. Nadia had vaulted to the deck below and was sprinting across the lawn, legs pumping, arms still handcuffed behind her.

"Get the woman!" Jun shouted. The officers downstairs flooded onto the deck and raised their weapons.

"Stop running or we will shoot!" one yelled.

Nadia didn't even slow down. Had she been in their shoes, she would have taken the shot, but she knew they wouldn't shoot—not at an unarmed suspect in a residential neighborhood. Reaching the fence, Nadia hopped up and pulled her hands forward and beneath her legs. Her arms now in front of her, she leaped at the fence and grabbed the top beam. She latched one foot on top of the fence and used her momentum to roll herself over it, falling to the ground on the other side. She stood up, smirked, saluted the police on the deck with both hands, and took off running in the other direction.

"She's gone—through the backyard!" Jun yelled. "I repeat, the female suspect has escaped!"

Jun ran down the stairs and ordered her officers after Nadia. Grabbing her radio, she barked into it: "Attention, all units. Female suspect on the loose near Loyang Lane. Tall Caucasian, blonde hair in a ponytail."

Outside the cottage, Collins and the other CIA agents were getting into their car. Jun went after them.

"Jeff! I'm not done with you. You can't take evidence from a crime scene."

Collins rolled down his window.

"Jun, if you have any objections, talk to Harden. But as far as I can tell, the crimes here are breaking and entering and assaulting a police officer. Nicholas's equipment isn't part of all that. Hey, if it makes you feel any better, we're going to use his information to help Singapore, and the rest of the world. Don't you want that? See the bigger picture, Jun."

"It's not right."

"You want what's right? Catch that Russian snake—that'll do your country right. We're your allies, Jun. Dryovskaya is the enemy. Don't let her get away. That wouldn't be good for you or for Singapore."

# 24
## ASHLEY AND JUN

Monir, Tong, Mae Mae, and Dominic spent several hours at CID headquarters after leaving Changi Cottage. Each of them was questioned individually, and then Jun brought all four together to hear their story one more time. Jun asked them a number of questions about Nadia, demanding to know if they had any information about where she was now or where she might go. Monir answered truthfully, emphasizing Nadia's experience with countersurveillance tactics. When asked whom else Nadia was working with, Monir said he had no comment.

It was early afternoon when Jun said they were free to go, with the understanding that they would make themselves available for further questioning. Monir and Mae Mae were cleared of any wrongdoing but were warned not to evade the police again. Dominic was assured that he and CID would be talking very soon about his newfound enthusiasm for explosives.

"Hey, Dominic," Monir said as they walked out, "I meant to ask you, what was with all that 'blow this place to kingdom come' stuff you were shouting back there?"

Dominic coughed and blushed. "I was trying to be dramatic to buy Tong some time. All I could think about was how the characters talk in American action movies."

For his part, Tong gave Jun's analysts a thorough briefing on exactly what the CIA had taken.

\*　　\*　　\*

Later that day, Monir met William Tan for dinner at a renowned sushi restaurant.

"You know, Monir," began William, "Chijmes is a historic building complex, one that had humble beginnings—"

"As a Catholic convent," finished Monir, a broad smile on his face. "I did my homework. I wanted to suggest a restaurant that would be meaningful to you."

"That was very thoughtful," said William. "I've heard the sushi here is excellent."

"The freshest fish in Singapore, according to one review."

"We'll find out for ourselves."

A waiter arrived and poured tea for them.

"I assume you will be leaving again soon?" William asked. "Though since Cyprus has officially declared that it will partner with Singapore for the lithium, this time your departure will not worry us."

"I'm glad to hear that, William. This situation with Tong and China certainly had a bearing on the decision," Monir said. He grinned. "Though the president of Cyprus is still trying to figure out how he can convince Adrian Valencik to invest in the country. But actually, my wife is coming here for a week. She had some vacation time at work, and after the events of the last week, if she doesn't see me soon, this time there really will be a family emergency."

"Ah, wonderful! When does she arrive?"

"Tonight around midnight. She's flying a Greek airline to Frankfurt, and then Singapore Airlines into Changi."

"You must give her a tour of all the locations you've visited. Your adventure has made you something of an expert on Singapore. You said you two live in the mountains of Cyprus?"

"Yes, a little village in the heart of the largest mountain range. It's not far from where the lithium was discovered. By the way," said Monir, "the official I've been working with in Cyprus, Christakis Savvides, wanted me to convey the president's desire for a state visit, perhaps a small delegation from Cyprus that would meet with your government's leaders."

"I am confident that our PM and his cabinet will be pleased to host the Cypriots. Speaking of delegations and such, I've been wondering about our talk on the phone the other night," said William. "I heard on the news earlier about an incident at Changi Cottage. Apparently the police were called for a break-in. Several arrests were made and fatalities were reported. Were you in any way...?"

"Involved?"

"I was not quite sure how to ask that. Violence at Changi Cottage is so rare—anything occurring there is rare, to be specific. To my knowledge, nothing major has happened there at all since Mr. Lee's brief stay in 1965. I could not help wondering if your friend who saved us at the restaurant was...."

"Involved?" Monir chuckled. "I am familiar with the events you're referring to. Maybe we'd best leave it there. As for my friend, let's just say time has a way of bringing things to the surface."

"Or burying them deeper." William shook his head. "I guess we'll have to wait. You are one interesting individual, Monir Young. And so is your mysterious friend."

"He is indeed. Oh, here comes our sashimi platter."

\*    \*    \*

Monir shook hands with William and left the restaurant, planning to catch a cab to the famous Taka Jewellery at Eunos Tech Park, where he wanted to buy a pair of earrings for Stalo. Then he would return to his hotel to take a nap before picking her up at the airport.

Almost immediately after William rounded the corner, a silver sedan screeched to a halt directly in front of Monir. The passenger door opened and a man sprang out. Monir felt a flash of panic before recognizing Jeff Collins.

"You sure have a gift for dramatic entrances," he said to Collins, who was grinning. "Does the CIA pay you extra for it?"

"Hi, Monir," Collins said. "Can we give you a ride? Anywhere you want to go."

"You know me, always happy to accept a lift from strangers." Monir got in the backseat of the car, where he was introduced to a man with a shaved head and muscles that bulged beneath his suit.

"Monir, this is David Canon. He's with the Department of Justice. The driver is one of ours as well, so we can speak freely."

"Hi Monir," said Canon. "Thanks for coming along."

"Canon? You didn't have someone keeping an eye on me in California, did you?" Monir asked, thinking of the green sedan at the San Francisco airport.

Canon reached into his pocket and took out a small white card with a cannon embossed on it. "I'm afraid so. You were given one of these, if I'm not mistaken."

"Yep, that's it," Monir said, turning the card over. "Cute."

Canon chuckled. "With a last name like mine, you have to have a little fun with it."

"I'd hate to see your business card if your last name was Trebuchet."

"Listen, Monir," said Collins, "we know your interests here in Singapore have been different from ours—the lithium and all—

and believe me, we are glad Cyprus and Singapore will be working together."

Monir frowned and was about to ask a question, but gave up. It didn't matter how they knew. They wouldn't tell him anyway. "Go on."

"Frontfacer is *our* interest," said Canon. "Naturally, after what Nicholas Tong revealed, we want to go after Adrian Valencik for his involvement with Zhang Wei, the Chinese government official who was involved in the backdoor. But first we're making sure we have all the tools we need to do it."

"Speaking of tools, what happened with the backdoor?" Monir asked. "Did Tong get the second password he needed to close it?"

Collins and Canon exchanged a glance.

"The second password was sent to Tong's private e-mail server, yes," Collins said slowly.

"So the backdoor is…closed?" Monir said.

"Not yet," Canon said smoothly. "But we have access to it, which is a solid bargaining chip for us when we start to make life very uncomfortable for Valencik."

Realization dawned on Monir. "You aren't going to close it. You're going to use the backdoor yourselves."

"Monir, you know how things work. You've been around. Legally speaking, we aren't sure Valencik did anything wrong. We're starting a thorough investigation into his relationship with Wei. There's a lot more to this than just the backdoor."

"Legally speaking," Monir echoed flatly. "Tell me, what else is part of it?"

"Well, our larger foreign policy with China, trade deals, various other economic concerns. The world is pretty big, and despite Frontfacer's prominence, it's just one part of that world. We know Wei was acting without the Chinese government's consent, which could be something we can use to our advantage."

250

"Good luck with that. Hey, driver," Monir called to the front of the car, "I'm going to Eunos Tech Park, please. Picking up a gift for my wife."

"We were hoping you would help us with Valencik," said Collins. "For whatever reason, he likes you, and he seems aware that you have a connection to us."

"*Had* a connection to you," Monir corrected. "Gentlemen, I'm tired. I've been shot at, followed, poked with a knife, and nearly blown up by a bomb that didn't exist. All I want right now is to see my wife and sleep for a few days. And sleep *with* my wife for a few days. What I don't want is to have anything to do with what you're describing."

Collins and Canon exchanged another glance. Collins nodded.

"That's too bad," said Canon, reaching into a seat pocket. "Because in return for your continued help, we were going to offer you something we thought you might want." He withdrew a manila folder and handed it to Monir.

"What is it?" Monir asked. He opened it. Inside were two pictures of his parents. One was a courthouse photo from the time of their trial. The other was his mother and father in front of a house he didn't recognize. The date on the photo was three days earlier.

"Recognize the happy couple?" Canon asked.

"How did you get this?" Monir demanded.

"I'm with the Department of Justice, remember? We work with Witness Protection. Your parents are in our custody. I took that picture myself."

Monir was noticeably shaken. He held the picture tenderly, as if he could actually touch his parents' faces in it. *Canon saw them just days ago...*

"They miss you, Monir," said Canon. "They told me there's a lot to explain and atone for. Maybe you have a few words to say to them as well. Think about it. In exchange for your cooperation, we are willing to reconnect you with Derek and Suhir Young—and to expunge their criminal records. Would you consider that?"

Collins put his hand on Monir's shoulder. Monir was too stunned to shrug it off.

"It's time, Monir," said Collins. "Time to go home."

\*   \*   \*

After narrowly avoiding arrest at Changi Cottage that morning, Nadia had run through a patch of trees west of Loyang Lane, emerging on the eastern side of Pasir Ris Drive. She'd continued west until she reached Pasir Ris Park. Then she'd run north for a few hundred meters until she hit the shores of Serangoon Harbour. She'd walked along the edge of the beach for a few miles until she'd reached an industrial park west of Pasir Ris Park. Pulling out her phone, she'd turned it on and tapped out a message.

Jael had come to Nadia's rescue, bringing her to the safe house, cutting off her handcuffs, and helping her with a disguise. The plan was for Eli to stop by shortly to debrief. He would provide Nadia with a new passport and identity, and with a new cell phone. Nadia would remain at the safe house for a few hours, leaving on a flight to London at 23:00.

After a quick nap, Nadia had showered, dressed, and packed. Surprised that no one else was at the safe house, she'd made coffee and eaten a banana. Just before leaving the condo, Nadia had gotten a text on the new phone Eli had given her: *Wait in the lobby until a white car flashes the lights twice.*

Now Nadia was sitting in a plush red leather chair in the lobby of the safe house's building, a small suitcase at her side. Peering through a pair of sunglasses, her eyes were scanning outside the building for her ride to the airport. She pulled out her passport and took one more look at the picture page. A lock of brown hair broke loose from the rest and swung down in front of her right eye. She pushed it back and kept reading:

*United Kingdom of Great Britain and Northern Ireland*
*Surname: Griffith*
*Given name: Ashley*
*Place of birth: Northampton*
*Nationality: British citizen*

\*　\*　\*

Jun had left Changi Cottage in a hurry that morning. Singapore police, having arrived in numbers, had taken over the processing of those arrested, as well as the removal of bodies from the premises. Jun had rushed back to headquarters, having several intense conversations along the way over her radio and phone. All communication had been centered on one thing: finding Nadia. The last call, one Jun had placed to police headquarters, had proved to be the most significant.

Jun had instructed her team to watch the airport for any passengers booking last-minute flights out of Singapore for the next few days. The Russian would not be hanging around Singapore, waiting for Jun to arrest her; she'd be trying to get out as soon as possible. Jun had heard and seen enough to recognize that they were dealing with a very dangerous individual. Nadia would disguise herself and use a different passport. It would be European or American, but not Asian.

By the time Jun had finished interrogating Monir and his friends, Jun's team had collected fifty-three names, only six of them not Asian. She'd had immigration check the disembarkation cards that recent visitors had submitted upon entering the country.

Only four of the six names had documentation. More investigation on the remaining two had turned up a man of European origin who had been a Singaporean resident since 2006—and a woman from the UK. "Ashley Griffith" was heading to London at 23:00 that night. She had not submitted a disembarkation card at Changi, and there was nothing for her at any of the Malaysian border checkpoints.

Jun Ai Boon had issued an APW for that name immediately. CID, working with a small army of Singapore Police Force personnel, had contacted hotels and condo rentals, as well as limo services and taxi and cab agencies. If any booking was made for Ashley Griffith, the business was to report it immediately.

Half an hour later, LionDrive Limousine Service, an airport limo service, reported a booking for Ashley Griffith. The dispatcher said the caller had been a man with a Middle Eastern accent, and the address was a condo in Tampines.

Jun took it from there. She had memorized the footage of Nadia's getaway from Highline Residences days earlier. A white Infiniti had picked up Nadia moments before police had arrived on the premises. Wanting to catch Nadia off guard, Jun told her team to find her a white Infiniti.

\*   \*   \*

The vehicle arrived just before 19:00. The driver flashed the lights twice and Nadia made her way to the door. It was a white Infiniti. *That will be Jael*, she thought as she walked through the building's sliding doors.

The Infiniti's rear door opened for her, but no one stepped out. Instinctively, Nadia paused on the sidewalk, steps away from the vehicle. What happened next was too fast for her to react to, but her training made it play out almost in slow motion.

The car's passenger door and driver door swung open, guns appearing at the edges of both. From the passenger side, a woman's voice shouted, "Put your hands where I can see them. Do it now!" From the open rear door, two police officers emerged, guns pointed at Nadia. Several police cruisers roared into the area, lights flashing and sirens blaring.

Nadia put down her purse and let go of her suitcase.

"Eli," she growled, raising her hands.

*    *    *

It was a small gathering, in comparison with the feat that was being celebrated. Director Low personally escorted Jun to the room. He stood outside the entrance and extended his hand, motioning Jun to enter. She walked into the room to the applause and cheers of her colleagues, each of who personally congratulated Jun and shook her hand. The SPF chief and his deputy had come across town to honor her. Director Low had even arranged for Jun's mother and uncle to be present. Jun held back tears when she saw them smiling at her proudly.

Director Low walked behind a small podium and tapped the microphone to get everyone's attention.

"A few weeks ago, we experienced one of the most horrific crimes in Singapore's history. The shooting at Demetra Bistro and the events that followed shocked us. We found ourselves in the middle of a multifaceted international fiasco. We have been challenged and tested to the core, both as law enforcement officers and as citizens of this great nation. Today, thanks to all of you, order and peace have been restored in Singapore. The perpetrators are dead or behind bars, facing trial. The shooter herself will most likely receive the death penalty for her actions.

"On behalf of CID and SPF, I am pleased to give special recognition to Officer Jun Ai Boon, who has led the investigation with exceptional diligence and fortitude. Through her leadership and tireless efforts, we were able to successfully close one of our most historic cases, and we have shown our people and the world that violent crimes will not be tolerated in Singapore."

\*　\*　\*

When Monir heard the circumstances of Nadia's arrest, he called Eli and demanded to talk in person. Eli seemed surprised that Monir was upset.

"How could you abandon her like that, Eli? Singapore is going to execute her for something you told her to do! She was your agent, and you threw her to the wolves. You recruited her, you assigned her the shooting. You don't just walk away."

"There are decisions I have to make in my job that don't make sense from your vantage point. Perhaps this is one of them," Eli said, his eyes never leaving Monir's.

Monir wasn't done. "Not to mention your constant oh-so-polite requests for updates on my work. I don't know, Eli. I fully admit you've helped me in the past—"

"I believe 'saved my life' is the phrase you're looking for."

"I don't work for you! I'm not a part of your spy agency over there in Israel. I can only imagine what you'll put Aileen through."

"Monir!" Eli raised his hand. "Stop. Enough. You aren't happy with our arrangement. I thought we were friends, but I get it. I get it. But we did what we had to do, and once again we prevailed. Can't you be thankful for that?"

"I need some time. Too much has happened since I met you." Monir took a few deep breaths to calm down. "Listen, you're a good man. Thank you for everything. But we're finished. I'll go back to Cyprus soon, and you go wherever you're headed next."

Monir reached out for a handshake. Eli gently grabbed the bottom of Monir's wrist instead.

"I don't believe we are finished just yet. You have been very useful to us. Gina and I may need your assistance again."

Monir twisted out of Eli's hold. "No, I think this is goodbye for me. So, goodbye." He started to walk away.

"And what of your parents, Monir?" Eli asked.

Monir turned around and looked at the katsa in disbelief. "Really, Eli? You're doing this right now?"

"I hear the prospect of you seeing them again is suddenly on the table. We can help you with that, if you wish. Gina has been making preparations." Eli smirked at Monir. "After all, what are friends for?"

*   *   *

Tong sat around a dinner table with Mother N and Father N, his old friends from the faith group.

"I cannot quite believe things worked out the way they did," Tong said. "Not exactly according to my plan, but not entirely far away from it either. Thank you for the access to the cottage."

"We are glad you are all right, Nicholas. But thank Mother over here," Father N said. "I simply inherited the privilege. She and her family are the ones who always had it."

"Is that true?" Tong asked Mother N. "I did not know that."

"Yes, my father was blessed to serve Mr. Lee and his family on his security detail at Changi Cottage," Mother N replied. "We were very happy to extend the blessing to you, Nicholas."

"And we must thank you, Nicholas," said Father N, "for taking such great risks to expose the schemes of criminals. Our nation, and the world, owes you a great debt."

"Unfortunately, that may not be true. The men I thought were trustworthy proved themselves to be other than that," Tong said. "My efforts may have been in vain."

"Doing what is right is never in vain," Mother N said. "Never forget that."

Tong smiled sadly. "Thank you for those words, Mother. I hope you are right. For now, all we can do is hope—and eat." He pointed across the table. "Father, would you pass the durians?"

\* \* \*

After cooling off from his talk with Eli, Monir called Aileen. She picked up on the second ring. "Hey, Monir! I've been meaning to call you. How's everything in Singapore?"

Monir caught her up on the last few days, the end of the clue hunt, Tong, Jun, Nadia—and Eli.

"Wow. I hadn't heard the full story, though Dominic told me some of it."

"Did he tell you he's become a real-life action hero?"

"No. What do you mean?"

"Ask him," Monir said, grinning.

"Believe me, I'll be doing that as soon as I hang up. So the lithium is all squared away? That must be a relief. When do you leave for Cyprus?"

"Stalo and I are spending a week in Singapore first. After the last couple days, I'll have a chance to enjoy the city for once. What about you? What are your plans?"

"Funny you should ask. Remember those tinfoil-hat-wearing weirdos you met?"

"How could I forget?"

"It sounds like I may be joining them. Siena is vouching for me. We'll see."

"Interesting. I wouldn't have pegged you as a…Clandestiner? Clandestinite? Is that what you want, to be a vigilante hacker?"

"To help people on a global scale, yes. If not for Tong and people like him, we never would have known about the backdoor. Someone has to protect us from the powers that be. Given the way things are going, it's a job that'll only become more important. I was searching for what I'm supposed to do, remember? I think this could be it. You might call it my Clandestiny."

Monir groaned. "That was literally painful to hear."

"No worse than yours."

"You've got me there. What about Valencik?"

"We seem to have an understanding. Our goals aren't the same, but this job could give me an opportunity to do something that really matters. I want to see where it goes. Maybe it'll work out, maybe it won't. Only one way to know."

"Wise words. Glad things are going all right for you, Aileen. And don't be a stranger. I may be out there again soon, and I'll make a point to stop by San Francisco."

"You're coming back to the States? What changed?"

"Long, long story. I'll tell you when I see you."

"Gotcha. Looking forward to it."

"Same here. Let's talk soon. Take care of yourself, Aileen."

"Thanks, Monir. You too."

\*　　\*　　\*

Monir caught a glimpse of Stalo through the glass doors of Changi Airport while she was waiting for her luggage. He always missed her when he traveled, but the intensity of the last few days had accentuated the feeling. He couldn't wait to show her the parts of Singapore that fascinated him: the *Kinetic Rain* sculpture in that very terminal, the rain trees along the ECP, the CBD skyline, the Botanic Gardens in the morning, and, above all, the view from the observation deck at Marina Bay Sands.

Monir went off his Cyprus budget and splurged on a room at the hotel. The splurge continued with an afternoon at the spa, the rooftop infinity pool, and a feast of modern Asian cuisine at the deck's restaurant, CÉ LA VI.

*It couldn't be better than this*, thought Monir. Everything was finally exactly the way he'd dreamed it when he, Dominic, Mae Mae, and Nadia had been looking for clues. It felt good to not be dodging security cameras for a change.

As the colors of the sunset settled over Singapore's business district and Marina Bay, Monir grabbed two glasses of wine and led Stalo to the very spot he'd stood in days earlier. Stalo was enchanted.

"This is so beautiful, Monir. I've never seen anything like it."

Monir pulled his wife closer and remained silent, letting the view do the talking.

"Clearly, Singapore is who Cyprus needs as a partner," Stalo said. "I need an excuse to come back here."

"Then you're a lucky woman," Monir said, "because we have an excuse whenever we want for the foreseeable future."

Stalo kissed Monir on the cheek. "I am a lucky woman, and not only because of the view." She took one of the wine glasses from Monir. "I'm very glad the lithium is done with. All thanks to your efforts, my love."

"I can't take all the credit, unfortunately. I had help, and as the priest in your village would say, it wasn't just from the people around me. Maybe I have friends in," Monir raised his eyebrows at his wife, "heavenly places."

Stalo smiled. "Maybe you do. And the development with your parents—you get to see them again!"

"I'm not settled on going back yet, to be honest. I...I think I want to see my parents, but the government wants something in return. That's a decision for much, much later. How about we take it one moment at a time, at least for tonight. Deal?"

"Deal." Stalo linked her arm through her husband's and held up her wine glass. "Now, a toast—to new friends, to good wine, and, most of all, to our first vacation together in far too long."

"To all of those things," Monir agreed. They clinked glasses and watched the sky take on shades of gold and orange, then red and brown, then blue and violet, until the sun had sunk below the horizon.

# AUTHORS' NOTE

Apologies to all Singaporean locations and businesses where criminal activity takes place in the story. In some instances, we changed the names of the businesses. Singapore has been and continues to be one of the safest cities in the world.

Changi Cottage does not exist as we describe it in the story. The Lee family took refuge at the Cottage in 1965—that part is accurate; however, the property has long been part of the Aloha Changi resort.

There is indeed a faith gathering in a Tiong Bahru home, and it is led by a couple similar in character and demeanor to Father N and Mother N. Much appreciation for their encouragement and support over the years.

Cyprus's lithium is, of course, fictitious. Cyprus was chosen symbolically and for sentimental reasons.

–M.E.


There's a lot of scary, complicated stuff happening right now at the intersection of surveillance, privacy, and technology. We wanted to write a book about why those things matter, based on current events, but we also wanted to write an entertaining story. If you made it this far, I hope that means we did both.

–J.O.

# ACKNOWLEDGEMENTS

Many thanks to: Captain Sergejs Kurnikovs for input on cargo ships and the trade route between Cyprus and Singapore. Tom Sanders for consultation about submarines and personnel transfers at sea. The real David Canon for information on U.S. federal law enforcement and for consenting to us using one of his old operational code names. Jason Hackley for IT support and technical advice in the area of cybersecurity. Mark DeJesus for formatting the manuscript. Elijah Ngiam and the real Nicholas Tong for research and consultation. Sergio Barrera for the cover and website design. All who resourced this project financially. Family and friends in Cyprus and Singapore—their support has been phenomenal, and this book is a tribute to them and their nations. My parents for always having my back. My wife and three children for their patience and encouragement. Last but not least, the growing fan base for Trace Evans books. We are just getting started, everyone—enjoy the journey with us!

–M.E.


Thanks to the real Casey Margaret, who for two years in a row has put up with me vanishing during the final stages of these books. Thanks to the many writers—among them Roberto Bolaño, Willa Cather, Elizabeth Bishop, and Frank O'Hara—who made me want to write a book. And thanks to Jon Hopkins for providing the soundtrack to this one.

–J.O.

**Trace Evans** is the pen name for two authors who live in the northeastern United States. *The Cargo* is Trace's second book. His first, *The Trade*, was published in 2015. For more, go to www.TraceEvans.com.

72375350R00149

Made in the USA
Columbia, SC
20 June 2017